PELHAM FELL HERE

Praise for the work of ED LYNSKEY

"Ed Lynskey's new novel PELHAM FELL HERE is a delight. With a plot as complex as your grandmother's crocheted doilies, Mr. Lynskey creates a portrait of the rural hill country that rings as true as the clank of a Copenhagen can on a Pabst Blue Ribbon can, as does his handle on guns, love, and betrayal. This is a novel well worth the read and makes me want more."

—James Crumley, Hammett Award winning author of THE LAST GOOD KISS

"Ed Lynskey's PELHAM FELL HERE is as hard-bitten and hard-boiled as they come. The dialogue crackles with such sharpness that you'd swear sparks were jumping off the pages. And P.I. Frank Johnson is a character cut from the Tarantino mold: tough, wounded, conflicted, and bad-ass. Pick up a copy today!"

—James Rollins, New York Times bestselling author of THE JUDAS STRAIN

"PELHAM FELL HERE is a gritty, fascinating thriller with colorful characters, snappy dialogue and plenty of plot twists. Ed Lynskey has created an interesting hero with Frank Johnson, a man with a mission who becomes a man on the run after killing some crooked cops. PELHAM FELL HERE kept me guessing—and on the edge of my seat."

—Kevin O'Brien, New York Times bestselling author of ONE LAST SCREAM

"Nobody captures rural America like Ed Lynskey...a thoroughly engrossing and satisfying read."

—Anne Frasier, USA Today bestselling author of PALE IMMORTAL

"Ed Lynskey writes in a voice utterly unique to the crime genre. His language cracks like a whip. His dialogue pops like fireworks on the Fourth. In PELHAM FELL HERE, he's crafted a story Indiana Jones would kill for, full of humor, action, neo-Nazi thugs, and the marvelous countryside of rural Virginia. If you haven't read this guy, drop everything right now and do it. You'll be very happy you did."

—William Kent Krueger, Anthony Award winning author of THUNDER BAY

"Ed Lynskey's followup to THE BLUE CHEER is another lean, tough slice of rural noir. Lynskey reminds us that for every mean street in the city, there's an equally mean dirt road out where the buses don't run. The writing is pure joy to read; he can evoke more powerful imagery with a single perfectly chosen phrase than most writers can with a half page of descriptive prose. Strong stuff, but always satisfying."

—J.D. Rhoades, author of SAFE AND SOUND

"PELHAM FELL HERE bears the richest nicotine and bourbon stains of the hardboiled genre, yet also bristles with vitality. The plot sings, the characters are twisty and textured and the violence brutal but inevitable. All of these elements would be more than enough yet Ed Lynskey offers so much more in the form of a perfectly pitched prose style that swings effortlessly from back-country grit to Appalachian poetry and back again."

—Megan Abbott, Edgar nominee author of QUEENPIN

"Ed Lynskey's PELHAM FELL HERE is top drawer PI fiction. Lynskey has a stark, original voice and he is not to be missed."

—Jason Starr, Barry and Anthony winning author of THE FOLLOWER

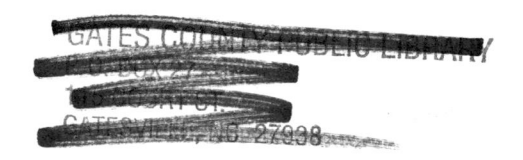

PELHAM FELL HERE

A PI FRANK JOHNSON MYSTERY

ED LYNSKEY

Mundania Press
Cincinnati, Ohio

Pelham Fell Here Copyright © 2008 by Ed Lynskey

All rights reserved under the International and Pan-American Copyright Conventions. No part of this book may be reproduced or transmitted in any form or by any means, electronic or mechanical including photocopying, recording, or by any information storage and retrieval system, without permission in writing from the publisher.

The scanning, uploading and distribution of this book via the Internet or via any other means without the permission of the publisher is illegal, and punishable by law. Please purchase only authorized electronic editions, and do not participate in or encourage the electronic piracy of copyrighted materials. Your support of the author's rights is appreciated.

This is a work of fiction. Names, characters, places and incidents either are the product of the author's imagination or are used fictitiously, and any resemblance to any actual persons, living or dead, events, or locales is entirely coincidental.

A Mundania Press Production
Mundania Press LLC
6470A Glenway Avenue, #109
Cincinnati, Ohio 45211-5222

To order additional copies of this book, contact:
books@mundania.com
www.mundania.com

Cover Art © 2007 by Anna Winsom
Book Design, Production, and Layout by Daniel J. Reitz, Sr.
Marketing and Promotion by Bob Sanders

Trade Paperback ISBN: 978-1-59426-401-6
eBook ISBN: 978-1-59426-400-9

First Edition • August 2008

Production by Mundania Press LLC
Printed in the United States of America
10 9 8 7 6 5 4 3 2 1

Warning: The unauthorized reproduction or distribution of this copyrighted work is illegal. Criminal copyright infringement, including infringement without monetary gain, is investigated by the FBI and is punishable by up to 5 years in federal prison and a fine of $250,000.

For Heather, with love

"Pelham fell here leading a charge—the exact death he would have chosen"

John Esten Cooke
Hammer and Rapier, 1898

Chapter 1

"That's all I've got, sir."

At a covert glance, I took note of the new sales girl wearing a crisp, white blouse. She was speaking to a hunter.

"The hell you say." The tendons corded in Sugg's neck. His sun-chapped face had a menacing look.

She tilted her chin at the boxes of shotgun shells on the glass countertop. "That's it. I've rechecked. We've sold out. Sorry."

"The hell you say," repeated Suggs.

Shifting in closer, I propped my elbows on the beveled edge of the glass countertop and pretended to study the Luger out on display.

"You must stock extra number 8 lead shot." Suggs' hands crushed the boxes. His inflection cut with a harder edge. "Well, don't you?"

She folded her tan, bare arms on her chest, a defensive gesture. I saw goose bumps on her arms. "Cody has Fed Ex'd more. The truck will be here tomorrow morning." A perfunctory smile creased her lips. "I'll call you, if you'd like."

Suggs snorted. "I'd like you to call Cody." He jabbed a finger as a pointer. "Go get him."

I started to say something but she spoke.

"Cody left for the day." She tapped the cash register keys, aloof to his adversarial glare. I saw her nipples emboss her blouse fabric, and Suggs' dropped gawk did, too. "With state sales tax, the total is $64.65," she said.

"Have Cody buzz Suggs Pella. We're old pals." Leaning on his elbows over the countertop, Suggs reached and cupped his hand on her right breast. "Think he'd share you with me?"

She trembled for a second, and then slapped him across the nose.

"Ouch!" His hands flew up to nurse his bloody nose. "I'll tie your tits in a knot, bitch."

"Yo, Suggs." I slapped him on the shoulder like good ole boys do. "How's the shooting? Besides with your mouth, I mean." The odor of creosote staining his bibs warned me he had muscles from hard labor. He might win a scrum, but the bourbon I also smelled dulled his reflexes.

"Huh?" Dealing me a scowl, Suggs dabbed at his nose. "The doves are flying, but I'm stuck here jawing with you." Seeing the blood on his finger deepened his scowl.

"Some days are real pissers." My hand clapped his shoulder again. "Pay the lady and go get sober."

"I'm sober enough. Paw me again, I'll show you." Suggs slapped down the money and brushed by the rack of shotguns. "Trailer trash," was audible before the door clanged shut behind him.

His accolade didn't sway my attention on her straightening the key chains sold in a basket. Anger and maybe disgust pinched her eye corners and mouth.

"What might you want?" Her inflection grew wooden. "Like I said, we've got no more birdshot."

"Uh-huh."

"Thanks for running interference."

"Uh-huh."

"Cody has left to buy more guns."

"Uh-huh."

I identified her smoky lilt as a Virginia Tidewater native's, probably on this near side of the Chesapeake Bay. What awed me was her hair—cider-brown, curls swept back, and held by two barrettes. Her clean, soapy fragrance was a close second. She stood at average height, but this was no average package. Off the bat, I liked her but I browsed too long. Her eyes, sad and blue, flitted to check the wall clock.

"I'm no hunter," I said. "I like guns but not like a fanatic. I target shoot for sport."

She now had to wonder at my sudden garrulity.

"You're not a local." I paused, unsure. "Or are you?"

"Sort of. Randall Van Dotson is my dad. I'm Rennie." After tossing her head that coy, sweet way girls do, she gave me a candid appraisal.

"Randall owns that tract of oaks. I've blasted mistletoe sprigs out of them. With his permission, I mean." Self-conscious, I quit talking. No wedding ring sparkled before her hands slid into her jeans pockets.

"Is it lunchtime?" Rennie craned her head and saw the clock hands hadn't moved.

But my best chance is slipping away, I thought. She'd just smacked Suggs for pawing her and might resent my overtures, but I went for broke.

"Would you mind if I dropped by again?" I asked. Some broke.

"Why should it matter to me?" Rennie scratched on a smile, her first.

Satisfied, I turned and left the gun shop. Sitting in my truck cab I realized something.

"Guess what, Johnson?" My palm thumped my knee. "She doesn't know your name." Then I cracked a grin. "Yet."

Chapter 2

That afternoon, chilly under a zinc-gray, overcast sky, I worked bush-hogging an ironwood thicket. Next spring in the new century, the Mormons wanted to seed this bottomland by Mosby River in corn or, quite possibly, they'd sell out to a developer. Regardless, my task was to mow off the scrub ironwood.

The clanky John Deere tractor lacked fenders. Dead animal bones and chunks of snakes flew up, lashing my boots. Every so often, the bush-hog's twirling steel blades mauled a pile of flint, raising sparks, and a din that failed to dent my reverie.

Who was Rennie Van Dotson? Was she married? Widowed? Single? Did she date? She acted older. Was that a problem? The comical sight of Suggs's bloody nose evoked my smile. I pictured her dad Randall on patrol, brandishing a Coleman lantern and 12-gauge shotgun, watchful to nail any mistletoe poachers. He blasted away at any noise, a dubious practice known as a "sound shot".

A half-hour shy of dusk, I mired the John Deere in a bog. I might chain its axle to my truck's winch to extract, but I wanted to hunt up my cousin Cody Chapman to glean a little information. I knew where to catch him, too.

∽∾

Fluorescents brightened the windows to Leona's Bar & Grill in Pelham, Virginia. I saw a white Chevy van at the traffic signal make an illegal left on red. The V.F.D.'s whistle erupting made me flinch—autumn's first cold snap caused fires to ignite in dirty chimneys. The greasy whiff I smelled promised steaks on Leona's grill.

Inside, Cody, 350 pounds in his sock feet, had commandeered a booth by a curtainless window. Cody almost lived at Leona's. His signature Cherry Swisher cigar smoldered in the ashtray, and folded under it I saw *The Pelham-Democrat*. Cody had been admiring his weekly hunting-and-fishing newspaper column I seldom took time to read.

He motioned me over to sit opposite him. "How's the turf farm treating you, cuz?"

"I quit. It was convict labor. Monday I started bush-hogging for the Mormons."

"Good for you. I bought some Marlin rifles ready for your magic."

Our fight, what had goaded me to quit working for Cody, in retrospect was asinine. Cody wouldn't pay me overtime, just straight time, for my 60-hour workweek. We'd jawed over it; he wouldn't budge; and I stamped out hotheaded. That was that.

Later crunching the numbers, I saw I cleared more on his sales commissions than I did with OT. He probably knew it, too. We smoothed things over, but I never worked at his counter again. Every few weeks I'd crate up Cody's defective weapons, and he overpaid me for my gunsmithing.

"I'll fix them this weekend," I said.

"You do that." Cody set down his fork before finger-tapping the ash cone off his cigar stub. "Leona, bring my cuz a bowl of split pea soup before he devours my supper."

"Coming right up," said the bony lady slicing a tomato behind the counter.

"Mind if I mooch a smoke?" I asked Cody.

Cody shrugged. "They're the brand we geezers smoke."

"Skip it. I quit." I pocketed the cigarette I'd shaken out of his pack.

"Bully for you. I might next week."

Now I shrugged. "You gotta die of something."

Cody took his coffee 100 proof, spiked by the bourbon pint wedged between his thighs. The bourbon flushed down his steak cubes, mashed potatoes, and butter beans. Leona's split pea soup tasted passable, and I talked between spoonfuls.

"I stopped by the shop. Keep that Luger. I'll swap you, maybe for my Beretta." Then after a swallow, I dropped in with casual ease, "Your new counter girl is a looker."

"Uh-huh." Cody tweezed a tobacco fleck from his lips twisting into a grin. His draw down sparked the round glow to the cigar stub. Eyes on Leona's ceiling fan, he spewed out a banner of smoke. I repressed a throat tickle to cough. Smokers weren't reviled at Leona's.

"You pups always come sniffing around."

"Is Randall her dad?"

"Yeah, but Rennie grew up on her mama's place down in Tappahannock." A belch interrupted his gossip. "Her mama, I heard tell, was out pinning up the morning wash. Next thing, she keeled over dead. Heart attack. I didn't know women got them, did you?"

"You gotta die of something." I ordered a beer from Leona and flexed my knees cramped under the tabletop. My boot bumped Cody. "Didn't Randall do some time?"

Grunting, Cody moved his boot. "He got into a property line dispute with a neighbor. Things heated up. Randall threw the first punch."

"But didn't he go to jail?"

Anger hardened Cody's face. "Don't you ask Rennie about it."

My palms heeled up. "Cool by me. So, what's her story?"

Cody butted his cigar stub in the ashtray. "Randall sent her to me. I don't know squat on her love life. She's a class act and a hard worker. I wouldn't like losing her. Got it?"

My lips quirked. The beer tasted like soy sauce. I set down the bottle and peeled off its label, stalling. Cody seemed overprotective. Was he sweet on her? "I heard you."

He used a paper napkin on his mouth. "Why do I sweat it? I'd bet that Luger you didn't say 'boo' to her."

"Wrong. I'm not that pathetic."

"Wrong. You are. Quit slinking around like a whipped hound. I'm sick of it."

I'd already lined up a righteous payback for Marty my ex, but I didn't share that mission with Cody. He'd try to dissuade me. "Marty cheated on me. Didn't you catch her red-handed in bed?"

Cody studied me through the cigar smog, his eyes shrewd. Candor was his strong suit, why I valued him as a friend. "So I did. But 'fuck 'em and chuck 'em' is my motto. Why beat yourself up over Marty?"

"I'm a sucker for heartbreaks and sluts."

"Christ, you're hopeless. How's Chet?"

"Crazy as ever," I replied.

"You ain't said shit. Chet dodged a bullet at his trial. Too bad Briones didn't dodge Chet's bullet. But Gerald is the psycho in that brood."

Gerald, Chet's older brother, was my age, mid-twenties. "Gerald is cool. Just don't cross him."

Cody grunted. "Gerald is one big, crazy-ass nigger."

I frowned. "Watch it, cuz. He's my friend."

"Blood is thicker than water, I always say."

"No matter. Gerald is solid by me."

I saw out the window the same van, now a white blob in the semi-darkness, brake at the traffic light. Why was the van circling the block? The engine backfired, died, and the repeated ignition cranks couldn't restart it.

Cody's interest was also piqued. A flash of surprise lit up his face before he resumed talking. "Rennie will be off soon. Her Aunt Erin offered to pay for her college up north. Rennie's somewhat mature, but there's no better time to hit the books." He screwed the top back on his bourbon pint.

"What's to entice a smart girl to live in Pelham?"

Cody's gaze held mine. "Go get laid, cuz. It'd do your cynical attitude a world of good."

"Thanks, doc, but my attitude feels fine."

"Suggs waltzed in here bragging he'll wax the deck with your ass."

"It's just the booze talking." I saw the van's driver step through Leona's doorway. He wore a befuddled expression and a Confederate cap, the stars-and-bars flag decal pasted on its beveled front.

"Listen, my cuz is a tough guy."

"Rennie's tough. She smacked Suggs for copping a feel."

"Good for her. I told you she takes no shit. Finish your beer and give that stranger a hand. I'll get this mess. You fix my Marlins, and we'll call it even. Deal?"

"Deal. He looks lost." I nodded at Rebby Cap eager to flag down a Good Samaritan.

Cody's chuckle sounded forced. "He's looking for something."

I strolled up and offered my aid to Rebby Cap. He eclipsed me by an inch and had blank grommets for eyes.

"You bet. My cell phone is busted," he said, his voice slow and sinister. (I think my alternator is shot"

Introductions were superfluous, and we headed out into the October chill. The jumpstart turned into a production. First, Rebby Cap chiseled $10 off me for "gas money". Second, the van's radio blared out acid rock. Third, he had no jumper cables, and we improvised with mine.

Antsy to be off, I butted my truck's grille against the van's front bumper. I saw the headlight, driver's side, was out and a Conquistador decorated the van's side. My jumper cables just did clamp on our battery terminals. Rebby Cap's sneakiness irked me. He cracked the van's side door and hoisted in one leg at a time to prevent my glimpse of his jailbait waiting inside. The van windows and side ports had a tinted opaqueness. He rolled down his window.

"Turn down the music!" I yelled at him inside.

Rebby Cap complied.

"Crank and give her a little pedal," I said.

Rebby Cap spurted his engine to life and raced it until my battery had juiced his enough. The glass pack mufflers exploded like a grenade from under his chassis. Rebby Cap wiggled out his door, unclipped my jumper cables to fling aside, and climbed in to rocket off. I'd heard no thanks, just gotten panhandled for a sawbuck.

But I felt relief after he left. Rebby Cap smelled like trouble in spades, something I didn't need.

Chapter 3

The next morning was a cloudy, raw Thursday. I used my truck winch to drag out the John Deere from the bog, and I bush-hogged a larger parcel of thicket for the Mormons. A drizzle saturated the bottomland enough to wet down the dust. By early afternoon, the overcast sky broke up a little to let in slivers of sunlight.

Before long, the sun heated the breezeless day into a rotisserie, and pesky deer flies stung through my t-shirt. The incessant *pap, pap, pap* to distant shotguns pounded the doves though only a few tail feathers ever fell to the ground. I yearned to start my own hunt, but like a working fool, I pressed on.

I charged a catbrier patch, its thorns clawing at my shins. I finished there and took five. Grateful for some quiet, I drank a cup of water dipped from an icy cold spring. It left a chalky aftertaste as I walked through the sumac stobs to board the John Deere. Bunching up, the dark clouds returned.

The rain soon pelted me, and the temperature plunged by fifteen degrees. October's weather was unsettled. The John Deere waffled before it conked out, and I had to laugh at my snakebit luck. My grinding couldn't kick over the engine. Soaked to the skin and clattering teeth sent me to my truck. The motor belched, and the heater's blower wheezed. There had to be easier ways to make a living.

I witnessed the red clay churn into puddles of blood like those staining a combat zone. Not that I'd seen much live combat during my MP stint. Fort Riley in Kansas had been my home station. I'd hunted elk and quail there. Saw bald eagles and the rolling prairie. I did a few overseas deployments including one furlough in Ankara, a majestic city but without a drop of Kentucky bourbon for sale in it.

Rennie's sad eyes resonated in my mind. So she was off to college. Chewing on that snarled my mood. I put on the radio. A signature bluegrass tune extolled this enchantress taking a guy down a notch, then ditching him "like a fox on the run". I'd hummed along to The Country Gentleman singing a thousand times before, and now the lyrics spirited me back to see Rennie. I pinned the accelerator.

At quarter till five, Cody's gun shop, a low-slung brick structure with a flat asphalt roof, hadn't yet closed. I braked in front of the Grumman canoes racked on shelves under a tin roof pavilion. I sat in the cab and, my eyes closed, used visualization to plot my approach. I'd go in and strike up a conversation.

"Hi. It's Rennie, right? I never forget names. What's say we go out tonight?"

Inside the gun shop was quiet as the familiar synthesis of gun oil and khaki tanged the air. I glanced left to right. A young couple—she wore cornrows and he kept a hand on her tight ass—picked through a bin of Civil War spurs, breastplates, and belt buckles Cody had out for sale. A photo gallery of his pals' trophy game kills lined the knotty pine wall panels. The dead bears exhibited more grace than their scruffy hunters did. My gaze shifted. Today Rennie looked radiant in a cranberry red cardigan, snug but tasteful.

"May I assist you?" Her second look recognized me. "Oh...it's you again."

"Johnson." I switched on my most winning smile. "Frank Johnson."

"How may I assist you, Frank Johnson?"

"Just Frank, please. I hoped we'd go out tonight."

"Sorry, Frank. My employer enforces a no-dates-with-the-customers rule, and I like my job. But thanks for asking."

"I'm no customer. I mean Cody is my cousin and he won't

mind." I gushed like an acne-scarred teenager.

Rennie allowed a guarded smile. "Persistence wins out, I suppose. Okay, I live at the old Shepherd place. My apartment is upstairs, first one on the right. There's no number on the door. Come at seven and no earlier, please. See you then, Frank."

"I look forward to it," I told her, waving.

Back in my truck cab, I watched the young couple traipse out. They laughed. They were in love, and I'd been in that state once. Or so I'd thought.

I drove to the doublewide trailer where I lived in a trim mobile home park. A navy shower and two pats of Brut put me in high stride. My brief hiatus from the dating scene hadn't dulled me. Why, I'd shake off the rust and charm the girl out of her melancholy airs. My heart thudded way up between my jaws.

※

By quarter to seven, I was speeding down Rogue's Road—muggers had waylaid naïve travelers here in Colonial days—and hauled by a sprawling copse of oaks. Garm Castle, the top of its yellow brick parapets towering into view, sat couched further back among the oaks.

Garm, a homesick Scotsman, had erected the castle in the late 1890s and then sent for his new bride. They lived in the manor over a happy interval, but then Mrs. Garm contracted tetanus from pricking her finger on a rose thorn and died childless. They said Garm went insane and followed her to an early grave. The disused castle became Pelham's most exotic landmark, and its imperceptible driveway offered our teenagers a lover's lane. I'd parked on it.

I recalled when proud Sears homes and shady maples had flanked our town streets. Blondes wearing hot pants and flawless tans lounged on porch gliders, sipping on colas through bent paper straws. Cannas bloomed red as claret above the wrought iron fences, and the swept sidewalks sat even. But Pelham had turned shabby at the edges, and so had I. Here a few months shy of the new millennium, I'd fallen short of the brass ring. This truck and the leaky doublewide represented my sole wealth.

I passed a road sign advertising a new housing tract and frowned. Like I said, Pelham had turned shabby.

Eight minutes early, I docked across the way from Rennie's apartment building, my truck engine idling to run the heater. The old Shepherd place squatted on the desolate end of Main Street. The out-of-town landlord had diced up the Victorian two-story into four cubbyhole apartments. The Shepherd's oldest boy, Whit, had played star shortstop (a scholarship to Arizona State waited in his future) next to my serviceable third base.

My disaffection with Pelham started when Whit ran his VW off the rain-slick pavement into a telephone pole, died of his injuries, and his parents sold the house. I never saw the Shepherds again, but they were better off—bailing from Pelham offered a shot at redemption.

Not long afterwards, I'd also left to serve in the Army MPs. MP work wasn't sexy, but it was satisfying enough to take pride in doing well. After graduating from Military Police School, my beat was Fort Riley. I patrolled its gates and streets, writing up tickets (even for the brass) and arbitrating domestic disputes. Something of a barracks rat, I read a ton of pulp paperbacks. Prisoner escort duty sent me on trips throughout the mainland to fetch AWOLs back to face court martial. Most were scared kids, not much different from me.

The main rub was the lack of RnR and I burned out. Three years and three stripes later, I ejected from the MP Corps, vowing I'd never do police or criminal investigative work again. Instead, I returned home when I should've learned better. Lonely, I'd next tried marrying and then divorced the two-timing Marty. I curbed that unpleasant memory.

No lights blazed in the ground windows to the apartments rented by the old widows. The bright upstairs window had to be Rennie's bedroom. I could picture her at the mirror dabbing on perfume before debating, then leaving her top blouse buttons undone. I grinned at my wishful thinking.

The truck cab had grown stuffy. I cut off the heater, slid out, and heaved the tool chest into the bed. The unscrewed gun rack went under the seat. The half-empty pint (I'd had no drinks all afternoon) fit in the glove compartment.

Whistling, I tuned in to WKQK, the last old-time bluegrass radio station in Virginia. Vintage Jim & Jesse, Reno & Smiley, Flatt & Scruggs, and Mac Wiseman wailed those mountain ballads pinching your heart in a forceps of woe and misery. Were they that far off the beam?

The night of my parents' fatal auto smashup had brought a young deputy sheriff knocking on my aunt's door. A few years older than me, Cody was off at summer camp. Sending a uniform to give a notification of death, I later learned, is standard police procedure. I hopped out of bed and beat her to answering the door.

The deputy sheriff had slouched in a yellow slicker on the stoop. The torrent drowned out his words until my aunt in her robe invited him into the foyer. He smelled of motor oil and dripped rainwater from his yellow slicker to pool on her terrazzo tiles. Stammered words spelled out the tragic reason for his visit—

A cant of my head saw the upstairs window blacking out. Rennie came skipping downstairs and through the door. Wearing no scarf or hat left her pretty face distinguishable. She'd dressed in a parka over a short, plaid skirt and black hose. Only she wasn't alone.

Turning, she peered down. Two small children trailed her.

"For Christ's sake, can you believe this?" I muttered.

Rennie tugged down the stocking caps over their ears. Their breaths created miniature haloes in the frosty air. The longhaired, little girl pointed at the glitter of stars. With a nod, Rennie glanced up. She clutched their small hands in hers and led their parade to the streetside Prizm. They piled inside it. The tailpipe smoked and the taillights reddened. I saw her take off and turn at the next block.

She'd scoot back in a few minutes—"seven o'clock, no

earlier please". Did I take off like that fool of a fox on the run? Maybe. Cody's sly omission of Rennie's kids angered me, but I'd had a stomachful of moping. I cuffed off the radio, ranged out, and paced across Main Street to the apartment building's porch. Waiting, I fished out the cigarette I'd bummed off Cody and lit it.

I exhaled the smoke, looking up at Orion the Hunter poised in our town's night dome and marveling how a mother of two could stay so damn trim.

Chapter 4

My mind had grown flighty as the doves. I lounged in bed, back to chain-smoking filterless Camels, using a coffee can for an ashtray. The portrait of Jesus and His Sacred Heart on the wall gazed down chiding me. My plans, now all but foiled, had been to wait by a chopped cornfield, my eyes lifted skyward, set to bag my game limit of twelve doves.

What were my future prospects for romance? Last night at Leona's from the get-go had been a calamity. Talk had petered out over our steaks. Rennie frowned at my Black Label. (Or was it a frown?) I got a terse "thanks" whispered at her apartment door but no good night kiss. (Why not?) She gave me a subtle squeeze on the forearm. (Significance?) Then I tailed her to the babysitter. (Two kids?) That confirmation was still a bit much to swallow.

I grew fed up with my self-pity and threw on a pair of Levis jeans. The sweatshirt was ragged but clean. My hands mashed in the jeans pockets as I schlepped into the kitchenette. My orange cap and dove decoys sat by the paperbacks stacked on the countertop. Cody's hand-drawn map to the latest dove jackpot protruded from the camo vest pocket. My Fox 12-gauge stayed racked in the truck cab. I decided over a yawn to skip breakfast and hitched to the door.

Naturally the phone squawked. My glance out the window saw a distant combine chopping silage. I snatched up the handset. A dove terrorized by my neighbor Mr. Farok's tomcat exploded with screaming wings from the blue spruce. My hopes for the dove hunt rekindled.

"Johnson."

"Hello? Frank?" The lady's gasp stunned me. It was Rennie. "I'm at the gun shop. It's awful."

"Awful?"

"Cody…" She heaved in for a breath.

"Slow down. Please." The thumb callus I gnawed on hurt. "Okay, Cody. What about him?"

"I came in." I heard her sniff. "Cody had been shot. Sprawled in a pool of blood—"

"Blood? Christ. Sit tight. I'll be right there."

The handset clunked to the drainboard. I sprinted outside the doublewide and didn't think. The frosty grass was slick. I spanked the truck engine and slammed out of the mobile home park. The truck bucked over the blacktop, and my hands strangled the steering wheel. Gory red images seethed in me. Cody had been shot? Impossible. Murder had no place in Pelham. The gun shop lurched into the windshield and my gut wrenched—it was a bad scene.

Four deputy sheriff cruisers flashed their red-and-blue roof bar lights. My scan didn't spot Rennie. My braking halt was a skid. Rennie lashed out her legs from the Prizm. Her hair mussed despite the barrettes, she hurried over to me at the gun shop door.

"My stomach is tied in knots."

"Hang tough," was my reassuring cliché as we moved inside.

Sheriff Dmytryk and the uniforms focused downcast gazes to the floor. Murmurs came from set-face nods. Rennie squelched a cough and I held her hand. Red crime scene tape cordoned off ground zero, but I was bad with boundaries. The crouching Stonesiffer, our county coroner, rocked back on his haunches. I knew his platinum hair was a rug. Rising, he whistled between his teeth.

"A 12-gauge fired at point-blank makes sausage. Pity." A folksy twang flavored his speech.

I dug deep for the grit required to view my best friend

and cousin in death. The rusty odor from his corpse infused my nose, but I didn't pull my look. Coppery blood had oozed beyond the edge of the poncho liner covering Cody, but the Wolverines belonged to him. Few, if any, men I knew laced up a Size 13 boot.

"For the record, is he, sonny boy?" Stonesiffer kicked Cody's boot sole as if it bore a "Goodyear" imprint.

"Is he what?" I asked.

Stonesiffer tilted his ink pen. "I'm asking you if the deceased is Cody Chapman. Can you make a positive I.D.?"

"Obviously he is," I replied, giving Stonesiffer a drop-dead look.

Sheriff Dmytryk scribbled down notes. "I need an inventory ASAP to track any missing firearms. Include the serial numbers and calibers."

"That shouldn't be a problem," said Rennie.

"Did Cody work late last night?" asked Sheriff Dmytryk.

"I believe so, yes. He often stayed late," replied Rennie.

"He had a business to run," I said.

Sheriff Dmytryk didn't react to my sarcasm. "The cash register has been jimmied and robbed."

"We keep a small amount of money on hand to open in the morning," said Rennie.

"The killer emptied the till to stage a robbery," said Stonesiffer, his jaundiced eyes favoring me.

Sheriff Dmytryk also shifted his hooded gaze to me. "The killer sure had to know the layout."

Rennie refocused on the facts at hand. "When was Cody shot?"

"Body temperature and stage of rigor indicate, oh, one a.m. It certainly was no later than two," replied Stonesiffer.

The deputy sheriff armed with a digital camera caught Sheriff Dmytryk's glance. "Woodrow, snap me plenty of close-ups. Shoot from all angles. You others, scour this crime scene. I want you to bag and tag anything of evidentiary value."

"Cigarette butts?" asked the rookie deputy sheriff looking all of eighteen.

"As I just said, get everything."

They whirled into action. Rennie and I moved behind the red tape and out of their way. When the Fed Ex truck lumbered up, we went out to unload the shipment, including the boxes of new shotgun ammo. Too bad Rennie's clean, soapy fragrance and my busy hands weren't enough to divert me.

The jagged finality of Cody's loss was touching home. The timing was ripe to ignite another episode of my depression. Was I up to weather it? My indecisiveness turned to fear. I'd battled depression after booting out Marty and even dubbed it "The Jet Jackal". What a dark time. I never shaved or showered after my day job went by the boards. I vegetated in front of the idiot box. Life was 110% shit, and only Cody gave a damn. Now that he was gone, who'd throw me a lifeline?

"Hey, Frank." Sheriff Dmytryk was jabbing his ink pen at me. "Account for your whereabouts last night."

"Huh?" As I looked up, my mind hit static.

Stonesiffer acted haughty. "The sheriff wants your alibi."

"Why? Am I a suspect?" I asked.

"You might be," said Sheriff Dmytryk.

Rennie threw me a lifeline. "Frank was with me last night."

I looked at her.

"At one in the morning?" said Sheriff Dmytryk.

"He stayed the night. Is that against the law?" asked Rennie.

Not quite repressing a leer, Sheriff Dmytryk shrugged. "I suppose not among consenting adults. Okay, let's transport the gunshot victim."

Stonesiffer after backing up his stationwagon unlatched the tailgate and offloaded a gurney to wheel it between the bystanders. I bumped Stonesiffer aside to kneel and lift Cody from the shop floor to place on the gurney. Three hundred fifty pounds was a lot of freight.

"Play it smart, Frank," said Erskine, the one deputy sheriff I actually liked. "I don't blame you for being PO'd. Cody was a stand-up guy, but it'd be expedient to reel in your horns."

"Dmytryk can bite my ass."

"My point is a little tact greases the skids," said Erskine.

"Let's do it," I said.

We guided the loaded gurney back to the stationwagon, Erskine and me on each end. As we put in our human cargo under the poncho liner, a couple rubberneckers on the highway tapped their brakes. I wanted to flip them off but I didn't. Could be Erskine's advice had started to sink in.

Stonesiffer's eyes singled out my truck. "Don't you carry a 12-gauge, sonny boy?"

To deny it was lame—the whole town knew I did. "A Fox is on a sling."

"You'll voluntarily consent to a lab analysis. Otherwise I'll have to wake up the cranky judge to obtain a warrant," said Sheriff Dmytryk.

"That won't be necessary," I said.

I removed my Fox shotgun from behind the truck cab seat and thrust its gunstock at Sheriff Dmytryk. He took it and gave its chamber a careful sniff. "No cordite smell and probably no residue dirties the bore either."

"Sonny boy is a squeaky clean killer," said Stonesiffer.

"I can't imagine Frank's murder motive," said Rennie.

"As the next-of-kin, he inherits the gun shop worth something given today's property values," said Stonesiffer.

"All right, that's enough. You're finished here," I said. "You said this is now my place, so beat it."

"You don't order around the law." Stonesiffer and I traded toxic gapes.

"Let's head back to the station. We've got a homicide investigation to run," said Sheriff Dmytryk.

"Just stay reachable, sonny boy," said Stonesiffer.

"You know where I live," I said.

"He's right, Frank. I want you nearby," said Sheriff Dmytryk.

Hearing his gruff tone, I caught the whiff of a Miranda recitation on the breeze, and I nodded once. "You know where I live."

The deputy sheriff cruisers, their red-and-blue roof bar

lights splitting the morning gloom, mounted a crawl to Pelham. Stonesiffer's bald stare from the tail-end car hit me. How long was it before they tagged me with Cody's murder?

Today was Friday. The weekend loomed and I realized a ton of shit could hit the fan. The autumn wind flapping the old paper targets on the firing range behind the shop sent a shiver through me.

My apprehension subsided as I turned analytical. Was Cody's murder a thrill kill? Most likely not, I reasoned. Too up close and personal. Had Cody made any enemies? No especially disgruntled customers came to mind. Robbery, even for chump change, was a possibility. Meth fiends craving a score ripped off Nikes to sell. I envisioned the script to the robbery.

The stick-up punk in an unbuttoned trench coat had swaggered into the shop. Maybe he was a little beetle rubbed raw because he thought the world owed him a living. Whatever, but he demanded the cash drawer's contents.

Cody would've chuckled. "Beat it before I stomp your ass."

The stick-up punk's sawed-off shotgun levered up from under the trench coat. One blast had decked Cody. The morning sun scudded under a bank of leaden clouds as I replayed the thud of him striking the floor. Smelling a whiff of Rennie's soap fragrance soothed me. She reached and took my hand as a shriek rolled over the countryside.

Stonesiffer cracking the town limits had goosed his siren. The trailing deputy sheriffs chimed in like a medley of off-key bagpipes. Cody in death was a free man and a cynical part of me envied him. Given enough time, I'd age into a bitter, old fart while Pelham would link youth and vigor to Cody's name.

"Frank, you look cold." Rennie hooked her arm in mine. I liked it. "Have you had breakfast?"

"I'm not hungry," I replied.

"Me neither," said Rennie. "But we living souls still have to eat."

Chapter 5

I followed Rennie across the highway to McDavid's, a fatty food shack built in the configuration of a big computer monitor. An elderly Hispanic in a black apron with squeegees and a pail to clean the windows got the door. Rennie smiled our thanks. The smell of Pine-Sol invested the damp-floor lobby.

The counter guy, a wiry, young black man in a blue smock, jotted down our orders. Chet Peyton had lent me a hand at gunsmithing duties, and we became friends despite our age and pigmentation differences. His older brother Gerald and I also hung out, and I liked all the down-home Peytons.

"Sheriff Dmytryk came over for a cup of coffee and gave me the skinny. Sorry about Cody. That's tough." Chet tapped his pencil eraser on the order pad. "I can help you."

"Go on." I peeled back the tab to my coffee cup's plastic lid.

"Last night I saw a van cut into the parking lot over there."

I sipped. The coffee had a corrosive bite.

"Its mufflers rumbled, you know, like he ran glass packs. They popped off shotguns and played loud stoner music." Chet chomped down on a hot fry. A timer buzzed and the fish patties swimming in the hot grease were edible.

Rennie gathering napkins and plastic utensils leaned near. "Frank, is everything okay?"

"We're just catching up. Give me a second."

Rennie, nodding, left to claim a table.

"Then the same van pulled in here. I was alone and

hightailed to the backroom and found a meat cleaver." Chet jiggling the fish patties tray dropped one into the hot grease. He ignored the fish patty, and I knew his manager would give him shit later.

"What then?" I asked.

"They'd jetted off by the time I hustled back up front."

"I gave a white Chevy van a jumpstart. Its left-side headlight is busted, and a guy wearing a Rebby Cap drives it."

Chet nodded. "That's got to be mine."

"Why didn't you tell Sheriff Dmytryk this?"

"I'm not doing his work for him." Chet pantomimed a phone with his fingers. "If you need me, you've got my number." I regarded the bantamweight grinning at me. "You better deal in Gerald, too. He's always up."

Chet's idea jolted a chill through me. Gerald, a human forklift, was the last kick-ass assistance I wanted. But then I felt the riptide to Cody's murder dragging me under.

"Hang loose. This is on the bubble and something will break soon," I said.

"Solid. Are you dating the Van Dotson girl now?"

"Shit Chet, she found Cody's dead body and called me. That's all."

"Solid. You call me. I already talked to Gerald and he's amped."

"Gerald stays amped."

Rennie sat at a window table. We picked at our unappetizing stack of hotcakes, butter, and syrup. My mouth opened to thank her for providing my alibi, but I felt too embarrassed. We hadn't even kissed.

"Killing a man for less than twenty-five dollars stuns me," said Rennie.

"The cash drawer theft is a red herring," I said.

"Do you actually think so?"

"I do. Somebody wanted Cody dead," I said.

"Any idea who did it?"

"No real suspects yet," I replied, pushing aside my food tray.

"Or why they did it?"

"Motive is a tougher nut," I replied.

Rennie fished her car keys from her purse. "Do you mind driving? I'm sure my babysitter has heard, and she's bouncing off the walls."

My eyebrow arched at Rennie. "Babysitter, you say?" Rennie zipping up her parka just nodded, and I played it cool. After a morning like this, facing two energetic kids couldn't daunt me. "Just steer me the right way," I told her.

Chapter 6

I hit it off with Buddy and Gin who, like their mother, were also brunettes. When Rennie introduced me as her "new friend" with a laconic smile, I liked how it played. Eyes bird-bright, they appraised me, and Buddy extended his sticky, waifish hand.

"Put it there, partner."

I saluted him with our handshake.

Gin giggled at us.

"Did you do any fun activities this morning?" asked Rennie whose morning had been anything but that.

I edged Rennie's Prizm from the babysitter's driveway. School kids at the bus stop waved as we accelerated off, making for Pelham.

"We used Play-Doh, and I made a dinosaur," said Gin.

"I made a space shuffle until Frankie Shreeve sat on it. What a dork," said Buddy.

"Space shuttle," corrected Rennie.

"*Frankie is a dork*," said Gin. "*Frankie is a dork, Frankie is a dork.*"

Rennie twisted around in her seat as if she meant business. "Remember we use good manners around guests."

"Yes ma'am," was their refrain.

She looked at me. "They're wound up from eating too much C-A-N-D-Y-C-O-R-N this morning."

"What does that word spell?" asked Buddy.

Rennie and I just laughed.

We passed day laborers in hoodie sweatshirts milling in a church yard hoping to catch a job. I parked and Rennie let us into a plain but tidy apartment. The faint scent was Pine Sol. Sunlight slanted through the spotless windows to highlight the linoleum. It along with her stove, refrigerator, sink, and countertops were avocado green, a décor plague surviving the 1970s. But her rooms, five all counted, had a coziness the doublewide lacked.

The rest of the day crawled by, and we didn't mention Cody's murder around her kids. Rennie and I took a stab at playing Scrabble. She asked if I'd enjoyed MP work, and I replied I'd liked it okay enough. Then she asked if I missed doing it. I shrugged in reply and asked her why she'd moved to Pelham, of all places.

After her mother had the fatal heart attack, her father Randall forwarded the suggestion, and she knew he wanted to help with the babysitting chores. She wondered if I liked living in Pelham, and I confessed it was my hometown. She turned to look, assuring we were alone in the room.

"You were a cop, Frank. Who'd want to murder Cody?"

"I don't have a good read. All I know is this can't go unsolved for long."

Rennie heard my forceful tone, and her curly lashes lifted. "But isn't this strictly a sheriff matter?"

Not with me pinned on the his radar, I thought but I shrugged.

We fussed at our nuked frozen pizza dinner before she ran me over to McDavid's. As I drove my truck back, Rennie's fib on my alibi came up. I wondered if my ex Marty would lie for me. Fat chance. Did Rennie like me enough to spend the night? I was clueless. Then I debated how long before Sheriff Dmytryk cracked my alibi (Had any witness last night seen me leave Rennie's apartment, or pull up at the doublewide?) and collar me.

                                                    ✎

After Buddy and Gin trooped off to bed, Rennie and I sat

opposite each other at her kitchen table. A cop siren yawping along the murky edge of town jarred me. Not noticing, a pensive Rennie hooked an errant hair strand behind her ear pierced by a sapphire stud.

"Sheriff Dmytryk's murder motive for you is flimsy," she said.

"Don't worry, he'll make it stand up in court. Thanks for covering my time last night."

Pinkish rouge darkened her cheeks. "So now we're even. But I can't work in that mess on Monday. I'll go wipe down the display cases and scrub behind the cash register. The floor could stand a stiff brush, too."

"No, I'll bring in a cleaning crew over the weekend. You did more than run the cash register, but this isn't in your job description."

"Is the gun shop yours now?"

Rennie's innocent query disturbed me. The gun shop, now my new responsibility, daunted me as too complicated to run.

"It appears that way. Cody's lawyer—his name, if I recall it, is Gatlin—will work on all the legal angles."

"Robert Gatlin?"

"That sounds right. Do you know him?"

"I know *of* him," replied Rennie. "He has a practice set up in Middleburg, and I've seen him on *Court TV*. The commentators liken him to a young F. Lee Bailey."

My head shook. Middleburg is the bucolic playground the rich and powerful conspire to keep pristine and aristocratic for their pleasure. "Cody liked to hang with the fat cats."

"Gatlin is a self-made multi-millionaire who defends the little guy. He does it pro bono and just accepts cases that interest him."

"No kidding. Maybe Gatlin has some integrity."

"I'd say so. Now Mr. Stonesiffer will release Cody's body post-autopsy. When will you make funeral arrangements?"

"Forward thinking stumps me right now."

"Can your other family handle it?"

"I'm afraid not. No close family is left. Cody's mom died

from breast cancer. Earlier my parents died in an auto smashup."

"Goodness. What happened?"

"An inebriated CPO humping back to Norfolk ran a red light and T-boned them."

"I'm so sorry."

"Thanks, but don't be. It was ages ago."

"How old were you?"

"Just turned seven." I regretted my sharp tone.

Rennie's sad eyes retreated to the dark window. "Then should I call Fincham's?"

"That'd be super. Try to get a maple casket. Cody would like that." Reminded of Cody's claim made at Leona's, I ran a visual sweep, but no suitcases or bags sat in her kitchen or hallway. "It's not my business, but have you packed?"

"Packed?" Rennie's smile was quizzical. "Why on earth would I?"

"You're moving, right?"

She resurrected the Yellow Pages from a cabinet drawer. "Moving where, Frank? What are you talking about?"

"You're off to college. Cody sprang the big news on me."

"Oh that." Rennie flipped the directory pages. "Cody and I concocted that rumor to discourage the guys from hitting on me."

"It made me think twice. Why didn't you use the line on me?"

"I didn't want to." She smiled for me. "Cody was okay for a boss. What sort of a person was he?"

"Just a regular guy, sometimes too stubborn for his own good."

"Did you trust him?"

"Absolutely. Look, we squabbled over his not paying me for overtime. He was tight-fisted, too." Jay Leno's monologue on the TV behind us elicited a tepid applause. I thought his predecessor was wittier. "Are you divorced?"

This time Rennie's tone sounded sharp. "Yes I am. Is that a problem?"

"Not at all." I thought but didn't add, "Since I'm in the same boat." We were establishing boundaries, our divorces declared off-limits for discussion.

"I'll call Fincham's in the morning."

"Right and I better shove off." It sounded as if I was rushed when that was the furthest from my mind. "Can I call you later?"

"Sure. Do. I'd like that." Rennie gave me a subtle squeeze on the forearm, and this time her simple gesture befitted the occasion.

I shivered my way outside her apartment building to my truck. The dark roads I took home to the doublewide conjured up Rebby Cap piloting the white Chevy van. I suspected a sawed-off shotgun rode strapped under the van's dashboard.

Was Rebby Cap a deranged killer? Did he gun down Cody? If so, why? I also knew Stonesiffer stroked a hard-on to bench me on death row. No telling what bullshit evidence he'd counterfeit in his morgue. I felt as if I should do something to help myself, but I didn't know what that something was.

Headlights speared their high beams in my rearview mirror. The air horn bleated, and I slacked off the gas, and a tractor-trailer roared by me. It towed a bevy of corn-fed hogs to make bacon at the packinghouse. Their caustic shit stench made me cough. My blackening mood heaped pity on them. They rode to their doom encrusted in their cold shit on a still colder night, and I couldn't imagine a grimmer fate.

Chapter 7

Early Saturday morning, I put away my dove hunting stuff to try again next season and worked the phone. Our exchanges ended on the same crabby note, and I had no takers. Understandable since I couldn't stomach scrubbing away Cody's gore either. My egg lady hit on an idea.

"I know, hit up Leona's nephew. He's saving to go on a tour of the Holy Land, and the working fool's name is Lenny Curtis."

"Thanks for the tip." I pecked in the numbers she gave me. "Lenny? This is Frank Johnson."

"To what does Lenny owe this honor?"

Lenny referring to himself in third person left me with doubts, but I presented my quandary.

"Maybe you've already heard, but last night Cody was killed at the shop. It was senseless. I plan to reopen because that's how Cody would want it. A minor snafu, however, might delay me."

"You need a custodian, Frank."

"You must be a psychic. A C-note is in it for him."

"Lenny hears two. Three rings even truer."

"Sorry Lenny, but I'm not rich. One C-note is my best offer. Take it or leave it."

"You're a mule trader, but Lenny hears a higher voice whispering in his ear. Lenny agrees to your terms."

"Excellent. It shouldn't take long."

Ten o'clock was good for us. I raced through a tub of

laundry between the annual battery changes in my smoke detectors. I hoisted up my windows to invite in a ventilating breeze. Not until my clean socks were paired and stuffed in their drawer did I take a break. If I played my cards right, I'd entertain an overnight guest at Castle Johnson.

I savored that hope until Mr. Farok's tomcat squalled outside my door. I went out and set down a saucer of skim milk. The tomcat was a muscled, brindled, and scarred terror that grew on you. I flumped back down on the sofa to read until a new racket returned me to the cinderblock porch.

Next door Mr. Farok, balanced atop an extension ladder, shot a leaf blower through his gutters to hose out the stray leaves. That was odd. Few trees grew here on the lip to the old limestone quarry. We'd no dirt. Even reviled Johnson grass put down no roots. Our alkaline yards chocked with rocks behind white paling fences resembled a lunarscape. I walked over to Mr. Farok's doublewide and held the ladder steady for him. He nodded down his thanks. His leaf blower quit wailing and Mr. Farok scuttled down.

"When are you taking back your tomcat?" I asked him.

"That turd factory? Ha! Don't say I never gave you anything, Johnson."

"You're all heart. Is your wife still AWOL?"

"I haven't heard a peep from Lois in over a month." Mr. Farok scuttled up his extension ladder again and adjusted an awning. "You can keep her along with the turd factory."

"You've exiled everybody," I said.

"So I have. Sorry for your loss." Mr. Farok clattered back down the extension ladder. "Cody was a decent sort."

But was he for real? "Thanks," I said. "Do you need another lift to the periodontist?"

"Thanks Frank, but I've nixed getting any further gum grafts. Life is too short."

My clothes dryer honked and with a wave I returned inside. I piled my final bundle of laundry into the basket. Clean sheets stretched over my mattress. I was lugging out the bags of rubbish when the ringing phone vied for my attention. Sheriff Dmytryk was tenacious.

"Hi, Frank." Rennie's breathy salutation surprised me. "You didn't call. Are you busy?"

I exhaled, glad not to hear more bad news. "Right and I lost track of time."

"Fincham's called me back. They're ready to move ahead."

"Where does that put us?" I felt a little self-conscious allowing Rennie to arrange Cody's funeral. Still, if she was willing, it spared me the hassle of dealing with the irascible Fincham.

"Okay first, I put it on my charge card."

"I'll pay you back," I said.

"This is what we discussed. Cody's viewing is on Monday. His service and burial are the following day." Rennie hesitated. "We should get together and talk some more."

"Does four o'clock suit you?" I asked.

"See you then."

As we hung up, I spotted out the window a cruiser skulking along my cul-de-sac. A police presence wasn't unusual here, but this time Sheriff Dmytryk gloated. I knew. Badge-heavy town sheriffs relished flexing their authority. I receded into the doublewide as he cut in to park on this side of Mr. Farok's yard.

I tracked Sheriff Dmytryk in his low, white snap-brim hat maneuvering through my rock lawn to the doublewide and scuffing up the cinderblock porch steps. His Masonic ring tapped on the door glass. Trying to figure why he'd driven out, I let an edgy moment drag by, and then another. His second rap was crisper.

"Johnson, I know you're home. Don't make me come in there."

Had he come armed with a warrant? But he'd delegate any dirty work like effecting an arrest to a diligent flunky. Then Mr. Farok, no pal to cops, yelled over.

"You're too late. Frank heard you coming and took off. That boy is too smart for you."

"Bullshit. His door is open and I see his truck. Johnson,

answer me. I'm losing my patience."

I yawned, poked out front, and my befuddled look regarded him. "Sorry Sheriff, I was catching a nap, but the door is unlocked."

Sheriff Dmytryk stepped inside from the sunlight.

"Have you taken Cody's killer into custody?" I asked.

After removing his hat, Sheriff Dmytryk used his hand to smooth down his hair. "Our investigation is barely off the ground."

"Has Cody been post-mortemed?" I asked.

"Why do you ask that?"

"Because I'm Cody's closest family," I replied.

Then Sheriff Dmytryk surprised me. He tugged at his basket-weave holster and dropped his antagonistic demeanor. "Frank, I came to tell you something. This is off the record, and I'll deny saying it. Hire an experienced trial attorney before this shit storm flattens you."

"Why the advice?" I asked.

"I knew your dad. Harmon and I laid a lot of track together before your time. It's terrible what happened to them."

"Did you know the deputy sheriff who told us the bad news?" I asked.

"He quit long before my watch. The drunk skated and that was wrong." Sheriff Dmytryk gazed out at his parked cruiser. "That was so wrong…"

The presiding judge had tossed out the drunk's vehicular homicide charge on an arcane technicality even now I didn't quite grasp. My parents seemed like obscure figures. Aloof, curt, and humorless, my dad hadn't left much of an impression on me.

Harmon worked long hours as a local plumber, something tangible he could bend and control. By contrast, my mom was an outgoing, affable lady fond of wearing yellow ribbons and bowling in her weekly league. Old photos showed I favored my dad's looks, but I attributed my curiosity to my mom's inquisitive bent. She always asked questions, lots of questions.

"Don't bank on the drunk's dumb luck for your day in

court. Get a lawyer ASAP," Sheriff Dmytryk was telling me.

"You sound as if you have somebody in mind," I said.

"Well." Sheriff Dmytryk rubbed the wedding band strangling his knuckle. "Bob Gatlin up in Middleburg, I hear, is a heavy hitter."

"I've heard the same. Gatlin is Cody's lawyer."

"Then there's your in. Did your inventory flag any stolen guns?" Dmytryk had resumed the clipped speech of the town sheriff, ending his counseling session.

"We're still pulling it together," I said.

"Call me when you're finished. I'd be surprised if a few handguns didn't disappear," said Sheriff Dmytryk before he ambled back to his cruiser.

My suspicions fixed on Cody's autopsy as Sheriff Dmytryk scorched a tire burn on the cul-de-sac. Stonesiffer planned to twist my Fox 12-gauge's ballistics to nail me, and then the shit storm would blow at full gale. He'd hassle Rennie over lying to alibi me. Despite his advice, I felt Sheriff Dmytryk's crosshairs centered on me, and Gatlin just might bulletproof my ass. The lit desk lamp showed my $4.20 checkbook balance left me solvent enough to spring for a long distance call.

A modulated lady's voice picked up. "Hello, Gatlin Law Office."

"This is Frank Johnson. Mr. Gatlin handles my late cousin Cody Chapman's estate and I'm the executor."

"This is his answering service and Mr. Gatlin is away."

"He's away?" My heart nosedived. "When is he expected back?"

"I'm not sure. He's in Hong Kong at a symposium on the preservation of the Nepal Snow Leopard."

"Listen, my cousin was murdered last night. The police are tossing me hard questions. I need legal advice like yesterday. Follow me?"

"That's scary. Let's try this approach, Mr. Johnson. I'll relay your message, and Mr. Gatlin will get back to you."

My firm, deliberate voice gave her the phone numbers where to reach me. "Stress to Mr. Gatlin my urgency."

"I'll pass on your message."

"Look, I can't afford another long distance call."

"Your message will be relayed. Good day, Mr. Johnson."

Gatlin lobbied for the preservation of the Nepal Snow Leopard? I thought, setting down my phone receiver. *How about the preservation of Frank Johnson?*

Getting blown off ticked me. But Rennie had said Gatlin took cases pro bono, and I might swing an affordable deal so I played along. Restless, I couldn't wait around for Gatlin's call. Stuff needed repairs. The doublewide's sheet metal skirt had buckled loose. I scared up a claw hammer and a fistful of nails and ventured out. The intact metal skirt blocked gusts from blowing under the doublewide and making my oil furnace burn. I pounded more on my thumb than the nails and lost interest.

On my way inside, I picked up a .69 caliber Yankee Minié ball lying in the rubble and dropped it in a flowerpot with its cousins I'd collected. We lived on an old battlefield. Mr. Farok came over and grabbed me. The old lady down our cul-de-sac had a flat tire. I changed it and refused her token payment. Washing up at the sink, I saw I'd less than three minutes to go let in Lenny Curtis. I hoped he wasn't punctual.

Chapter 8

I chuffed up to the gun shop where Lenny waited in his Datsun. He pinched his eyes shut and raised his hands as if imploring an angelic uplift. So, I'd let in Lenny with his cleaning stuff, putter around, and lock up after he finished. No, first I'd inspect Lenny's scrub job, and we'd disappoint all the future rubberneckers.

Lenny Curtis popped open his eyes. The misshapen young giant wearing a black turtleneck sweater climbed out, and I nodded at him to forgo his bone-crunching handshake.

"Frank, Lenny expresses his condolences."

"Thanks, I appreciate it," I said.

I undid the door and toggled on the fluorescents. Sheriff Dmytryk hadn't assigned a deputy sheriff to babysit the crime scene, or else his guard dog had hit on a diversion.

"Just duck under the red tape," I said.

Lenny appraised Cody's death spot purpling the floor by the cash register. "This will take at least an hour."

I fingered the jagged edge to the cash register's drawer. The tool marks indicated a screwdriver or switchblade had jimmied it. I opened the drawer and not one red cent lay in its coin bins. The jangling phone back in Cody's office interrupted us.

"Grab that, Frank, and Lenny will jump on this mess."

"Take your time and do a good job." Cheesed at the interruption, I went in Cody's office and barked into the phone receiver.

"Is this Mr. Johnson? Frank Johnson?"

The man's urbane timbre ruffled me a little. "Speaking," I replied.

"Robert Gatlin returning your call."

"Thanks for getting back to me. It's just Frank, too."

"Certainly, Frank."

"Have you saved the snow leopards yet?"

"Sarcasm is counterproductive, Frank."

"No, I'm asking if you can help me now."

"Talk to me."

"You've heard the bad news?"

"Regarding Mr. Chapman, I did, yes. It was tragic. Such a senseless act defies logic."

"Excuse my curiosity, but how did Cody find you?" I asked.

"I owed a mutual friend a favor, and Mr. Chapman wanted to write his will. So, we met twice at my office. That's all I can say on that. Now, how can I assist you?"

"Sheriff Dmytryk has all but given me the Miranda spiel for Cody's killer."

"Sure, you're the easiest mark."

I warmed up to Gatlin's direct tact. "I'm not your client but..."

"You're the executor of Mr. Chapman's will, and I'll handle its legal aspects, and that qualifies you as my client."

"Okay so we're set, but I'm floundering here."

"I can see that. Regrettably I won't be back in the States until Monday, but my counsel is simple enough: don't get arrested."

"How do I pull that off? Turn rabbit and run?"

"It's the only way, Frank. You're facing a big-time frame job. Any interrogation with the cops is a no-no unless your rabbi is present. If I'm not there, you're sunk. They'll fabricate an elaborate false case and spin the media. Even I can't pull you from that quagmire. Are we clear?"

"I hear you." His bluntness sobered me. "How do I stay in orbit?"

"Why, utilize your native wits. You can do it," replied

Gatlin.

"Sure, utilize my native wits. Then I'll see you first thing on Monday a.m." My thoughts reeled as we disconnected. Who had enough native wits to evade a noose already snug around their neck?

Lenny's tin pail clattered over the floor, and I recoiled at the tingly fumes to his Clorox bleach. A scratching brush accompanied Lenny's bassy rendition of an old hymn and I grinned. Having some time to idle away, I felt my old nose problem flare up.

I toed away the flatiron Cody used as a doorstop and nudged shut his office door. The singing Lenny paid me no mind. I did a 360. Cody's small office featured a low drop ceiling and a rectangular window above a row of filing cabinets. A green patio carpet lined the rat slab floor while an executive chair and a walnut desk rounded out the furnishings. Through a doorway was a second larger room with a single brass bed, tarnished floor lamps, and a chest of drawers. I gave Cody's bachelor digs a quick toss in vain and returned to his outer office.

A thought struck me as peculiar. Wouldn't the 350-pound horse Cody prefer more stable space? Not if he had a big secret to hide. I moved the folded edition of *The Pelham-Democrat* from the chair's seat and flumped down. The filing cabinets where Cody archived newspaper and magazine clippings were a low priority. His scheme had been to use his research to author a bestselling outdoor adventure series. That facet of Cody—always the big dreamer—I knew all too well. Squeaking back in the chair, I rubbed my gritty eyes before they landed on the fake grass carpet.

Tired, I'd been up and down the previous night. I'd racked my brain, charging Cody's homicide from every conceivable angle. We criminal investigators are schooled in the trinity of means, opportunity, and motive, so I tackled the last one, motive. Why had the killer shot Cody? To rob him? The cash register, Rennie had said, held fewer than twenty-five bucks. Was the murder a case of bad blood? No, Cody hadn't made enemies like by snaking another man's wife.

We were both Pelham natives so I scratched any clandestine past. Extorting money from Cody was as preposterous as the likelihood of suicide. The only one benefiting from his death was me, and I shunned the onus to operate a gun shop. A reason to explain his murder had to hide somewhere.

My riffling through the desk drawers turned up nothing of consequence. I found Cody's emergency cashbox and scooped up the last five banknotes. Then I reared back again, lowered my eyelids, and my thoughts drifted till I snared a past conversation. Cody at Bud's Creek Raceway in Maryland had revealed a secret.

"It's all in my office floor, Frank," he'd told me, slurring his words.

"What's all there?" I asked.

"Some bling. Worth thousands."

"Bling. Okay, so why tell me?"

"I want you to have it. It's not in my will. Even my lawyer Bob Gatlin has no idea. You'll also inherit the gun shop. Don't you wish I'd hurry up and die?"

"Sounds like the Grey Goose talking," I'd said, dismissing our exchange until now.

Again my eyes dipped to the floor. Sighing, I arose and dragged Cody's desk to the wall. My flip of the unglued fake grass carpet bared the concrete underneath. Sure enough, pavement saw marks cut in the rat slab outlined a square section, and it was detachable. I saw a cigar box in the carved out niche. The box's lifted top emitted a cherry scent, Cody's tobacco brand.

The baggie in the cigar box held an extravagant lady's pendant. It baffled me. Cody hadn't been one whit sentimental. Why did he go to such elaborate extents to conceal this? Had he lavished upscale gifts on his paramour? But I was sure he would've bragged to me if he had.

I undid the twist tie and fingered the pendant before my caution not to destroy any latent prints. The pendant had a valuable sheen. Gold (was it real?) held a starburst daisy of freshwater pearls with a pea-sized diamond (was it a bauble or cubic zirconia?) in the center. No visible initials or marks imprinted the underside. Before I puzzled over it any further, I heard a shout ring out.

"Hey Frank, Lenny has completed his task."

"Be right with you, Lenny."

I pocketed the pendant, restored the cigar box, and smoothed down the fake grass carpet. Cody's desk went back before I opened the door and headed out to Lenny.

"How did you get up the dried bloodstain?" I asked him.

"Trade secret. If you find more, just call Lenny."

I peeled out the five Andy Jacksons from Cody's cash box to grease Lenny's palm. "One hundred was our negotiated agreement."

"May the Lord bless you, Frank."

"Your effort is also appreciated." The outdoors had a nippier bite to it as I keyed the lock shut.

"Lenny enacts all his brothers good deeds," he said, folding into his Datsun.

Especially if the price is right, I thought.

The glittery "PTL" fish decals on Lenny's vanishing bumper left me musing. I hoped he reached the Holy Land, and it was what he anticipated, but I had my troubling qualms.

Chapter 9

I sat in my truck, thinking. That rusty corpse stench had clotted in my nostrils where nothing could erase it. Murder fouled the air, and some creep had killed Cody. I inhaled, bit my lip, and let out my breath. Raw grief blistered my insides.

My Beretta's firing pin had snapped but going unarmed with a demented shotgun killer on the rampage was dimwit logic. I tromped back into the shop and by the photo gallery of hunters and their bagged trophies next hauled to the taxidermist, by now rich as Trump.

I felt like a kid in a candy store. Light bathed the handgun counter displays under the tempered plate glass. The dinky .22s and .25s designed to tote in ladies' handbags didn't sway me. The .32s and .38s, old standbys, felt undersized. This time the Luger didn't hold the same allure. The .44 and .45 Magnums amounted to field artillery. My sight affixed on the Browning 9 mil made in the USA. Smiling, I undid the rear panel, and my fingers groped the 9 mil's polymer grips.

I aimed the 32 ounces in a classic stance, squinted down its target sight, and dry fired—the 9 mil unloaded with no bullets—in six clicks. Contented, I nodded. Cody and I had disagreed. He was a purist babying his belt guns from the second they came into his possession. Preserving their looks was vital—he chased a potential sale. But I adopted a pragmatic view. Firing a hand weapon, dry or live, honed a shooter's reflexes. What's more, I felt no guilt over dry firing his handgun now.

The 9 mil's magazine holding 13 cartridges popped out,

and I couldn't strap a better handgun on the mean streets. My rummaging through the shelves for high-velocity ammunition found a hand-lettered poster, "Cody's Ten Commandments for Shooting Safety".

Commandment #1 caught my eye: "VERIFY THY TARGET PRIOR TO SQUEEZING THY TRIGGER." A shadow skulked across my mind's eye, and I knew what evil boiled in its heart. Rebby Cap armed for bear in the white Chevy van was now my foe and target. I needed protection, but I sensed my shooter dynamics were out of synch.

My tramp behind the gun shop ended at the firing range. Cody had bulldozed up the dirt berms to serve as backstops. Pewter-gray clouds portended snow, and the wind in my face had a brittle snap. Weather conditions seesawed from warm to cold and back, typical for October in Virginia. A far-off siren yawped, tensing me. It abated. I went on a short leash our local law could yank in when they pleased.

My fingers, jittery to play death's agent, slid out the cartridges from the Styrofoam tray to fill the magazine. I tapped its butt, seating the load, and fitted in the magazine. I detested wearing earplugs. The paper target went up. I returned to take my mark, chambered a round, and pivoted in a half-turn.

It's Fort Riley all over again, Johnson.

My two-handed Weaver stance held the 9 mil and I took my aim. I breathed in and my conditioned reflexes activated. I drew a bead on the paper target, and my finger mashed the trigger. My motions were fluid enough, but my round hit off-kilter. I'd only dinged the paper target's outer circle.

All my rounds punched a wobbly pattern high and right. My old bugaboo, flinching to soften the handgun's kick, diluted my accuracy. I banged off that box without hitting the bull's eye. I didn't spot any nosy deputy sheriffs lurking on my trip back to the shop for more ammo.

I refined my shooting technique, slowing my moves despite the autumn cold gnawing at me. This was a do or die business. I busted off the next ammo, and my slugs started to nip the paper target's inner circles. As I reloaded the magazine, a thread of memory unraveled back to the fateful afternoon I'd confronted Marty.

"Where did you two hook up?" I asked.

Marty latched her suitcase shut. Her glance out the window directed mine to see her blue-and-white checkered taxi whisk up. "What the hell difference does it make?"

"I guess my ego wants to know," I replied.

"We met in a chat room. There. Do you feel better?" Marty dragged her suitcase off our former bed. The cabbie bleated his horn.

"But why?"

"My taxi is waiting."

"You owe me the decency of an explanation, damn it."

"Christ, do I have to spell it out? I'm bored. And I see us being called 'trailer trash' for the rest of our lives. It's all too much."

"It takes money to move up."

"No, Frank. It takes ambition, and I know you're perfectly content to rot right here. But I want bigger, and better."

My head shook. "I had plans for us."

"Yeah, I bet."

"You could've gone back to work."

"Guess I will now. I gotta go. My taxi is waiting."

The cabbie leaned on his horn, and the sandy-haired Marty rolling her suitcase on its coasters breezed by me. She slammed out of the doublewide. Later that first night alone in bed, I replayed the march cadence count of the soldier serving away from his wife at home. We'd used it at Fort Riley: *"Ain't no use in goin' home,/Jody's got your girl and gone..."*

Now I finished reloading the 9 mil, drilled the paper target dead center, and pumped my celebratory fist in the air. My hand calluses throbbed, my wrists burned, and my ears bled, but I felt "perfectly content", to borrow from Marty. I'd read somewhere gunslingers in the Old West went deaf before age forty from plying their noisy trade, but my gunfire roared in my ears. From a crouch, I rehearsed my snap draw. Feeling more confident, I collected the spent brass around my feet.

I returned to Cody's office and spotting his desk phone stimulated an idea.

Chapter 10

Dreema Atkins had skipped one grade ahead of me and, to her credit, had ejected from Pelham. She was a striking brunette with hazel eyes, and I'd judge an inch taller than Rennie. A criminal justice major, Dreema had graduated with top honors from Virginia Tech. By the next autumn after a disastrous summer job as a dog groomer, she accepted a lab technician job with the Virginia Department of Forensic Science down in Richmond.

We'd kept in touch. I wasn't clear on why. The term best characterizing our relationship was "platonic" since I'd never even asked Dreema out to dinner and a movie. Perhaps her drive and ambition left me a bit awed and hesitant. Truth was, I couldn't imagine not picking up the phone and chatting with her. Costs be screwed, I now placed a call to Dreema's apartment and brought her up to speed.

"Wow, Cody shot dead...what a bring-down...how are you handling it, Frank?"

"It's still sinking in," I replied.

"That's rough. Where are you working now?"

"I'm mowing bush at the Mormon farm on Mosby River."

"That would be like me still being a dog groomer, Frank. You need a career path. Might I make a suggestion? My lab partner has a kid brother who works as a part-time private detective. He tells her it's not a job but an adventure."

"Uh-huh."

"Weren't you an Army MP?"

"Uh-huh."

"That work experience qualifies you for a license."

"Uh-huh."

"You've even got the P.I.'s speech down pat."

"Too bad my analog brain can't untangle clues to solve puzzles."

"Don't sell yourself short, Frank. You're nosy as a goat and can pry around to nab Cody's murderer."

"I hear the P.I. field is pretty glutted."

"But there's only one P.I. Frank Johnson. Think about it. Now, how can I help you?" Dreema, as always, said it as if she meant it.

"Sheriff Dmytryk is running the science on my Fox shotgun. Can its ballistics be rigged to implicate me?"

"What are we talking about, a one-ounce slug load from a 2-3/4-inch shell?"

"No, double-aught buckshot killed Cody."

Dreema laughed to quash my jitters. "Shotgun ballistics are inconclusive. The lead pellets blown through a shotgun's smooth bore encounter no rifling to striate the pellets with identifiable tool marks. Also, the shell's plastic wad helps to shield the lead pellets from the bore. Sometimes the ejected plastic wads can be matched to its shotgun. Did investigators recover any at the crime scene?"

"Not that I saw," I replied.

"It sounds as if your anxieties are unfounded." After a pause, Dreema varied topics. "Sorry to hear about your divorce. When it rains, it pours."

"Thanks. Marty got to be high maintenance."

"Uh-huh. I've always heard it cuts both ways, Frank."

I drew in a breath, ticked by her comment. Maybe it held a kernel of truth, but I'd never cheated on Marty. By the next moment, I felt my irritation evaporating. Dreema was my long-time friend.

"Frank, are you seeing anyone?"

Dreema's glibness caught me off-guard. "Life has been a bit hectic for romance," I replied.

"What time is better? Didn't Rick fall head over heels for Ilsa in *Casablanca* during wartime?"

"Things aren't that bad," I said.

"Not yet anyhow." She laughed at her quip. So did I. "Call any time. You know we always love you down here, hon."

"Thanks, Dreema."

I checked for any phone messages left recorded at the doublewide. A sincere-voiced lady from a Catholic charity solicited a donation for earthquake victims in Peru. I saved that message. A slick realtor wanted to push a McMansion in a new gated estate dubbed Brigadoon. That pitch got hosed.

On my way out of the gun shop, I requisitioned a Hobbes cleaning kit with a brass brush, two ammo boxes, and a leather shoulder holster. The new gun shop owner wouldn't bitch. My truck crossed the highway to McDavid's. The manager, a paunchy, thirtyish man named Cleburne, gave me an earful.

"Chet Peyton, shit." Cleburne's fists rode on his hips. "He comes in smelling like a brewery, and he's sloppy with my food inventory. I'm a red cunt hair away from sacking his ass."

"Is Chet on duty today?" I asked again, glancing past Cleburne for any sight of Chet's handy meat cleaver.

"He's my closer on Wednesday. Are you ordering anything?"

"No, I ate at Leona's," I replied.

The dour Cleburne waved me out of the lobby.

I made a mental note to buzz Chet and pushed my truck toward Pelham. My new pal, the holstered 9 mil, rode under the seat with my trusty tire iron. Along the way, I did a double take out my window, and what I observed festering on both highway sides galled me to the bone.

Our rural paradise was transmogrifying into a concrete-and-neon gulag. The skeletal shells to new McMansions had mushroomed overnight in the hilly pastures where livestock had once grazed. The soaring prices for new McMansions ran you a kite-tail of zeros. The soulless McMansions cramped together resembled pyramids of skulls. Had the Khmer Rouge just skipped town?

Developers had gouged a labyrinth of streets through the bluegrass fields. Hustling carpenters were ants. Skil saws whined. Hammers clanged. Tractors dragged landscape rakes over the yards. Once nested, these latest homeowners would begin to beat the drum to curb any further development. But less and less about

Pelham County was country. Residing in a McMansion had jazzed Marty, and she'd dropped a thousand hints I'd tuned out. I'd rather die than live in such a monstrosity.

Twyman's Jewelers was shoehorned between a camera shop and an acupuncturist in the Persephone Strip Mall. Soapy music, overstuffed chairs, and wheat-hued tapestry inside Twyman's lulled the starry-eyed chumps into believing love endured for eternity. I'd been one who'd dropped a mint on Marty's diamond wedding ring. The wizened Twyman, his hair coppery gray at the fringes and harassed by a right leg limp, sidled up to my elbow.

"May I assist you, Mr.—?"

"Johnson. I bought an expensive stone here. Now I'm back for an appraisal on a different piece."

"This is a slow time."

The baggie holding my pendant from Cody's office came out. Twyman snicked on his counter lamp and subjected my pendant to the loupe he'd lodged in his eye socket.

"By definition, any appraisal is inexact." He whistled as if wowed. "But this lavaliere is 18-karat gold, chain and pendant alike. The three-karat solitaire stone is flawless and the pearls are, well, dazzling. Do you mind if I ask about its origin?" He popped out the loupe.

I blurted what first flew into my head. "I bought it at an estate sale on a hunch."

"Always trust your hunches. I'm no final authority, mind you. But I'd assess its value at thirty-five to forty thousand dollars."

I almost whistled in awe. "Was it made in the U.S.?"

Twyman bagged the pendant. "West European, I'd say. Scarcity is what drives up its value."

"Is your consignment pretty standard?"

"60-40 is how I cut that melon. I'd go as high as 55-45 on this choice piece."

"Fine, but let's keep it mum until I decide what to do."

A shrewdness ruled Twyman's reaction. "Absolutely, Mr. Johnson. I pride myself on discretion."

"Thanks for your time," I said, leaving.

I rotated the truck key when I heard Twyman's shout. His right leg trailing, he hobbled out to the truck and clutched my side mirror for support.

"One moment please." His Adam's apple hitched. "I thought that distinctive pendant struck a chord. This fellow brought in one just like it."

"When was this?" My heart banged high in my chest.

"One, two months back. He was an out-of-towner and drove a van."

"What model van?"

"White van. The side had elaborate artwork, a knight mounted on a horse."

The white van with the Conquistador design had to be Rebby Cap's. Did this revelation link Cody to Rebby Cap? I kept my suspicions quiet and face deadpan. "What was his name? What was he after?"

"He gave no name and I didn't think to ask. But like you, the pendant's value interested him. But that's not all." Twyman's laconic face flushed. "My old friend in the trade some years back gave me a sketchbook of jewelry designs. Zanzibar told me he'd found it in a small shop at Calais. This was after the Second World War. Your pendant compares favorably to the sketches. I just checked them."

My brow lined in furrows. "I'd like to see your sketches, but right now I'm in a hurry." I reclaimed my truck door.

Twyman limped back a step, and my truck belched plumes of smoke. He rapped on my window and did a roll-down gesture. I did so. "I'm here all week, even on Sundays."

"Maybe I'll have a wedding ring to sell you back."

Twyman's smile took a sardonic twist. "Your marriage crashed on the rocks. Join the club. If your ex returns the diamond ring, I'll buy it back."

"Thanks, but don't hold your breath." I left Twyman standing in front of his shop. My opinion of him had altered. He didn't act as smarmy as the day I'd come to buy the diamond ring for my ill-fated marriage.

Chapter 11

For days I'd hashed it over, my enraged decision growing ever momentous. I caught myself in lax moments relishing the precise second the fatal bullet flamed out of my hit man's .22 handgun and pierced Marty's cheating heart. Or his silencer muted the just as deadly hit.

I told nobody, not even a hint to Cody. This was my private vendetta. I vowed to go it alone and avoid any pressure to stop me. Marty as a rabid she-wolf had to be put down. Letting her live subjected the next guy to the same grief her extracurricular romps had brought me. I felt too weary to justify it all again. Marty had screwed me, and I'd screw her, except on a grander scale. It was simple payback.

Marty and I had met through mutual pals at the Fredericksburg duck pins alley where our proximity touched off sparks, and she was an ace between the sheets. She stood cute and compact, a sandy blonde with a full top drawer and an elliptical smile. In the summer days after our Virginia Beach honeymoon, I thrilled to streak home from the gun shop to ravish her. Marty didn't work. Big mistake. She made some noise about resuming her floral design courses at the local community college, but she really only puttered.

She tried needlepoint and stuck up bluebird boxes. No bluebirds nested there. The zinnias browned in the milkcan planters I painted sunflower yellow. We strolled around the mobile home park's 1.3 mile oval. Our marital joyride zipped along on cruise control until I keyed on rumors of Marty's indiscretions. I dismissed the rumors as small-town gossip. Life was never better since I'd left the Army.

Then Cody Chapman dropped by the doublewide to see me about fixing some Walther PPKs, and instead he caught Marty *in flagrante* with the stud she'd met online. She moved out, and the last I heard, the stud had left the state, a prudent move.

Not much later, I sat watching a *Rockford* rerun and fixing a .44's firing pin one evening. The rap at the door was my hit man. Locating him hadn't been difficult. Bexley, an old school pal, had survived a bloodletting divorce. The town consensus was Bexley had turned flaky but I didn't care. I'd shared my sordid tale with him, and Bexley posed a tidy payback.

This guy Bexley knew did a nine-to-five as a tool-and-die machinist but moonlighted doing murder for hire. After his second rap, I hid the .44 and let him into my kitchenette. The angle of light detailed his face, a pitted, lumpy mass of flesh. It reminded me of a limpet, a clingy shellfish moving on a snail's foot I'd seen caught in fishing nets. We plotted at the table. His name wasn't relevant—he was Limpet to me.

Limpet went straight to business and rasped in a two-pack-a-day voice. "Who's the target?"

"It's my ex. Do you have a rule against doing women?"

"I don't discriminate. Who's the target?"

The photo recorded Marty shoving a wedge of wedding cake through my goofy smile. Limpet pinched the photo between his oily thumbs, squinted at it, and then over at me. He may've smiled.

"Did the target get some strange?"

"Habitually."

"Yeah, I hear that everywhere. Damn pity. Now the deal is I proceed at my own pace. So if you're raring to go, I'm not your man."

"Just do it."

Limpet's fingernail tapped the photo. His glassy eyes looked me up and down. "Does the target reside in the area?"

"The last I heard she lives and works in the northern end

of the county, but she still hangs here on the weekends."

"Then just list the target's favorite watering holes."

That part was a cinch—Marty haunted the local dives. I noted them down and gave him the list.

"How do you prefer to package the hit?"

"I'll defer to your expertise."

"Let's rig it as a mugging gone sour in a remote alleyway. The optimal time is late night after the bars shut. No, in a burg as Pelham such a hit might whip up the citizens' anger. What if I arrange it as a hunting accident?"

At one in the morning? I wondered. "Whatever. Just make it count the first time."

"I always do. But first, are you all-fired certain? You strike me as a bit tentative. It's irrevocable, see? My clients too often don't grasp that fact lucidly enough." Limpet had a stilted smile. "That's a bummer. I can't offer any store returns."

Limpet used a smooth patter a little too pat. My mouth felt parched. Was he an undercover cop setting me up? I'd researched how offenders pulled five years for the solicitation of capital murder, but my thirst for revenge blunted my sense of wariness, and I plowed ahead.

"Just do it."

Nodding, Limpet pocketed the photo. "Once I duck out that door, you don't know me from Adam's off ox."

"I hear you. How will I know when? I'd like to hang somewhere public and sew up an alibi."

"Sharp thinking, but I can't say precisely when because I go when it feels right. One morning over your coffee, you'll rejoice at reading it in your newspaper. Where's my down payment?"

I unsnapped the plain, black attaché case as per his instructions. Limpet's fingers nimble as a card shark's shuffled the corners to the C-note bundles. They tallied to $25,000.

"It's all there," I told him.

"You just better hope so. The balance is due once I do your hit. My delivery instructions will follow."

My reply snapped through my teeth. "Just do it."

We didn't shake hands—I didn't wish to get blood on mine.

Limpet, chuckling, halted on the cinderblock stoop. "Enjoy it, Mr. Johnson. You stand on the threshold of a new existence."

Fabulous, I'd hired a philosophical assassin.

After six wakeful nights and drams of Maalox, I curbed my obsessing. What did I expect? Revenge exacted its exorbitant price. What was Bexley's favorite credo? "Don't get mad, get even."

I'd borrowed the fifty Gs from Cody, and he knew I was good for it, even if it took me years to repay him. Fifty grand was the going rate to get even. That's how I justified dropping that wad of cash. Cody and I had sat down at his office desk. He stacked the paper, five hundred C-notes, in twenty piles. We called it a loan at a measly two percent interest.

"Why do you ask me for this much money?" asked Cody.

"Um, I lost my shirt on some gambling debts," I replied.

He sent me an askance look. I moved to elaborate when Cody raised his hand. "Save it, Frank. You need the money, so there it is. Take it. We're family. No more questions. Pay me back whenever."

By then our ill will had evaporated, and I figured Cody's generosity stemmed, in part, from his guilt over our spat on my OT pay. It didn't matter. I crammed the C-note bundles into my game pouch and left the gun shop, ecstatic I now had the means to dispense my personal justice on my ex.

Chapter 12

My truck ate up the pavement to Rennie's place. I turned up my wrist. 3:15 wasn't fashionably early as we'd agreed on four p.m. My first swing by her apartment building on Main Street jutted my jaw. An orange Nissan, its rocker panels corroded out by road salt, blocked her Prizm. I brushed the brake and recognized the license plate, "Wild, Wonderful West Virginia".

A clear plastic sheet held by duct tape patched the missing rear windshield. It's just another tenant's clunker, I told my miffed feelings. Then why did the orange Nissan box in Rennie's Prizm with her parking lot otherwise vacant except to trap her?

I looped the town block, figuring the Nissan belonged to Rennie's ex. I didn't know him, but knowing he was in her apartment poured acid on my smoldering nerves.

This wasn't my fight, I reminded myself. Rennie could demand that I leave. She'd have the right, too. I cursed my innate nosiness for making it a losing argument. My hand grappling under the seat for my 9 mil ratcheted up my pulse. The shortcut alley between the old bank and drugstore brought me to Main Street. I moored several car-lengths down from her apartment building. Stealthy and well-armed were my assets.

I tucked the 9 mil into my waistband, edged out, and scurried to the apartment building's rear entry. I hoped no busybody saw me and phoned Pelham's Finest. My vision adjusted on a washer and dryer. A load of clothes bumped at a tumble dry, and a detergent box with Rennie's name on it sat on the washer. She was more trusting than me—I knew riffraff who'd steal your clothes. I surmised her ex had braced Rennie when she hurried downstairs to check on her laundry.

A man's yell sent me up the stairs to a landing. I stood, my ears attentive. An object thunked off the wall in Rennie's apartment. I heard broken shards pepper her floor. I eclipsed the stairhead and flattened against the wall at her door ajar by three inches, affording me a narrow view.

"This is my weekend." The guttural words, male, sounded drunken.

"I know they're safe away from you. Now go. Please."

"They're my kids. You broke the law. I won visitation rights. I'll exercise them, no matter what you say, or do."

"Lower your voice, Virgil. Please. My neighbors will hear you."

"Fuck your neighbors."

"I'm warning you, Virgil. Stay away from me. Quit throwing my stuff."

Virgil snorted. "I'll throw what I goddamn well please."

"You're a sadistic bully."

"I'm their father. You can't change that biological fact. Unlike you, I teach them mental toughness."

"Newsflash: Virgil. Discipline isn't taught with a barber's strop. You're abusive, and I'll take out a restraining order. Now, leave."

Rennie's defiance lit Virgil's fuse. I saw him through the door crack lunge to strike her across the face. Yelping, she stumbled to the floor. If she hadn't writhed there in pain, I'm certain she would've brained him with the cast iron wok I saw on the stovetop.

I'd already watched her clip Suggs across the nose. She was assertive and scrappy. I liked that. But right now she was down and Virgil stomped her. Bile flushed up low in my throat, always a bad sign. I'd seen enough.

Rennie's door swished inward. Virgil with his back to me lifted a bottle to dish out more abuse. I avoided the pieces of broken crockery littering the floor before my 9 mil screwed straight into Virgil's ear.

"Make still, asshole," I said.

"Huh?" Virgil's brain failed to register it fast enough. "Who the hell are you?"

His feet shuffled away from me. The bottle he held sliced up to clout my head. Keyed on its arc, I lifted my forearm to buffet his hit and it struck me, radiating splinters of pain up my arm to my shoulder. I relied on my practiced crouch and snap draw.

The 9 mil round smoked out, its deafening report amplifying off the kitchen walls. Virgil, shrieking, grabbed his knee, both hands white-knuckled. The dropped bottle rolled to the kick plate, and Virgil did a gravity check.

"Fuck, you shot me."

I grunted. A piercing whistle filled my ears.

"Frank? Frank?" Rennie leveraged up to prop one elbow under her. Her hair was disheveled, and I saw her blouse had been ripped across the front. "What did you do?"

"Shot a rat. Can you make it to the sink?"

"I guess so. Did you hurt Virgil?"

I smiled.

"What will my neighbors think?"

"If Virgil's rant didn't freak them, I doubt if hearing a gunshot will," I said, hoping they didn't lodge a noise complaint with the sheriff.

Rennie let out a dry sob and I felt like a total shit. I hitched a hand under each arm and craned her up to sit in a kitchen chair. Her sinewy muscles under the blouse fabric felt taut. She cradled her forehead in her palms.

"Frank...I asked you if Virgil is hurt."

I snatched the dish towel from the refrigerator handle and wiped her gashed forehead. Her wince made me wince.

"Give me a straight answer," she said.

My glance fell on Virgil lying sprawled against the wall. No geyser of blood indicated he'd taken a flesh wound. Virgil overreacting to win Rennie's sympathy could bag an Oscar. Or maybe he smelled the long green to a lawsuit. If so, he was in for more pain.

"Try to relax," I said to Rennie. "Virgil is more alive than dead."

"Call him an ambulance. Use my cell phone."

"He'll do okay. What's say we patch up you."

When I didn't fly to Virgil's aid, Rennie acquiesced. She buttressed an arm on my shoulder, and we hobbled down to her hall bathroom. She nudged shut the door, the ceiling fan whirred, and tap water gurgled in the sink. I returned to the kitchen, avoiding the broken shards.

I felt Virgil's baleful eyes track me. A shade over six feet tall and cadaverous as Karloff, he was red-faced from working out in the elements. My second look realized his ruddy features derived from a weakness for bourbon.

"Didn't you hear my wife? Get me an ambulance." Sweat beaded in a ragged line above his predominant brow.

His reference to Rennie as his mate torqued up my temper. I saw his wedding band and lost it. My kick toppled Virgil to his side and exposed where my bullet had perforated the sheetrock. My 9 mil round had only nicked him.

Virgil swiped a sleeve over the sweat line and glowered at me. "You'd better..."

My 9 mil's muzzle jabbed into his upper lip flanged in hatred. "Beat it, Virgil. Don't return here. Ever."

"Are you now her bodyguard?"

"Better watch out. I'm also her private eye," I replied, enjoying my joke.

Snarling oaths through his yellow kernels for teeth, Virgil fumbled but gained his feet. He staggered over the broken shards out the open door and into the hallway. I stood outside Rennie's apartment door and watched him.

Virgil's shot-scraped knee supported him with no trouble. He gimped down the steps. At the newel post, he twisted and hurled an obscene curse at me. I laughed. It rang as hollow as his curse. He shambled down the hallway, making for the rear door. Waiting for a moment, I ensured he didn't sneak back to waylay us.

Chapter 13

Rennie had brushed her hair. She downed three Excedrin I dug out of her medicine cabinet. She collapsed into her pillows, her eyes closed and soon her breaths evened out. I hauled in a kitchen chair, straddled it backwards, and held vigil over her. Shaker furniture, utilitarian but elegant, adorned her small bedroom. The shadows grew oppressive, and I grew restless. Marty my ex tried to highjack my thoughts, but I didn't let her ruin this intimate moment.

I went in and picked up the broken shards off the kitchen floor to trash. Next time, I promised myself, they'd be Virgil's teeth. Rennie was still supine on her bed. I cracked a window for some air and noted Virgil's orange Nissan had split. He'd driven a fair piece from West Virginia. Or did he flop in a roach coach outside of town to lick his wounds? My commotion made Rennie stir on the pillows.

"Please pass me that box of Kleenex." She put a wrist on her temple.

I obliged. "You took a licking."

"Yeah, but I kept on ticking." Rennie scraped the Kleenex at her bloodstains. "Damn, it's a new blouse, too." Her sad eyes alit on me. "I've survived worse. Did you hurt Virgil?"

"All I can say is the half-drunk bastard has left. Shouldn't you see a doctor? File a police report? I'll take you to the ER and stationhouse."

"Thanks, but I'm not made of plastic."

"It's your call, but at least let's try some first aid."

"Okay, if you say so." Rennie fluttered her hand. "Is the dryer still running?"

"Don't worry about that."

Back in the kitchen, I yanked the ice tray's handle and swaddled ice cubes in a clean towel. Her bedroom had grown dimmer like inside a confessional.

"Here, it's probably too late but try numbing your lip."

Rennie cringed at dabbing the icepack at her swollen mouth. "Nothing can change Virgil."

"I'm no hard man, but using a niner on a bully trumps getting slugged by him."

Irony tinged her response. "Can I use yours? It seems to work pretty well."

"I can give you shooting tips, sure. Why did you want to meet at four?"

"No actual reason. Just to talk is all."

I used that as an invitation to get personal. "Is Virgil your ex?"

"Right. Our marriage was poison, too. Out with my girlfriends at a bar is how I met Virgil. My dad had him pegged from day one. If only I'd listened, but isn't 20/20 hindsight great? Marriage sucks. Do I sound bitter? I do. Sorry. Anyway, I reclaimed my maiden name after the divorce." Even, white teeth bit her lower lip before she tacked on an afterthought. "But I do have two beautiful children by him."

I took back the icepack and gave her cotton balls wetted by the witch hazel also from her medicine cabinet. I wanted to say life was a little sugar and a little shit based on the good and bad choices we made, but it sounded too condescending. "That's something." I put on the nightstand lamp, and her eyes cowered in the crush of light.

"Yes, it sure is."

Rennie sat up, undid her torn blouse, and shucked it off a shoulder. I watched. One hand held up the front while she swabbed the cotton balls on her bruises. Her natural tan offset her white bra strap. I saw the mahogany freckles sprinkled over the swell to her mango breasts, and I colored in the dusky suggestions of her nipples. My twitch was natural as I finished disrobing her and joined us to set fire to the sheets. Seeing her bleeding welts ruined the erotic effect. She was conversing in a husky, confidential admission.

"I fell hard for Virgil. He was wild, and at first that was exciting, but it ended quickly. His hair-trigger temper, hard drinking, and harder fists saw to that. God, I hated the violence."

"Give yourself credit. You had the wits to eject."

Rennie rebuttoned her blouse and swiped her bent wrist at the tears welling up in her eye corners. She fell to the nubby bedspread and buried a sob in her pillow.

"The drunk's rape got me pregnant with Gin," she said in a strangled confession. "Pathetic, isn't it? Some days back then I wished I was dead."

"That's crazy talk. Gin inherited all that's good in you." Brave words but I felt ill at ease sitting in her bedroom taking in all this. I turned practical. "Buddy and Gin are safe, right?"

"Yes, they're at Dad's. I knew Virgil was due by and ran them over early. He won't go there." Rennie wiped the Kleenex on her face. "I don't want to talk about it."

I tugged out the baggie from my pocket. "Does this look familiar? I found it in Cody's office."

Intrigued, Rennie sat up on the edge of her bed. The gold-braided chain gleamed in her slim fingers. A fleeting suspicion flared in me: had she killed Cody? She was too petite to trip off a 12-gauge. Besides, I couldn't analyze a feasible motive.

"No, but it's intricate." Rennie fiddled with the clasp. "It's also a toughie to undo. This heavy weight might mean it's gold."

"Twyman says it's solid gold," I said.

"He should know." She let the pendant drop into my outstretched palm. "How did you obtain it?"

"Cody had cut a hole in the concrete pad under the fake grass rug in his office. I found the pendant salted away inside an old cigar box."

"Weird. Why were you in Cody's office?"

"A clue exists somewhere and I'm on the prowl to find it."

"I've never seen the pendant before now. Did I overhear you tell Virgil you're a private investigator?"

"I was just busting his chops."

"You could use a P.I. right now."

I nodded at her insight reinforcing Dreema's but said, "Cody claimed some Marlin rifles came in. Did you inventory them?"

"Not yet. Where were they shipped from?"

I shrugged. "Cody didn't say."

"I'll start Sheriff Dmytryk's inventory tomorrow."

"Skip making the inventory. It's a made-up distraction until Sheriff Dmytryk lowers the boom on me," I said.

"Maybe I can help you. Mysterious arms shipments have arrived over the past months."

"Exotic arms jazzed Cody," I said. "Collectors acquire any rarity and brag it up. You know, who owns the sexiest Kalashnikov rifle. The novelty wears off, and they resell, usually coming out ahead."

"I've seen Cody's exotic buys, but this was different. Cody bought in bulk and kept it off the books. How these shipments came in is anybody's guess."

"Truckers deliver at off-peak hours with less traffic."

"But manifests cover even those deliveries."

"Didn't these arms have manifests?" I asked.

"No. They offloaded the crates to store behind the shop near the firing range. I peeped under the blue tarp and saw unmarked crates. Then they'd disappear a day or two later."

"Cody never did that when I worked there."

"He gave no details on their destination or customer." Rennie eased back into the pillows. "Ouch. My head throbs. You can talk and I'll listen."

I recounted my phone conversation with Gatlin. Rennie reared up again, dangling her legs over the bedside, her shoes stirring the dust ruffle. Appearing vulnerable sitting there made me want to hug and protect her. But I just watched her sitting on the bed. The silence lagged. The oil furnace downstairs squawked on, awaking the pipes and studs to vibrate behind the walls. I felt a chill set on my back despite the heat rising from the floor registers and fought off a shiver.

"Doesn't running just compound your troubles?" she asked.

"I've got no choice. Gatlin says avoid the cops until he returns. He's right. First perceptions like my arrest as Cody's killer are near impossible to shake."

"Mr. Gatlin is the lawyer." Rennie leaned to the other nightstand, flipped on its brass lamp, and closed the cracked window. "Frank, are you wearing your running shoes?"

"I could be. Why?"

"A deputy sheriff cruiser just rolled up. I see its lights."

Chapter 14

I joined her at the window. Sure enough, the cherry topper's lights swirled in nervy red-blue glints. Two shadowy figures jacked out. One carrying a riot shotgun raced around to the front. My neck hairs prickled. The cops had come to collar me. We heard the deputy sheriff rattle the front door in its frame downstairs.

"Good, it's stuck again." Taking charge, Rennie hopped off her bed, snared my wrist, and towed me into the hall. She hit a light switch. Her eyes tilted to the ceiling where mine followed. "My landlord says a skylight vents to the roof. I've never been up there."

My pull on the dangling cord lowered the fold-down ladder, and the crawlspace's mustiness washed over us. The attic light cast us in its rectangle of sallow illumination. I banged my knee starting up the ladder.

"Wait, Frank."

My head turned to see her expectant face lifted. "Kiss me, first." Her lips pursed and her eyes shut and her spontaneity was sweet. Our first kiss was fast yet unforgettable. I resumed my ascent into the attic.

Rennie whispered up instructions after me. "Try to use the skylight to reach the roof. If you wiggle to its edge, you can drop to the fire escape. Slip down to the parking lot and escape in your truck. I'll divert them."

That should be a piece of cake, I thought, seduced again by the witch hazel smell and a longing glimpse of the mahogany freckles across the hemispheres of her breasts.

A body slammed the door below us. The deputy sheriff's cloddish shuffle on the stairs sent me scrambling. Rennie nudging up the fold-down ladder disappeared. The insulation encircling me carpeted the attic floor in fuzzy pink. My eyes clarified. A board path spanning the joists took me to Rennie's skylight as I heard a fist drum on her apartment door.

"Ms. Van Dotson, are you at home?"

The attic's light bulb snapped off, cloaking me in semidarkness.

"Hold on. I'm coming." I heard Rennie's response trail into the kitchen. "Who's out there?"

"It's Deputy Sheriff Lars, ma'am. Open up."

"Why?"

"Ma'am, this is official business. Let me in."

"Do you carry proper I.D.? I must insist on seeing some. I'm sure you understand."

"My badge is plain as day, ma'am."

I heard Rennie pull out her squeaky door.

"Christ, what happened to your face, ma'am?"

"I slipped and fell toting my laundry downstairs."

"We're after Frank Johnson. You told the sheriff he stays here."

"He did for that one night. But he isn't here now."

"Mind if I poke around?"

She'd delay Lars. Years back, I now recalled, Whit and I had explored this attic. Mr. Shepherd had installed the Plexiglass skylight as a fire exit, and his foresight now served me well. The skylight voided to a roof catwalk better equipped to support eight-year-old boys than a full-grown man, but I was trapped with no alternate way down.

My hands thumped against the Plexiglass skylight. It didn't budge. I unbuckled its latches and used my shoulder as a battering ram, but the skylight was stubborn. Animated speech filtered up to me. Deputy Sheriff Lars searched each room, his shoes tromping with purpose.

"What's this switch do?" I overheard him ask.

"Oh that." Rennie hesitated. "I'm not sure."

"Let's check it out."

I saw the naked light bulb over at the attic's entranceway fizzle on again.

"Isn't that your attic ladder?"

Rennie downplayed it. "I never noticed, Deputy. I'm just a tenant."

"You wouldn't mind if I ran a consensual search."

"You'll only find dust bunnies."

"Uh-huh. You don't want to face an obstruction of justice charge. Trust me, ma'am."

"Go ahead and look, if you must."

I squatted lower and hurled my entire bulk to strike the skylight. It snapped free. Cold, clammy tree leaves slapped into my face, and I spat them away. The puff of chimney smoke stung my eyes, and I stymied a sneeze. My hands lifted me through the portal onto the roof. I squatted and did a scan.

The slate tiles slanted off at a precipitous angle. I capped the skylight's cowl as I heard the fold-up ladder clatter down. Deputy Sheriff Lars carrying a riot shotgun came steps behind me. I crabbed over the slate shingles to stand on the catwalk. It bowed but didn't snap under my weight and ended two stories up from where I distinguished Rennie's Prizm in the cruiser's strobing red-blue lights.

My scrutiny turned to the second deputy sheriff crinkling wrapping papers. He flicked his tongue to wet the glue strip and scratched a match to light his hand-rolled. I heard garbled words punctuate the static over the cruiser's radio. Indifferent, the deputy sheriff relished his smoking break. Did I smell weed? He was intent on getting stoned.

My fingers groped at the lap to the slate shingles until I dislodged one and tossed it Frisbee-style. The shingle plinked down a few paces beyond where the deputy sheriff slouched in an I-don't-give-a-damn leisure.

I clawed at a row of shingles except these nails weren't as lax. But a careless roofer doing repairs had left behind his zax tool in the gutter. I threw the zax and slugged out the hatted deputy sheriff. His arms and knees crumbled as he foundered into a heap.

My awe that I'd hit him gave way to the terror I'd killed him. I hung by my fingers from the gutter tearing free from the fascia board until my toes grazed the fire escape. The gutter rented away a few more inches. I let go and landed flat-footed on the fire escape.

Slits of light peeped out from around Rennie's drawn blind. By now Deputy Sheriff Lars had bulled his way into the attic. I sensed his flashlight beam trained on the skylight, and I tore down the fire escape. My fingers planted at the unconscious deputy sheriff's neck found a pulse. Relief thawed my dread. I ransacked the cruiser, my hands frisking the seats, front and back, but I unearthed no arrest warrant.

From the corner of the apartment complex, I thrilled to see my truck on the dark side of Main Street. I lumbered over, plunged into the cab, and dissolved into the night.

Chapter 15

The assassin Limpet played the monster in my nightmares.

"Where's the rest?" he was asking me now.

I shrugged, not a heady move. *Whish*, a six-inch straight razor flared into view, slicing inches under my nose.

"Time to ante up, or die," said Limpet.

Turning greedy, I'd decided to welsh on paying him. My 9 mil elevated to vaporize him, but he leered at me.

"The only killer here is me."

Mystified, I saw my 9 mil's steel rod melt into a spaghetti of black eels slithering through my fingers.

His singing razor nicked my carotid artery, and a guacamole green blood excreted from his razor's slash mark...

My eyes snapped open. Confusion left me dizzy. This latest nightmare had seeded major doubts in my mind. Employing a hit man to rub out my ex bordered on lunacy. What was I thinking? My heartbeat ramped up even more as I tried to get my bearings.

My cheek scraped on the tweedy fabric. No, I wasn't tucked between my clean sheets at the doublewide. I sat up and gazed through the frost-patched windshield. The dawn's light sketched in the gray oak trunks, Confederate sentinels guarding their way of life. Red and yellow ornamented the foliage. Today was Sunday, and I'd ditched here after eluding the two deputy sheriffs at Rennie's apartment.

Last night I'd streaked down a maze of roads, my brain overheating to find a spider hole. Sheriff Dmytryk had staked out the doublewide. My other recourses? If I skated on the back routes, it was a matter of time before their dragnet hooked me. The gun shop under watch wasn't my haven.

Scratching those ruled out other hiding places like the old limestone quarry or lover's lane to Garm Castle. I rolled down the windows. Nippy air perked me up and my eyes monitored the mirrors, but my reckless clip didn't spook any cruisers to scream out and give chase.

Randall Van Dotson's face nipped at my mind's fringes. His mistletoe oaks, remote and defensible, were my sweet spot. Nobody went there for fear of his sound shots taken at poachers. My jump on the brakes wrenched me into a rubber-shrieking U-turn, and I took the road I wanted at the electric substation. My truck, no ballast in its bed, ricocheted between the shallow ditches.

I barged off the road to take a shrub-tangled trail. Navigation was done by the fog lamps. Grapevines thick and hairy as my forearm thrashed the windshield. My bumper glanced off trunks, and my tires chewed up the ruts. My oil pan and transmission scuffed rocks, and a low branch leveled my radio aerial.

Thumping in and out of a pothole smacked my crown on the headliner. Off to my right I discerned the grist mill's pile of rubble moldering by the inky Mosby River before the lane petered out. I geared down, ripped across a weedy plot, and gunned it through a rail fence. My flight at last halted in the mistletoe oaks. I keeled over on the tweedy upholstery and sank asleep, marauded by bloodthirsty deputy sheriffs and Limpets.

But now I heralded a new day. The autumnal morning cooled my feverish skin as I stretched out, gazing up into the branches at the furry, green clusters of mistletoe. A sweet spot, oh yeah. Squirrels scampered in the oaks, and a trio of deer scarfed up the acorns on the ground. The gaudy foliage, despite our dry spell, reminded me why October was my favorite month—

"Ow!"

A solid object had jabbed the tender area under my short ribs. I saw the black oxide barrel to a riot shotgun.

"You're trespassing, ass-wipe." The accusation issued in an older man's gruffness.

"Beg your pardon?" I said, a little dumbstruck.

"You're illegal, thief."

"Your mistletoe isn't why I'm here."

"I bet. My property is posted."

"I must've missed your signs." Committing no hinky moves, I asked, "Any heartburn if I turn around and make our conversation more civil?"

He dictated the terms. "Grab a little air. Slow. Or I spray your dumb shit brains over that truck fender."

"I hear you."

Arms up vertical, I rotated. The sun, a tangerine wafer, shined through the oaks' trunks to backlit a tall, gangly man at least twice my age. He wore faded jeans, a blue work shirt, and brush boots. A purple bandana knotted pirate-style held his lank, dirt-brown ringlets. His skin tone was dusky, suggestive of the Melungeon extraction, and his eyes, pale blue marbles, bored into me.

"Just who the fuck are you?"

"Frank Johnson." My eyes flicked down, then back up to him. "My wallet in that pocket vouches for me."

"The hell you say." The pale blue marbles tamped into slits before the 12-gauge unfastened from my chest.

"My apologies, Frank. It's these damn cataracts. Rennie called me with an idea you'd be by."

My arms lowered as my heart parachuted back behind my ribs. "I'm in a tight spot."

"Tell me about it. My cop scanner harped on your name all night. A couple of deputy sheriffs have been by and cut out already."

"Sheriff Dmytryk is fitting me for Cody Chapman's murder." I met Mr. Van Dotson's gaze. "I didn't kill Cody. Swear it. He was my cousin and friend."

"That shit ain't right. Dmytryk has a hard-on for you. If

Rennie says you're cool, I say welcome."

"Virgil socked her around last night."

"He's an asshole, but she's safe now."

"We pulled a fast one on the deputy sheriffs."

He grinned, his teeth even and flawless as Rennie's. "So I heard."

"Does your welcome include breakfast? I can pay."

"Pay me? Your money is shit here." Mr. Van Dotson rotated with a wave. "You're hungry, eh? Me, too. Just follow me."

Chapter 16

A soprano sax crooned on the MP3 player. John Coltrane, I believed, lightened the load. The incongruity of jazz played on a digital device wasn't as striking as Mr. Van Dotson's gourmet breakfast, including grits with sausage gravy and muskmelon. He flipped off the MP3 player and cop scanner.

"Frank, you're up to your nose in scorpions." Mr. Van Dotson reclaimed his chair. "What really happened?"

"Like every morning, Rennie came in yesterday to open up the gun shop. She flipped on the lights and spotted Cody lying on the floor. He'd taken a load of buckshot to the chest. She called me and Sheriff Dmytryk. I hauled ass over and no sooner had I arrived than Sheriff Dmytryk started to size me up."

"That's a no brainer. Frame job city. Dmytryk wants to wrap up Cody's murder or he gets voted out of a cushy job. Have you landed a lawyer?"

"Cody's attorney Bob Gatlin came recommended."

"Robert Gatlin?" The furrows striating Mr. Van Dotson's dark brows relaxed. "He's an ass-kicker lawyer I always see written up in the newspapers."

"I phoned Gatlin's office but he's overseas. What's his stellar advice? I stay on the lam until he gets home on Monday."

"Sure, it's harder to nail a moving target. Rennie said you've got some ideas who really did whack Cody."

"Chet Peyton saw a van in the gun shop's parking lot."

Mr. Van Dotson removed two cold Yuengling long necks from the fridge and handed me one. "A van, you say?"

"A white Chevy van has one headlight out, and a Conquistador scene painted on its side. A guy wearing a Rebby Cap drives it."

"I've never seen it. Does Rebby Cap look good for Cody's killer?"

My nod assented.

"That's not much to go on. White vans are a dime a dozen. A new headlight is a fast fix, and a coat of spray paint covers up artwork."

My voice fell flat. "I could ignore Gatlin's advice and take my lumps in a police grilling."

"Suit yourself, but I'd stand up and defend my good name."

Just then Buddy and Gin shuffled into the kitchen, both yawning and munching on candy corn from a new bag.

"Look all, we've got a visitor." Mr. Van Dotson hid the long neck between his thighs. I aped his action, suffering an instant case of jock frost.

"Why are you back?" asked Buddy, his jaw a small, red vise of anger.

"Mr. Johnson dropped by to chat is all," said Mr. Van Dotson.

"That's it." I nodded. "But I can't stay long."

Gin's slippers swished over the floor tiles to the window. She leaned to touch her forehead on the glass, where her breath clouded a small patch of condensation. "I don't see his pickup."

Mr. Van Dotson told a white lie. "He parked it behind the shed for me to put in a quart of motor oil."

"What got Mom so upset?" asked Buddy.

Before I could reply, Mr. Van Dotson cut in. "Mr. Johnson is late. Go wash up and get dressed for breakfast." He shooed them off, then adjusted his bandana. "I love 'em but some mornings they try the patience of Saint Patrick. Good thing Rennie will be by later. If Virgil shows, I'll take him off at the neck. Promise you. The deputy sheriffs sat on her place all night and he stayed away. Now, are you strapping iron?"

"I swiped a Browning niner from the gun shop."

"If Rebby Cap packs a sawed-off, you're toast. I have a 12-gauge in the bottom of my footlocker. Good weapon. Just ask the tough, old leathernecks from Guadalcanal."

"What do I owe you for it?" I asked.

"Didn't I say your money is shit here? I'll put you on equal footing with Rebby Cap by cropping its barrel."

"Not less than the legal eighteen inches," I said.

"I can lop off the butt, too."

"No, the shortened barrel will do." I tugged out the pendant in the baggie from my pocket. "This was in Cody's office. Ring any bells?"

Mr. Van Dotson's dusky face didn't alter its noncommittal cast. "No, but then I don't wear faggot earrings or necklaces. Is it gold?"

"Twyman says so. He appraised the lady's pendant for forty, maybe thirty-five thousand dollars."

Mr. Van Dotson set our breakfast plates and cups in the sink, ran the tap, and rinsed them off. "Did Cody hide a ritzy gift for his lady friend?"

I handed Mr. Van Dotson my empty long neck to trash. Sarcasm laced my voice. "Cody was too stingy. Shit, maybe it's just something else sneaky in our little town."

"Sneaky and our little town remind me of the Nazis." Mr. Van Dotson sat in his chair.

My surprise was a questioning smile.

"My father during the big war worked as a prison guard at our Nazi POW camp. Daddy hated it, but the paycheck was steady."

"But didn't he get drafted?"

"Daddy was too old, but he had his fill of Nazis right here. The most fanatical POWs stayed at the Pelham camp. Lucky us, eh?"

"Where did they come from?"

"They served in the Hitler Youth and boycotted any camp work for their keep. All the captured U-boat crewmen continued to fight us here at home. They remained defiant and waited for their Führer's rescue mission. He never made it this far.

"They also bribed Daddy to help them to escape. He would've done it, too, and then mowed them all down and pissed on their corpses, but his sergeant caught wind and kiboshed it."

"Did these Nazis stick around after the war?"

"Some old-timers swear a few did."

"What's your take?"

"I've never met one, but I don't dismiss the talk."

"This is the first I've heard of the POW camp."

"The Feds kept it hush-hush like the Roswell UFOs, and the alien cadavers on ice at Area 51."

I didn't take up that controversial debate by asking, "What became of their camp?"

"The Feds razed and buried the complex within days after Berlin waved the white flag. Daddy said a cargo plane in the middle of the night spirited the die-hard Nazis back to Berlin. The Feds coerced Daddy with jail time to sign an oath of silence. Dirty shame how he rambled in his sleep."

"Why all the secrecy?"

"Don't know. Maybe Uncle Sam doesn't want it known the worst of the worst Nazis were kept here."

"But that was a half-century ago."

Mr. Van Dotson canted his eyebrows at me as if I were an idiot. "This is the Federal government, Frank."

"How nearby was the prison?"

"The satellite farm stands there today. You know where? It borders Doc Edwards' family place."

"I've gone by the facility. Didn't Clinton shut it down?"

"I didn't vote for the lying shitbird."

Politics also not my bag, I let that remark hang fire. "Sorry, I was born nosy and something bugs me."

"I'm all ears, Frank."

"Didn't you do a stretch some years back—"

"Don't throw that shit up in my face." Mr. Van Dotson turned antagonistic. "My grandkids are here, man." An icy silence separated us until he dialed it back. "Damn Frank, we're all guilty of flying off the handle. My neighbor pulled a gun on me and I just lost it."

"I'm not judging you," I said.

"I know. Look, I did a short stretch. Let's drop it," said Mr. Van Dotson.

I nodded but the MP cop in me was leery of any ex-con's loyalty.

Chapter 17

Mr. Van Dotson reactivated the cop scanner. "Sunday morning listening is the pits, but thanks to you not this one."

Just then Sheriff Dmytryk's humorless voice crackled in its broadcast. "We beat the boonies from dusk to dawn but scared up nothing. All patrols are out on a hard target search." Mr. Van Dotson decreased the volume knob but there was more news.

"Is that other thing ready for sonny boy?" Hearing Stonesiffer's jeering tone grated on me.

"Indeed so. This arrest warrant charges Mr. Franklin Johnson for the homicide of Mr. Cody Chapman."

"What do you need?" asked Stonesiffer.

"Physical evidence, if you get my drift," replied Sheriff Dmytryk.

Stonesiffer sputtered out in a gleeful snort. "Drift received and understood."

Grimacing, Mr. Van Dotson cut off the scanner. "You better do as Gatlin says and blow before the deputy sheriffs return here. This might come in handy."

He gave me a quick and dirty on operating the cop scanner.

"You'll call Chet Peyton for me later when they're awake and up?" I said.

Mr. Van Dotson didn't try to disguise his misgivings. "But why call Chet?"

"Don't be fooled. Chet's a tough, smart kid."

"Since you're his pal, set me straight. Did he accidentally kill Briones? "

"The jury ruled it was a hunting accident," I replied.

Mr. Van Dotson's hirsute eyebrows tilted. "Of course it was a local jury. Now Briones is no big loss, granted. But Chet nailed him in the heart, and the deer stand was that many paces away. Man, that's a stretch."

"If it's too much, drop it," I said.

"I said I'll call Chet and I will. If Sheriff Dmytryk shows, I'll sic him down a wrong path. Do you favor organ donation or hooked to life support?" Mr. Van Dotson squinted at me. "I'd better ask you now."

"The odds against me can't be that lopsided."

"Keep rolling and stay one jump ahead of the law."

I left him with a dismissive wave, taking along the cop scanner, a knapsack of redneck caviar in cans, the sawed-off shotgun, and a carton of shells. My return to the mistletoe oaks tramped down the yarrow, ragweed, and goldenrod left soppy from the thawed frost. A piece of milkweed duff lifted on a breeze. The sun burning off the ground haze had tempered the dawn chill, and the deer gorging on the meaty acorns had meandered off into the ironwood thicket.

I righted my radio aerial and set the knapsack and cop scanner on the cab seat. The sawed-off shotgun fit behind the seat where my Fox 12-gauge, now at the forensics lab, had ridden. I fell under the wheel and juiced the V-8 engine. The 9 mil rode in my lap. Grabbing a gear, I muttered under my breath.

"Cody, I'll nail your killer. Swear it."

But then a jag of guilt stabbed me as I drove away from the oaks. My paid hit on Marty my ex didn't qualify as murder. No, no. She'd done me dirty, and I sought payback, and it felt righteous. I was in accord with my reasons to deal with her one final time. Nirvana for me was a life without Marty tracking her dirt through it.

Why then did a pain skewer my gut? Judgmental, bitter, and acrimonious was a shitty way to get through life. I debated if I could trust Mr. Van Dotson. Wariness cautioned me he might never deliver my message to Chet. I nudged aside my negativism. Events were careening too fast for me to veer off in my self-absorbed ruminations.

I reversed my nocturnal trek, following my tire impressions, and stamped on the brakes midway across the weedy plot. I unlimbered my sawed-off and fed shells, double-aught buckshot, into its chamber. Mr. Van Dotson had reamed out the plug and given me a full magazine's destruction. I jacked a shell into its breech. This time my sawed-off went under the bench seat within quick reach, and I put spurs to the truck.

Shooting the gap I'd notched last night in the rail fence set me to laughing. Imagine me as a desperado fugitive. My truck ran over something hard that I heard scrape underneath me. Next the oil gauge on the dash flickered to red. My rough flight had jarred the oil pan enough to spring a leak and lose motor oil. Wanting to inspect the damage brought me to a halt by the old grist mill's pile of rubble. I opened the truck door. Hearing the far-off freights clanking over the steel rails snapped free a memory.

The summer I'd turned sixteen, a new four-lane bypass had been constructed to sidestep Pelham. Earthmovers graded the pastures and pine tracts to pave a yellow-striped highway. No more through-traffic to stop at its antique stalls, fatty food dives, and service stations left Pelham, like many such humbled towns, to wither on the vine. All the while, the modern hydra known as "sprawl"—chain outfits, yuppies, and soccer fields—splurging all around us threatened to swallow up Pelham.

I dropped to the sand and wiggled under the truck. Hot motor oil had sprayed all across its undercarriage. Wrenches or bubblegum might fix it. Now what? I skimmed flat stones over the scummy river pools and let my mind hum away. Who'd killed Cody? And why did they? Rennie had seen the mysterious crates under blue tarps stacked behind the gun shop. Cody had procured big lots for some gun-happy customer. That might well tie in to his murder. Or maybe it didn't. The myriad of angles to analyze bummed me.

I'd starve earning my bread employed as a private detective. Riddles and enigmas bored me to tears. My personal schema of Hell put me shackled to its icy ramparts and slaving to fill in the blanks to crossword puzzles. Or Hell was gnashing my teeth over testing the endless machinations to solve a Rubik's cube.

Yet here I sat noodling clues around in my head as a P.I. might do. Cody's pendant put with the one Twyman had seen from Rebby Cap exceeded coincidence. Had Cody pretended not to know Rebby Cap at Leona's Bar & Grill? He'd told me to give an alleged stranger a jumpstart. Cody had never shaded the truth with me. Had he? I recalled the flash of surprise I'd seen pass over his face. What did that mean?

I groaned. Man, I wasn't here. I'd left Pelham, never to return. Rennie and I had moved to a classy suburb off somewhere, say, in the glorious flatland of Kansas. We'd made love and then grilled rib-eye steaks out on our patio—.

A deputy sheriff cruiser broke through the treeline, its tires muffled by the sandy lane. My startled glance took in its tinted windshield, big bull bar, and low suspension. It braked on a dime. Both doors wagged out. A pair of deputy sheriffs vaulted into sight. Their riot shotguns braced on the windowsills, both pointing at me.

But I was humping.

Chapter 18

With no verbal warning, they fired double rounds to pulverize my former spot into a crater. The din split my ears, caromed off the treetops, and bopped down Mosby River. They smelled blood. Mine. My momentum carried me by the cab door, and I scooped out the sawed-off. I expected a bullhorn to boom out directives.

"Pitch your weapon. Hands up. Kiss the dirt."

But no bullhorn blared—this was no routine collar. Their coinciding pumps—*click-clank*—cycled in new shells. Their next combo shots riddled my truck where shrapnel clawed up the upholstery and seat batting. I dove and hugged the ground behind a log. They were a few steps behind my truck now, prowling closer. The log offered me minimal cover. I heard their coarse laughter.

"Dale, did you smoke him? My round shanked low."

"He ate dirt. I saw him. So tops, he's down. I got first dibs."

"I hear that, soldier."

"I told you he'd use this back way. He's sticking that Van Dotson pooty." I saw Dale turn. "Search down to the river."

Lars did and emitted a coyote yip. "His 9 millimeter is still on the cab seat. Say hello to mop-up time."

"Sweet. But the coup-de-grace is all mine."

"Got it. Stay sharp, soldier."

"Do we radio for back-up?" I watched Dale's roguish grin cut to Lars. "Some soldiers are still at the farmhouse just up the road."

Farmhouse?

"Why? We've got this covered. Besides they went off on field ops."

Field ops?

"Huh? Nobody told me. I could use the practice, too."

"Tune up your shooting here on a live target, soldier."

I sprang up, desperate to take better cover.

Lars barked out. "That way, pull down!"

Their double-stoked shots boomed out. My reaction time was a bit tardy. I dove over a fallen tree as birdshot peppered my lower calf. I felt the fire rake my leg and stifled my yelp. Adrenaline suppressed my jolts of pain, and I knew that's why maniac gunmen were unstoppable. Riddle them with lead, and they bull-rushed you, supercharged by adrenaline. Behind the fallen tree, I felt a hot dose of that juice. Both tubby deputy sheriffs stalked in bow-legged stances. Their aviator green sunshades scanned to and fro, alert to grease any glimpse of me. My heart reeled.

I was road kill to them, but why? I knew Dale and Lars. We'd earned varsity letters in football. Hell, I smiled hello to their wives and kids in town. What pissed them? I choked my sawed-off. Yelling out to parley seemed ill-advised, if not unhealthy. They shuffled over the sand, their itchy fingers bent on shotgun triggers.

"He's near." Lars sniffed. "Smell it? He shit his britches. Told you he's yellow. Split up. I'll hunt our front, and you can seal off our rear."

Dale's finger enacted a throat slashing. "I'll cap him. My skull took his chunk of slate last night."

"Okay, Dale. He's yours. Drop it before I get ticked at *you*."

I saw Lars pad by my tailgate. Black splotches of sweat pasted his shirt to his armpits. His lips crimped in glee. Fear electrified my self-preservation urge.

One shot, one kill, I mantraed.

I yanked to my feet, braced one knee against the fallen tree, and thrust the sawed-off into my shoulder pit. Lars, well inside of my range, pivoted, and I saw his sunshades reflecting my visage in their mantis green lenses.

"Aloha, asshole." I tripped the trigger. My 00-shot batted Lars backwards. The ejection port spat out the smoky shell. Where Lars' five-pointed star had glinted, his lacerated chest now steamed like a pot of fresh lasagna.

Click-clank. Dale just aside the front tire jerked about to face me. It was like shooting skeet. "You wanted my ass, Dale. Here I am."

"You die."

But I beat him to the count. The sawed-off thundered in my fists. My volley bludgeoned him to the sand. His arm dangled limp, but adrenaline whipped Dale to his knees, and he jacked up his wobbly shotgun, but his burst of pellets shanked wide of me.

Click-clank. I adjusted my vector, and flame belched out. Pellets scalped him, flinging out morsels of white skullcap and grayish brain pulp. If I registered the horror, my body had grown numb to it. I racked in more ammo and stared long enough to verify they'd do me no harm. My sawed-off's stopping power was absolute, and its cordite saucing the air gagged me.

My teeth clenched and I forced a longer appraisal. The truck tire grazed Dale's leg hyper-extended at a cruel angle. His mantis sunshades sat askew on his chin, and his insect eyes riveted on the blue, empty sky. I marveled how it'd all flared by so fast.

The drone was a dragonfly wafting by me. Cody's mother had called them the "devil's darning needles". If true, the devil had knitted a hellish shroud from this blood-churned morning.

Chapter 19

I had two cop cadavers and one bloody mess on my hands. The clock was my enemy. Sheriff Dmytryk had bragged on my arrest warrant. I went through the cruiser's seats, console, and glove compartment. My irate breath came in jerks. Static blurted over the radio. The dispatcher used my now popular name twice. I smashed the radio quiet and spat through the cage on the rear seat where the misfits in cuffs sweated their futures. This one was still free.

"Pay dirt."

My arrest warrant was inside a plastic sleeve I found Velcroed to the sun visor. "Name: Franklin Johnson. Charge: Capital murder. Victim: Cody Chapman." Print made it official. I tore up my warrant, its shreds sent flying. Every cop weapon I recovered sailed out to splash into Mosby River.

I filched a smoke from the pack on their dashboard and put a hot match to the tobacco. Buoyed by the infusion of nicotine, I formed a plan. I leaned into the truck cab. Three-quarters full was more than adequate enough gas.

Had they radioed in their 10-20? What were their references to a "farmhouse" and "field ops"? No clue but I had an inkling Sheriff Dmytryk wouldn't miss combing here. Vultures within the quarter-hour would circle, a tip-off of fresh corpses. I envisioned the authorities at work. Wearing hi-viz jackets, they'd videotape the fallen deputy sheriffs (a chalk outline made in the sand was of little value). My heart lurched. I'd never outrun or outsmart their K-9 dogs.

Okay, calm down, I coached myself.

I knew any self-defense plea I made was futile. The news media's outcry of "cop killer" would lynch me in the court of public opinion even before my trial. Getting a change of venue was a joke. Gatlin on his most scintillating day arguing before a jury of my peers couldn't save me. I removed the cruiser's keys still in its ignition. The first aid kit I rousted from its trunk included a two-foot length of plastic surgical tubing.

My tank behind the cab seat made siphoning gas into a hubcap a cinch. I milked out a half-gallon before moving my knapsack and sawed-off a short distance away. But first I used a roll of cotton gauze and medical tape to dress my shot-speckled calf, proof I was no medic.

Next came the tricky part—Dale morphed into me. I draped him in my truck's seat and threaded his arms through the holes in the steering wheel. I'd rig the scene to mimic a harrowing shootout where I'd sat in my truck when it incinerated, leaving me as a crispy critter. Or if that ruse failed, I'd muck up the crime scene details enough to throw off Sheriff Dmytryk. Okay, so perhaps my logic was fuzzy, but I'd no time to refine it.

"Yo, what's this?"

The pendant I'd just frisked off Dale duplicated the one I'd scrounged up in Cody's office. I flipped over Lars and he carried the same dingus in a shirt pocket. Now I had three pendants, plus the one Twyman had seen from Rebby Cap totaled to four. Four pendants quadrupled the mystery, but they all linked up. My cop nose said so, but just how? I also had no time to dissect any fancy theories.

My sawed-off blew out the cruiser's four tires. Only ghosts of the dead could pursue me. Dousing Dale's corpse and my truck cab with the siphoned gas nauseated me. My truck was collateral damage. I dribbled a path of gas over the sand to a safe distance away, struck a matchbook, and ignited my crude fuse. The flames lapped down my trail of accelerant and lit up my gas-spattered truck.

I vaulted behind a tree and watched the fire whoosh into

a wall. Flames swamped my truck's frame, roof, and hood. The hot spectacle enthralled me until the lardy reek of scorched human flesh hit my nose and branded my memory. My gag reflex heaved up the sausage with gravy breakfast.

    I retrieved my stuff and booked as the flames snapped. My running boots pounded the sand, and trees blurred by me. The gas tank's explosion roared out. I heard the fireball hurtle up, but no rear glance admired my instigated mayhem.

Chapter 20

My thumb flicked the sweat off my brow as I rested against a loblolly pine. Smelling the greasy stink that'd seeped into my clothes sickened me. The deputy sheriffs' pendants, one in each palm, left me more perplexed.

Need to get more information.

I stood up stiff-legged, brushed off my ass, and gazed across the lethargic Mosby River. Locked in a drought since late spring, the river, if it moved at all, slithered over black rocks into scummy pools. Large-mouthed bass flashing coppery scales in the sunlight slashed up to snag airborne gnats.

The cop scanner hummed as I thumbed replacement shells into the sawed-off's magazine. No wonder military officers had carried them instead of sidearms in WW I. My 9 mil rode in the waistband at the small of my back. Redneck caviar—canned sardines packed in mustard sauce—went on the saltine crackers. Queasy again, I regretted eating. No humans yakked on the cop scanner. My geographical sense put me two miles west of Pelham, and the gun shop sat the same span northward.

Shock convulsed in me. I'd felt the dark vibes building all morning. *Let it roll,* I thought. Overwrought mental images accelerated in their onslaught. I slumped on the sand like a deep sea diver back on deck enduring the paralyzing bends. Shockwaves circuited through my arms and legs until my brain completed processing the recent blood horror. Then I turned practical.

Masking my scent from the inevitable K-9 dogs was a priority. I removed my boots and socks, hitched up my pants legs, and tipped a foot into the ankle-deep Mosby River. Muck squished between my toes before I waded upriver, adhering to the embankment shadows. A bobwhite chimed in the cattails, but its shy mate didn't respond.

Slosh, slosh. My sweat-oiled hands clamped the sawed-off's stock and fore-end. The knapsack gnawed into my shoulders, but my gait didn't let up. *Slosh, slosh.* The water striders like miniature catamarans glided over the surface. I enjoyed watching the blue gill and sun perch play aquatic tag. *Slosh, slosh.* A flat, scaly arrowhead protruded from behind a driftwood bole.

"Aw, shit."

Satan's split tongue flickered at me. Its pits at each serpent nostril detected my heat and stink. Hissing, it unhinged its jaws, and I beheld a throat stark white as a morgue sheet. Hollow needle fangs dribbled a green toxin.

"Aw, shit."

The water moccasin slashed out, its fangs grazing my jeans. I used my best defense. The sawed-off lowered and wailed out 00-lead shot. No more water moccasin. The drawback was the three adjoining counties had heard my gunshot, and deer season didn't open for a few weeks yet.

"Aw, shit."

Mosby River was no longer my ally, but I'd just about reached my departure point anyway. I tossed the sawed-off, muzzle end first, up on a ledge. After unlimbering the knapsack, I rested it beside the sawed-off and pulled myself up to the ledge. My anxiety over the deafening shotgun report proved well-founded. Somebody broke squelch on the cop scanner and animated chatter erupted.

"What was that damn racket?"

"It came from the river."

"Fan out!"

"We're on it, Sheriff."

"Just get Johnson."

I heard an auto engine strum up over the cop scanner. The next noise was clear as it was distressing. Just as I'd feared, excited K-9 dogs yawped, only they didn't howl over the cop scanner. No, the K-9 dogs worked the nearby woods. My reach for the knapsack brushed against the cop scanner, and it tumbled into the water. "Aw, shit." Rising dread touched off panic in me, but I knew the cop scanner had outlived its usefulness.

I rolled down my pants legs, stuffed on my boots, and ditched my knapsack in a hollow gum tree. My excursion came to persimmon trees, their branches studded by the puckered fruit. Hungry, I chewed one and spewed it out—too dry and seedy.

My trek bisected a stone wall erected by slaves when this riverbottom had been a nineteenth-century grain plantation. The slaves hadn't been paid one cent, much less for their overtime, and that'd been wrong. Rebby Cap and his flag decal came to mind. The much-lauded romance of the antebellum South struck me as anything but that right now.

The baying K-9 dogs crisscrossed a search grid to zero in on my spore, and I heard the K-9 handlers shouting out encouragement. I fumbled along parallel to the stone wall and wheezed for breath. My chances turned on Chet in his dad's '67 Plymouth Barracuda. He was supposed to patrol the state road up ahead, keeping a hawk eye out for me. Unless my memory was a sieve, this stone wall intersected a landfill where we'd blasted garbage rats. If Mr. Van Dotson hadn't phoned Chet, I was one of the bullet-pitted garbage rats.

Sticky spider webs cloyed my face, and I scraped them off. The morning had turned sultry, and I peeled off my jacket. My contingency plans were few. Plan A: Hide out somewhere. The humidity and heat might drive off my scent, flummox the K-9 dogs, and foil my trackers. Plan B: Build a spider hole in these rocks and shoot it out. Plan C: Keep my bony ass in gear. I opted for Plan C and, much to my relief, I met the landfill.

Virginia Creeper vines latticed the bathtubs, broken Clorox bottles, and generic rubbish. I rested on an overturned wringer-washing machine. The K-9 dogs' yelps had grown sporadic, and I speculated they'd divided up, one squad canvassing each side of Mosby River. They'd sweep downstream for a short ways, but when doubling back, the K-9 dogs would go nuts when they hit my scent. Local masons who'd constructed Garm Castle decades ago had excavated this sand pit, and our county government later made it a landfill. I bustled down the rutted lane away from the landfill.

No Chet driving a Barracuda appeared on the state road, but I saw a sandstone farmhouse where the state road leaned into a bend. One of many local family operations, the farmhouse crowned a knoll. I saw no vehicles parked under the trees and several outbuildings. No telephone wires stretched between the poles, but the lines might run underground. A cattle guard lay at the driveway entrance. My strides on the state road lengthened.

I didn't want to flip out any farmer, so I draped my jacket over the sawed-off. My shortcut across the field topped the knoll. Rusty hinges froze the wrought iron gate, and I stamped through it. No tenant had mowed the brown crabgrass in weeks, and I brushed by the arbor vitae hedge. My search of the outbuildings could wait. Duct tape patched the storm windows' cracks.

Standing aside to avoid taking a gut shot blasted through the door, I rapped on it. No host answered. My fist thumped louder. One eye stayed on the woods, and no baying K-9 dogs loped out. I jiggled the doorknob. Locked.

I found the rear door the same way, and I couldn't see too much inside. My first idea was to pad my fist with my jacket and punch a hole in the door glass, but I used my 9 mil's backstrap to chisel out the glass. My hand snaked through the jagged hole to scooch off the deadbolt. Advancing, I quartered the kitchen with my sawed-off.

"Hello. Is anybody at home? I need to use the phone."

Silence.

I penetrated further inside. The sink, stove, range hood, and refrigerator bore an avocado green. I preferred the same décor in Rennie's kitchen. The refrigerator light spilled on bottles of dark amber lager. German labels, I saw. Dishes and dry goods crowded the cabinet shelves. A fire extinguisher, dish detergent, and box-cutters lay under the sink along with a pile of old newspapers. I planted the phone receiver to my ear. My plan to remind Chet died with no dial tone. Cell phones didn't seem so lame to me now.

"Hello. Is anybody at home? I need to use the phone."

Pussyfooting on the balls of my feet, I cased the ground rooms. The ratty armchairs clashed with the new big screen TV dominating the cedar-paneled den. This lair catered to males. No family photos sat out, and cigarette smog polluted the air.

"Hello. Is anybody at home? I need to use the phone."

My foray into the foyer hit the stairs. What toys did our lads play with in the attic? A muffled crash from below brought me back into the kitchen. A door by the stove revealed a stairway leading down into the basement.

My hand flipped on the toggle switch. The bowed wood steps slanted below to a dark, dank place. I hated dark, dank places. Scratchy noises came. My nosiness superseded my paranoia, so I had to explore further. I expected mildew and cobwebs, but my eyes bugged out. The walls, floor to ceiling, bristled with 1940s Nazi paraphernalia. A cold, slimy lizard I knew as horror slid between my shoulders. Evil permeated the space. Revulsion jarred me. My intellect screamed: *Run!* But I couldn't. I had to know more. The proclamation stapled to the wood column summed it up.

> CONSIDER THIS, FELLOW AMERICANS!!
> History shows *jews* built a religion based on
> genocide and racism. It is true! Trust in those
> ideals Adolph Hitler set forth in *Mein Kampf*...

I got the gist and averted my eyes. A surge of puke burned low in my throat, always a bad sign. I tore down the poster to shred it up, and my need-to-know drove me to snoop some more. Framed photographs of haughty Aryan officers plastered the far wall. My eyes abhorred the portraits of half-nude women and children, agony carved on their faces, goaded by their armed captors to pack the ominous boxcars. My mind flashed to the trailerload of hogs I'd seen on the highway. Photographs extolled the assemblies of Brown Shirts and Hitler Youth, and I shredded up those as well.

A dehumidifier rattled on to run under a bookshelf. I went over and saw it was stocked with dreck by nut bag authors I didn't know or give a rat's ass. A folded map stuck out from a book. I found a red Magic Marker had circled the city of Washington, D.C. No notations suggested any reason just why.

My gaze traveled up front. A rostrum festooned with a red swastika glowered at me. I saw folding chairs stacked behind it. More than the one crackpot had colluded down here. A slinky, furry creature spilled off a mound of pamphlets, and I damn near vaporized a scared ferret. I could relate.

"You're trapped down here in hell. Good thing I found you."

I inserted the chatty ferret into my jacket pocket where it snuggled into a lopsided ball. I ventured back up to the kitchen and then on to the foyer. My edgy glance out the window verified no bogies were in sight. I still had time. My sawed-off led me upstairs to finish my tour of Hell House.

From the stairhead, I went down a short hallway. Steel bunks and footlockers sporting red swastikas furnished a barracks. The rumpled bunks looked slept in, but the footlockers proved empty. I went next door where my barking sawed-off ripped the padlock from its hasp. The ferret squirmed but it didn't squirt off. The room I entered smelled of fresh sawdust.

Somebody more adept at carpentry than me had erected gun racks from plywood. I read the labels created for handguns, auto-shotguns, and a trove of nasties. Fiery Waco popped into my mind. My curiosity had to ask where this armory had vanished. It'd take more legwork to find out.

My retreat went back downstairs. This was the nearby "farmhouse" the deputy sheriffs had mentioned. The "field ops" part still puzzled me. I'd heard of neo-Nazis, if that's what I confronted here, on the TV news. Who hadn't? Their ilk up until now had been relegated to the pages of history texts. However, seeing this direct evidence sobered me. Mr. Van Dotson had said a few Nazi hardcores had escaped, and I had a dire update for him—they were back.

I also knew violent rebellion had rocked this region in the historic past. Pelham, the town and county, had been named in honor of a fallen Confederate artillerist from Alabama. A local bronze historical marker recorded his heroic deed, what every local boy knew by rote:

PELHAM FELL HERE
Four miles southeast, at Kelly's Ford,
Major John Pelham, commanding
Stuart's horse artillery, was mortally
wounded, March 17, 1863.

Several Virginia belles from area plantations had turned out that March day in 1863, wearing jet-black mourning veils and weeping over the blonde, baby-faced Pelham. They decorated his caisson towed by a pair of black mules with mistletoe sprigs. But not all Virginians had shared in their theatrical outpourings of grief.

My descendents, Irish dirt farmers, had fled from the famine blighting the Emerald Isle in the 1840s. That March afternoon while the Virginia belles wept over the gallant Major John Pelham, I saw a somber tableau. My Johnson clan had grubbed on their hands and knees in the red clay, hustling to sew a potato crop.

Their marginal harvest with any luck was a hedge against winter starvation. They'd never shed a tear that March day. Who cared if Pelham fell here? They admired his valor, I'm sure, but the Irish were always an independent-minded bunch of cusses in the hilly region of the state harboring the most army deserters.

The neo-Nazi thugs would return to grab their swag, and

I should vamoose before then. Re-entering the kitchen, I sensed a bogie hard at my right, but the wallop crowned me. My arms threshed the air. I wobbled for a step. My teeth clacked as the taste of old pennies flew into my mouth. As I made my cut to black, my last thought was, *So this is death?*

※

Bit by bit, I grew aware I lay flaked out on the avocado green tiles. Dizzy and weak, I craned myself upright to slouch there, my hands braced on the countertop, a full three minutes before I stumbled ahead. The ferret squirmed in my pocket.

My assailant in a big hurry had left the same way I did. The sunlight blinded me cornering the farmhouse. My hand lifted to extract what had to be a hatchet buried in my skull, but the hatchet didn't detach. My excruciating headache raged on.

The sound of an engine drone drew my squint across the field at a black Barracuda, its fastback design unmistakable, trawling along the state road. The surge of joy I felt helped to clear my vertigo.

It was Chet.

Chapter 21

He'd overshot the farmhouse driveway. I screeched, waved, and fumbled in my small steps down the driveway. The woods at the landfill from which I was supposed to emerge attracted Chet's attention. Frantic, I pumped the sawed-off and reeled off three salvos, but hurting too much I couldn't manage a fourth.

My aggressive stunt did the trick. I saw no K-9 dogs, but Chet's brake lights flared on. The Barracuda notched a U-turn to fly back and scream up the driveway. I flipped out the Barracuda's door and eased my bones down into the black velour upholstery. I shut the door. The wiry, short Chet toed the gas and shot me a glance.

"Does the other dude look as bad?"

I took a moment to quiet my tremors. "I just got my bell rung. Was anybody else on the road?"

"Just some fool in an orange car. Is that a rat? My dad won't like rat shit soiling these new seat covers."

"Mr. Bojangles is a ferret."

"What are you doing with a ferret, Frank?"

"I found him at the farmhouse. He's the only good thing in there."

"Okay, but where were you?"

"I was right here. Mr. Van Dotson was supposed to tell you we'd meet at the old landfill."

"He did. He also said you tore off. What's up, dawg?"

"I left his place in my truck, bottomed out the oil pan,

and stopped at Mosby River to check it. Next thing I know Deputy Sheriffs Dale and Lars barreled up, their shotguns blazing to nail me. I did them instead. I doctored the crime scene to fake my death, and my truck is now charcoal. K-9 dogs and deputy sheriffs pursued me upriver, and I ran to that farmhouse."

Chet rimmed us on the periphery to a banked curve. "They came to whack you? But why?"

"I don't know but Cody's murder has raised a stink." I paused to link a few more distinct dots. "I patted down Dale and Lars. Their jewelry was the same design as the piece I'd quarried from Cody's office."

"Mr. Van Dotson said it was a necklace."

"A pendant," I said.

Chet snickered. "Could be they're fairies."

"Not fairies. Nazis."

Chet's snicker dried up. "Quit bullshitting me."

"I'm straight up. Inside that farmhouse"—my chin tip signified behind us on the state road—"it's like stepping back into 1938 Berlin. You should see it. Swastikas and photos are stuck up everywhere. I saw Aryan propaganda. Upstairs I found a weapons depot."

"Weapons like assault rifles?"

"That's it. Only now it's empty. Does a Nazi crew operate in our area?"

"Gerald may've heard a rumor. Nazis don't like our color. I don't like them."

"Me either. There was also a map with a red circle marked around Washington, D.C."

"Means nothing to me."

"Mr. Van Dotson told me the hardcore Nazi POWs during the Second World War were kept where the satellite farm is now."

"Our library might have a newspaper write-up on it."

"Uncle Sam kept the POW camp under wraps."

"Is it still there?"

"After the war ended, Uncle Sam flew the POWs back to

Germany and razed the complex."

"We better go see for ourselves." Chet shifted a leg to stand on the brakes.

"Not quite yet," I said. "Twyman has more information on the pendants. Swing us by his shop. I think he said he keeps Sunday hours."

"Do we risk a trip into town?"

"These pendants keep turning up, so they must be important. Everybody is at church or sleeping in."

Chet pointed us in the muscle car to Pelham. He and his dad had restored the Barracuda to its former luster. They had me beat as shade tree mechanics. I couldn't pull a dipstick without gooning up a head gasket. To me, cars were an anathema and since my long MP details chasing AWOLs over the Lower Forty-Eight, I detested driving. Travel hours endured on an Interstate were monotony. Neither could I understand pouring gobs of money into a luxury car. But then I got jazzed by watching NASCAR. Go figure.

Fields and farms sailed by us. Old Man Boggs in his combine harvester spewed shelled corn through the offloading tube into an idling truck. The combine harvesters scattering kernels and cobs over the stubbled cornrows lured in legions of hungry doves. I saw a startled covey flush up from the fencerow, their fierce wing-beat whistling in my ears. At the next family farm, I noticed a new gated community had germinated and I turned to Chet.

"Not much country is left to enjoy."

Chet's bony shoulders shrugged. "No problem, Frank. I'm just as easily a city cat."

"Is Gerald available?" I asked.

"He split early this morning for North Carolina on a bail skip." Chet's chin tilted at the windshield. "A roadblock is up ahead."

A sour grimace creased my face. "Are you for real?"

"You're a wanted man. Hide under that blanket, and I'll scoop the bushel baskets on top of you. But first hand me that ferret."

Not optimistic, I crawled in back and threw over the blanket—really a homemade quilt—as Chet hugged the final curve into Pelham. He reached behind him and pulled over the bushel baskets.

"Stay quiet."

"Keep it short," I said.

I heard the slowing Barracuda's tires chirr through the wheel wells, and Chet buzzing down his automatic window.

"Hi there, Chet." Sheriff Dmytryk used his gravelly morning voice, and his Masonic ring tapped on the Barracuda's metal roof. I heard the static on his handheld radio he must've used to direct my manhunt. "We need Frank Johnson for routine questioning on his cousin's homicide."

Sunday morning roadblocks are more than routine questioning.

"Don't you hang out with him?"

Chet didn't miss a beat putting on the guise of a kid eager to please. "Gerald and Frank are friends, and a few times they let me tag along, but I haven't seen Frank in over a week."

"What's up with the rat?"

"Ferret," Chet corrected the sheriff. "He's not vicious, or illegal. Just a pet I bought from a breeder in Sperryville."

"Uh-huh." Sheriff Dmytryk posed a cunning question. "Where are you off to on Sunday morning?"

I hoped Chet had a ready answer—one didn't pop into my mind.

"See my bushel baskets? I'm off to Mr. Birdsong's orchard to get apples."

"Sharp thinking. Go in early to beat the after-church crowd and before it gets too hot."

"All that and I brought my own baskets."

I could feel Dmytryk's laser eyes beaming through the Barracuda's large rear window comb over the quilt. The 9 mil in my waistband impinged on my sciatic nerve. My leg wound, courtesy of his deputy sheriff's shotgun, throbbed with each heartbeat. I had a violent image of shooting out the sheriff's eyes.

Sheriff Dmytryk sniffed. "Is that booze?" He gave a harder sniff. "Have you been sipping, Chet?"

"No way." Indignant, Chet undid the door handle. "Give me a breathalyzer. Look for any booze."

My nerves constricted. Chet's bluff eked too close to backfiring. Sheriff Dmytryk's shoes crunched on the gravel. I lay inert. My breath stayed trapped in my lungs, and my only moving body parts were my banging heart and my clenching fists.

"I'll let it slide, but if you spot Johnson, call me. Go ahead and take my business card. What's Gerald up to this morning?"

"He's not with Frank," replied Chet.

"Don't be so touchy. I didn't say Gerald was. I heard he's a full-time bail agent. How does he expect to make a living by doing that?"

"You better speak to Gerald. We never talk shop."

"I might do that. Give my best to your dad and mom. We went to school together."

"Will do." Chet toed on the gas. "I'll call you if I bump into Frank." I felt the Barracuda wheel to the middle of the road. Its rear end shimmied as the tires sped off. Chet's window whirred back up.

"Yo, Mister Armed and Dangerous, we're back in the clear."

Mr. Bojangles chattered as I threw off the quilt and bushel baskets. "Follow Edgar Street over to Wiley. Take the service alley behind Persephone Strip Mall and park us behind Twyman's."

Chapter 22

We invaded Pelham proper where the splashy hues of maples and beeches canopied its residential streets lined by modest ramblers and split-levels. Flame-tinged leaves eddied in our wake. A tall, thin man wearing a Walkman raked leaves away from a sewer drain. Chet blitzed through a stop sign and shipped into the service alley behind Persephone Strip Mall. My hand on his shoulder steadied him.

"Go at it easy, Chet. Let's not draw any looks from Pelham's Finest."

"I'm with you on that," said Chet.

I ticked off the store names stenciled on the doors as we rode by the various shops. A pair of grackles scavenged in the full dumpster for any food scraps to beat Monday's trash collection. Cutting the wheel at the last second, Chet swerved within a hair of grazing a pylon.

"That was too close for comfort. Dad would tar me alive for a fender bender."

"Didn't you ask him about taking out the 'Cuda?" I asked.

Chet shoved the gear shift into Park. "We'll be finished before Dad knows it."

"You better tell him," I said.

The service alley looked buttoned up. No delivery trucks had arrived to restock shelves for a new shopping week. We bounded out and pounded on the steel door until Twyman saw us through the peephole.

"Can I help you?" he asked, after pushing out the door.

"Frank brought some questions," replied Chet.

We went inside to the pasteboard boxes, a vacuum cleaner, and a cabinet of cleaning supplies cluttering the backroom.

"Stand guard up front," I told Chet before I looked at Twyman. "Last time here I brought in a pendant."

"I remember it. You requested an appraisal." Twyman polished a loupe on his apron corner. "Are you set to sell? I'll pay you top dollar."

I shook my head. "Just listen. Since then, two similar pendants have surfaced."

Twyman's brows wrinkled in dismay. "More pendants drive down the value."

"Forget the money. Their history is more important. Are your friend Zanzibar's sketches handy?"

Twyman's fingers combed a shock of coppery hair off his forehead as he motioned me to follow his gimp to a roll-top desk squatting in an alcove. Twyman inserted a key into the bottom drawer lock and snapped on the gooseneck lamp. The globe of light spilled down on the calfskin folio he removed from the bottom drawer. I produced my three pendants, the first from Cody's cigar box, and the two I'd skinned off the two deputy sheriff stiffs.

"How did you come by these pendants?"

"They're not hot so you can relax," I replied.

"Are there any additional ones?"

My smile was bland. "Let's focus on the sketches."

My pendants sparkled on Twyman's black velvet jewelry tray. He opened the calfskin folio and flipped through the sheaf of meticulous sketches. He gave a triumphant "m'm" and selected a sketch that, at a glance, I saw resembled my pendants.

"These pendants must represent a set," said Twyman.

"Did the same jeweler fashion them?" I asked.

"Probably, but not just any jeweler, Frank, because plainly this was a master craftsman. I'd surmise a customer ordered the pendants made to commemorate some big occasion."

"This customer had some deep pockets." I scrutinized Twyman's sketch, but the anonymous artist had left it unsigned.

"Their provenance is lost to history." Twyman subjected the pendants to his loupe. "I can observe one small disparity. The number of tick marks on each pendant's underside varies."

"But no tick marks are shown on the sketch," I said.

"Perhaps a later owner added them for I.D. purposes."

I wanted to examine the tick marks.

"Wrong way, Frank. Shut one eye and focus your seeing eye on the wall clock. Good. Now, pinch the loupe between your thumb and middle finger. Try and relax—this isn't brain surgery."

"Sighting through a rifle scope comes more natural," I said, fitting in the loupe.

"Do you observe the tick marks?"

"Yep, and you're right. The number varies. How many were on the pendant Rebby Cap brought you?"

"I missed noticing. The gentleman was rushed, but he left pleased after he learned of its value."

"Did you also try to buy his pendant?" I asked.

"Naturally, I'm a businessman."

"So, Mr. Zanzibar got these sketches right after the Second World War," I said to prime Twyman's memory.

"As I recall, it was somewhere about then."

"Can I pick Mr. Zanzibar's brain?" I asked.

"If he's still living, I'm sure. I haven't spoken to him in months. But I'll try to find his phone number and give it to you."

I jotted down my number on the flip side of Sheriff Dmytryk's business card with the proviso Twyman leave a recorded message if I didn't catch his ring.

Twyman studied his manicured fingernails. "The pendants are exquisite. As a collector I'd love to add them. Name your price, and I'll have no choice but to meet it."

"But you sell, not collect, jewelry," I said, suspicious.

"Not always. My vice is hoarding select gems."

"I prefer to keep mine a secret. I'll give you first crack if

I do sell," I said.

"My mouth is sealed tight."

Chet burst into the backroom, his eyes bright with alarm. "A cruiser just turned into the lot."

"Only a Sunday morning patrol," said Twyman. "I'll go piddle at the counter while you two duck out the back."

Chet and I exited for the Barracuda, and my hand clamped down on his wrist as he cranked the key.

"No flashy driving. Remember we're on a Sunday trip to the orchard."

"You're on the hook for murder, and all you got is for us to go pick apples?"

I crouched in the back seat. "You gave out this excuse at the roadblock. Find a phone, call your dad, and tell him you've got apples. That way if Sheriff Dmytryk comes asking, your dad will know what's what."

"Did Twyman give you any answers?"

"His sketches show the pendants as a set. An unknown jeweler probably made them in France before the Second World War," I replied.

"Is that significant?"

"I wouldn't rule it out," I replied, also intrigued by the pendants' Second World War connection.

West on Mitre Drive brought us to a near deserted mini-mart where Chet stopped.

"Did you eat breakfast?" he asked.

"Just get me a doughnut and ice tea. Make it beer nuts and bottled water for Mr. Bojangles."

"I don't cater to rats."

"Consider him as your furry guest."

Chet slapped the car door shut, grumbling what sounded like, "you can bite my furry ass", and strolled over to the pay phone. His expression turned serious as he detailed to his father what tied down our cover story. He went into the mini-mart, picked up our stuff, and a papa san shuffled over to ring up Chet's bag of purchases.

"Is your dad hip now?" I asked him back with me.

"He got the gist before he tore into my ass. This Barracuda is for auto shows and tooling around on sunny days, he tells me. If you can't drive a car when you want, then why own it?"

"Will he call the cops on us?" I asked.

"Not in a million years."

We headed off again. My ice tea and doughnut hit the spot. Traffic picked up as the churches let out, and I hid again in the rear seat.

"Did you hear me say Gerald is a bounty agent full-time?"

"Does it pay better than bush-hogging?" Mr. Bojangles nibbled the beer nuts off my palm, and I dribbled the bottled water into a yogurt cup for him.

"Gerald won't buy a yacht any time soon. Agents net ten percent of the bail plus expenses. His boss is a dragon lady, but he has to suck up to break into the business. It's hectic work, too. They juggle a bunch of cases and stay hooked to a pager 24/7. Gerald always takes off for North Carolina, Pennsylvania, or West Virginia on a skip trace."

"He must like doing it," I said.

"You bet because anything goes. Gerald wouldn't know a search warrant if it bit him. Bounty agents bust into your place, hang a riot shotgun in your ear, and march you off in manacles to see the angry judge."

My recon peering over the top of the Barracuda's rear seat worried me.

"Scope our rearview mirror. Is a tail on us? Two cars back is a big, chlorine blue model." Chet did as I instructed.

"Two suits ride in a Buick, maybe a Beemer."

"Plainclothes cops?" I asked.

"Can't tell. They're hanging back. Try this. I'll take a left...yep, they're still bird-dogging us."

"Nazis trick out in suits," I said.

"They're after us now?"

"Why not? We're after them." My sweaty hand squeezed the sawed-off as I powered down a window for a gun port, but then a more sensible idea weighed in.

"Pull us over," I said. "Pretend you're reading a house address number and see if they detour around us."

"What if they don't and open fire on us?"

"Fire back," I replied, slotting in more shotgun cartridges.

Chet again executed my plan, and I felt a large car's draft shipping by us.

"They're off to eat their Sunday dinner," said Chet, moving again.

"Good. Get us to the orchard," I said.

Riding over the town streets, I felt a twinge of guilt. Were my slayings of Dale and Lars on Mosby River justified? I rummaged around in my head to grab any Scripture okaying the use of self-defense. I tossed up a verse from Luke I'd learned in my catechism classes: *"But now if you tote a purse, take it, and also a sack; and if you don't own a dagger, sell your cloak and buy one."* For these modern times, I could substitute a sawed-off shotgun for a dagger.

How did you translate Saint Luke's true meaning? Men killed men in self-defense. Try as I might, I couldn't find another reason for the Bible to enjoin a man to sell a possession for the cash to buy a dagger. My hit man Limpet packed a .22 handgun, his version of a dagger, but I drew the line at citing any parallels between Dale and Lars gunning for me, and my hit man Limpet gunning for Marty. Then I didn't like mulling it over so I quit, but my thoughts took a darker twist.

My attention riveted on the Jet Jackal's last visit. He'd paid his respects after I'd booted out Marty. I was a train wreck. Everything in life soured, and the funk debilitated me. Then Cody dropped by the doublewide one morning while I sat at my table and obsessed over snicking the Beretta's trigger. A hollow-point bullet in the glass salt shaker ridiculed me to load the Beretta and play a bout of Russian roulette. Cody sat down and we talked.

"You want to hand me the Beretta, Frank?"

"I've got nothing left now." *Snick.*

"Marty is a slut. Believe me. I know her type. Flush her from your mind. Erase her from your memory."

Snick. "That's easier said than done, Cody." *Snick.* "She's bled me dry, and I'm left as a bag of bones."

"Your fiddling with that Beretta makes me sweat bullets." *Snick.* "What's say I take it off your hands?"

"I must've had shit for brains to marry her." *Snick.*

"I told you to re-up, Frank. Army life was good for you. You need a structured environment, and I can't fathom why you ever returned to Pelham."

"MP work bored me." *Snick.*

"What job is a thrill? I can't think of one. Just give me the damn Beretta. "

Snick. Snick.

"Please, Frank. I ask you as a personal favor, cuz."

How could I refuse Cody? I relented and handed him the Beretta. He put it along with the salt shaker and bullet in his pocket. Then over a short span, the Jet Jackal gnawed through its chains on me and sulked back to Hell's kennels. My depression lifted and my life perked up and I owed it all to Cody. That's why I couldn't believe he'd be mixed up with this scourge of neo-Nazis.

The blinker signaled our turn, and we cantered uphill over a crushed oyster shell lane to Birdsong Orchard at the summit.

Chapter 23

Chet halted in the fermenting apple musk, and Mr. Birdsong boosted up from the white cast iron chair. Lean and tall made him a Gumby figure, and his black-framed glasses copied Chet's except I saw the thicker lenses were bifocals. The aristocratic Mr. Birdsong in his beige poplin suit could've just ambled out of a small-town law office.

"Morning, gentlemen." Mr. Birdsong's forearm rested on our car roof as he gazed in and used a nasal tenor. "What's your pleasure?"

"My dad likes your Granny Smiths to put in his salads," replied Chet.

"The Grannies just came in. The dry summer has left my apples a bit smaller, but my customers say they're tastier," said Mr. Birdsong.

I saw the baskets stuffed with red and green fruit stacked on the shelves inside an old Sea-tainer behind us. Lethargic yellow jackets flitted through its open door.

"Sounds good. Just tell us where," said Chet.

Mr. Birdsong gave us the directions to go in his orchard. We left him and drove there. The Granny Smiths were at their prime, and we positioned a rickety stepladder under the nearest tree. The nimbler Chet clambered up into the branches and set to work as I held the stepladder. My inflamed gunshot wound brought back my deadly encounter earlier on Mosby River, and I started to feel antsy.

"Climb down from there," I told Chet.

"Take enough apples to make it look good."

"I need to make a phone call."

"Right now? Who are you calling?"

"You'll know soon enough. Hurry up," I replied.

We filled both baskets and loaded them in the Barracuda's trunk. When we returned, Mr. Birdsong sat at the white cast iron table. He arose and approached us.

"Chet, pay the gentleman. Meantime may I use your phone, sir?"

With a nod, Mr. Birdsong pointed. "It's on your right, just inside the door. Watch the bees."

My eyes calibrating to the Sea-tainer's interior dimness located the black rotary dial phone sitting on an upended crate. I doubted if the antique still worked as I swatted away a yellow jacket. The well-thumbed directory gave me the right number and ticking off the rings, I toed the door shut. Hearing Rennie's vibrant "hello" elated me.

"Frank here. How are you?"

"I'm better, thanks." Awkward pause. "Sheriff Dmytryk came here to Dad's with your arrest warrant." Longer pause. "Eddie Habib went fishing and discovered two dead men. The sheriff showed Dad horrid photos of a burnt corpse wearing a badge in your charred pickup truck." A longer pause came. "So Frank, what do you know about all this?"

I knew my sacrificial truck hadn't bought me much time. That didn't sting as badly as hearing Rennie's curtness, and I spoke in my defense.

"Both deputy sheriffs came with blood in their eyes. I had to stand and fight them."

"Don't do a snow job on me, Frank."

"God's truth, Rennie. It was me or them. They'd no intention to take me in alive."

Rennie lightened her brittle tone. "Tomorrow you'll go see Mr. Gatlin?"

"Just like we agreed," I said.

Her voice cracked. "You take care of yourself."

"You can bet I'll do my best."

My farewell trailed off, and we timed our hang-ups to coincide. I swallowed over the fork-in-my-throat lump, surprised Rennie's earnest plea affected me this way. I charged my next call to Dreema's apartment to my home phone tab, and she picked up, her greeting mushy from just awakening.

"You offered to help me," I told her.

"I did but this is sort of early. What do you need, Frank?"

"Do you have access to the FBI's NCIC database?"

"Through back channels, yes, I do."

"Run Cody Chapman through it and see what it spits out."

"That's doable."

"I'd like you to feed in Virgil Sweeney and Randall Darling, too."

"I've noted them down. Now it's my turn. Did you give our last chat any thought?"

"You mean the P.I. deal? I'm largely doing that now."

"But as a license holder, you'll get paid for doing it. Cool, huh?"

"Dreema, I'm not sold on liking this line of work."

"What else will you do? Bush-hog for the farmers in Pelham?"

I raked my fingers over my scalp. "Can you pop those names through NCIC?"

"Consider it done. I'll also send you the P.I. license application."

"Thanks, I think, Dreema."

I set down the phone receiver and nudged out the Seatainer's door to blink at the morning's brightness. Mr. Birdsong hitched one Florsheim up on the Barracuda's bumper and rubbed the back of his brambly neck.

"Mr. Birdsong knows something on Deputy Sheriff Lars," said Chet.

I gave Mr. Birdsong a questioning glance.

"Lars came with his family to the orchard. When he pulled up to pay, I went over, and he opened his trunk. I saw a red flag sticking out from under the baskets of apples. I thought it was the Stars and Bars, but when Lars went to fetch the checkbook from his wife, I tipped up the baskets. Well sir, the flag had a damn swastika on it."

"What deputy sheriff carries a Nazi flag in his trunk?" asked Chet.

"Maybe Lars had confiscated the flag," I said.

"No, the flag belonged to Lars all right," said Mr. Birdsong.

"I heard a Nazi POW prison operated here during the Second World War," I said.

Mr. Birdsong nodded. "The incorrigible Nazi fanatics shipped here. Lucky us."

"Did any POWs escape?" I asked.

"The head count before they flew home turned up a few short," replied Mr. Birdsong.

"Where did they go?" I asked.

"They stuck on American skins and slinked off to assimilate somewhere," replied Mr. Birdsong.

"How did they lose their German accents?" I asked.

"Oh, they'd stayed long enough to learn our lingo," replied Mr. Birdsong.

Chapter 24

"Where to, Frank?" asked Chet, stopping the Barracuda at the orchard's entrance.

"Head back to the farmhouse," I replied. "I'd like to set up a stakeout."

After arriving, we didn't spot any vehicles at the sandstone farmhouse, not a guarantee nobody was home. I came up with a ruse.

"Buck the car as if we've got engine trouble. Then stop, get out, and flip up the hood."

Chet grinned at me. "Stranded motorists can do a little accidental spying."

"Hopefully we'll see something useful," I said.

Chet rocked the Barracuda and edged over to the ditch a baseball's toss down from the driveway entrance. He popped the latch and went out to lift the hood. I saw no sign of my posse and K-9 dogs that must've moved on in their search. Chet played at thwarted repairs, smudging his nose, and after leaving up the hood rejoined me.

I knew Chet's dad enjoyed watching raptors and fished out a pair of binoculars from under the front seat. I trained them on the farmhouse. Mr. Bojangles sat preening on the transmission hump as we sat waiting, and watching.

"I'd go for some tinted windows. All this glass makes us too public," said Chet.

My magnified view saw nothing stir in the front windows patched by the duct tape. Our storm troopers, it would seem, had left their barracks for good. Seeing the kids' Hot Wheels toys left in the yard made their abandoned hangout all the more ghoulish.

"Did you call that Van Dotson girl?" asked Chet.

"Rennie. I did. She's upset over finding Cody shot," I replied.

"Uh-huh. This is a drag. I don't see how Gerald stands it. He tells me on stakeouts he pisses into a Pringles can and chews that nicotine gum to stay sharp."

"Sure, you make do."

"You dig this detective stuff, huh, Frank?"

I shrugged. "Right now I'm more interested in saving my ass. Let's give it twenty more minutes."

"We've got a nibble now." I saw Chet studying the rearview mirror. "An orange rice burner is chugging up."

I hit the floor mats and tugged over the quilt. "Motion them on. If they stop and offer aid, say a tow truck is on the way." Our weapons vanished under the quilt with me. Without fail, the orange rice burner screeched up to a stop. Why did country people always want to help you at the most inopportune times?

"Is your engine on the fritz, buddy?"

"My tranny crapped out," replied Chet. "The people across the way couldn't help me, but I'm okay. A nice, old lady called a wrecker service in town on her cell, and the hook will be by in a little bit."

The man's laugh issued as a bray. "I know the folks in that farmhouse. They aren't the helpful type."

That speaker used a familiar twang. He was Virgil Sweeney. He'd rejected my advice and stuck around Pelham. Bad move. I drew over the sawed-off, and my index finger nestled on its slick trigger.

"Did you go through a checkpoint back at the curve?" asked Chet.

"I sure did. The sheriff peeked through my windows and asked if I'd seen Frank Johnson. I don't know him. Do you?" lied Virgil.

"I just might," said Chet.

I eased out the opposite car door and lined the sawed-off over the Barracuda's roof. Virgil's eyes flashed to me, protruded in shock, and shifted back to Chet now loving him with the 9 mil's aim.

"Hands up, Virgil. Get out. Chet, park his car in front of us."

Virgil glanced around, saw no escape route without getting shot, and did as I said.

"Who are you?" asked Chet.

I made the introduction. "This is Virgil, Rennie's ex. We met at her apartment, didn't we, Virg? My bullet hole in his knee proves it. He just now said he knows who lives in the farmhouse, and he's up for giving us a personal tour and telling us all he knows."

"That orange Nissan is the same one I passed before picking you up," said Chet.

"Virgil's busy morning has included sapping me. Was your Nissan parked behind the barn?" I said.

"I don't know what you're talking about," replied Virgil.

"Didn't I tell you at Rennie's apartment to beat it?" I asked.

"I waited until this morning to drive home," replied Virgil.

"Where did you stay last night?" I asked.

"I bunked at a motel up the road," replied Virgil.

After shutting our car hood, Chet moved the Nissan and went back to rummage in its trunk. The roll of duct tape would truss up Virgil after Chet patted him down.

"Frank, is this similar to yours?" Chet dangled a fifth pendant on its gold-braided chain.

"What do these damn pendants signify?" I asked Virgil.

"I don't know, and I've never been to the farmhouse," said Virgil.

"Bullshit," said Chet.

Chet stuffed Virgil in the front seat and Mr. Bojangles snarled at him. Chet engaged the Barracuda and we kicked up the driveway's dust.

"Use the rear door I busted open," I said.

The Barracuda skated off the gravel driveway into the brown crabgrass before Chet braked. We exited and marched Virgil to the rear porch. Broken pieces of window glass from my hack job the last time crunched under our shoes. Roaches skittered over the kitchen's avocado green tiles.

"Downstairs." I motioned my sawed-off at Virgil. "You first." We descended into the neo-Nazis' nest of lies and delusions. This time the hornet buzz in my gut stemmed more from rage than the dread I'd experienced on my previous visit. The hot, muggy basement made Virgil roll up his shirt sleeves. I spotted his forearm tattoo of a Confederate flag overlaying a swastika. I also saw he wasn't wearing his wedding ring, a prop he'd used to play on Rennie's emotions. My sawed-off stuck Virgil in the side.

"I saw a map down here. Somebody had marked up Washington, D.C. Why?"

"Obviously it's somebody's destination," replied Virgil over a wince.

He acted too cocky for me. "I overheard Lars brag to Dale their pals went off on 'field ops'. I think you know. Where do they play their soldier games?"

Virgil shook his head, and Chet moved to restrain my fist drawing back.

"Hold on, Frank. Try this out. Pelham has grown too crowded with sprawl. That's why they decided to blow town."

Choking on my impatience, I nodded. "Okay, where did they move?"

"Virgil's car has West Virginia tags, and I know my native state has scads of hilly outback well away from prying eyes."

My sawed-off's jab cued Virgil. "Where are they in West Virginia?"

"I haven't the foggiest," he said.

I fished out his billfold, and his driver's license gave a Little Salem mailing address in West Virginia. "Did they pull out for Little Salem?"

"How should I know?" said Virgil.

"We'll go see for ourselves," I said.

We consulted a road map thumbtacked to the wall and found Little Salem in West Virginia's panhandle.

"What's upstairs?" Chet folded up the map.

"Their empty armory is a big joke," I replied, belittling the neo-Nazis.

Virgil snapped up the bait. "No joke. I heard they'd enough guns to outfit a castle."

"What else did you hear?" asked Chet.

But Virgil had clammed up again.

Chet pressed his 9 mil's bore at Virgil's temple. "Talk or I'll pop you like I did Briones."

I gave Chet a sideways look, uncertain if his shooting Briones had been a hunting accident. Next I wondered if Chet might pull a shotgun on Cody but dismissed it. Chet was my friend.

Miserable, Virgil recoiled and whined at us. "They're cagey talking around me and even if I did know more, I couldn't say it. These cutthroats will put a cap in my ass if I blab."

"I'll do it now. Did the Nazis go to Little Salem?" asked Chet.

Virgil only glared straight ahead, refusing to talk to us.

"I think the sniveler just admitted it," I said.

Chapter 25

"You're leaving their farmhouse intact?" Chet's disbelief, an exaggerated headshake, got my goat.

"What do you suggest?" I asked him.

"Rip a page from your playbook, and we burn the sucker, and show these punk asses we mean business."

Virgil had a hasty reply. "No-no, you don't. They'll kill us all."

I kiboshed Chet's plea and herded them back to the Barracuda. Chet patched Virgil's mouth, duct taped his hands and ankles, and I wondered why he blindfolded Virgil. Chet and I met by the trunk and saw through the windows our prisoner Virgil squirming in the front seat.

"I guess by now it's obvious," said Chet.

"I guess not. You better lay out what's on your mind."

"Cody was in thick with these Nazis."

"The hell you say."

Chet stood his ground. "You fished the same pendant from his office that you took off Dale and Lars, and now Virgil has coughed up one. They're all the same stripe."

"The hell you say."

"What further proof do you need? A signed confession?"

"Shut up and let's roll."

Chet dropped it. "Gerald dates a girl living in Apollo, not far from Little Salem."

"What sparked that romance?" I asked.

"Our shirttail cousins introduced them and they hit it

off. Sofia has even caught the bounty hunter bug." Chet ambled over to his side of the Barracuda.

"Call Sofia and ask her for a hand," I said.

"Will do, dawg."

I squeezed into the back seat. We rode halfway down the driveway where Chet locked up the brakes and tossed the shifter into Park.

"Why are we stopping?" I asked him.

Without a reply, Chet vaulted out his door, and my rearward gaze saw him race back to the farmhouse. The blindfolded Virgil muttered through his gag.

"Shut up," I told him.

I saw Chet hustle a gasoline can out of the tool shed and dart into the farmhouse where I could picture him in the kitchen balling up those old newspapers to wad up and stuff under the sink. He doused the newspapers in gasoline and lit a match. Sheriff Dmytryk had a limited chance to trace the fire to Chet.

The single point of origin under the sink suggested natural causes, not a case of arson. Insurance investigators, however, might detect traces of the gasoline accelerant. Chet returned the gasoline can to the tool shed. Bluish smoke wisped out a window as he scatted back to the Barracuda.

"Chet, what does this stunt buy us?" I asked.

The blindfolded Virgil let out muffled noises. Chet gassed the Barracuda to flail up blue stone and skipped any traffic check turning on the state road, and we slashed by the woods. I didn't see any K-9 dogs. A breeze fanned the flames licking up the tin roof, devouring its sappy pine joists and rafters.

The Pelham V.F.D. sat twenty long minutes away, leaving the farmhouse a goner. Seeing it aflame recalled the burnt human flesh on Mosby River. I heaved to puke and the knot on my head ached. Virgil's duct tape gag had detached. He mumbled obscenities until Chet patted the duct tape back down.

"Leave the orange rice burner?" asked Chet.

"The salvage yard will come and tow it," I replied.

"Okay I need some directions."

My finger tracing over the West Virginia map plotted a course over spidery roads to Little Salem. "Head north on Route 17 to Ashby's Gap, and then we hit Highway 50 west."

"It's under control."

I relaxed in the black velour seat, ignored my aches, and let my thoughts freewheel. The mysterious crates delivered to Cody off-hours at the gun shop bugged me. He'd always bought merchandise from international arms markets but why his underhandedness on these? A firearms beef landed you behind bars. Picturing the empty gun racks upstairs at the farmhouse iced the blood in my arteries. Who'd supplied the guns? But I stopped short of fingering Cody for equipping the neo-Nazis.

My eyes closed. This was unfair. Yesterday I'd mowed brush and today I was an alleged cop killer at large. Tomorrow I might go stir-crazy cooped up at the Red Onion Super Max. Or I'd end up Velcroed down to a gurney, a lethal cocktail mashed into my veins, then a second one injected as a precaution. Inside me, Merle Haggard sang the affecting lyrics of a condemned prisoner led away to his gallows. My eyes opened to dispel Dead Man Walking, but the bleak image lingered.

Maybe Cody had pegged it right—I was better off in the MPs. But law enforcement work drained me, and I just wished to go down the mean streets in my civvies, not garbed in a damn uniform. I yearned to blend in, just another joe in the crowd. I'd reached that critical point when I'd opted out of the MPs.

Late Sunday traffic was moderate on Route 17 before the Highway 50 turn at Ashby's Gap. The gradual ascent by the picturesque hamlet of Paris caused my ears to pop. Peterbilts, Wentworths, and Macks downshifted to a crawl to conquer the grade up Paris Mountain. Diesel exhausts spouted out ragged plumes of sulfur-rich carcinogens. Virgil had stopped writhing and sat quiet. I caught Chet's glance in the rearview mirror.

"My mouth is dry."

"Too bad the ABC stores don't have Sunday hours," I said.

I hulked over the front seat to see the speedometer. Chet had the hammer to the floor. A snapshot of my parents' fatal auto smashup played in my mind. Relieving Chet might be smart. We were in a different area code, and no highway cop patrol would recognize me, or so I hoped since cop killers were the devil's cum in all jurisdictions. Did it make any difference if Dale and Lars had been killer cops? Who'd believe my outlandish allegations they were in league with the neo-Nazis, frothing over my destruction?

My mood turned morose, and I cracked the window. Marty's duplicitous face reared up. Yeah, so I'd paid Limpet and my rancor at her ran that deep and dark. Cody's 25 grand had started the ball rolling. I could picture Limpet, crafty as a cheetah, out there stalking my prey, and I'd pored over the local newspapers, but I hadn't yet spotted Marty's obit.

Chet spoke up. "Keep me on the right roads, Frank."

"I'll tell you what turns to make," I said.

The recent time change—fall back an hour—left us with only fleeting minutes of daylight. We barreled through the hilly city of Winchester, home to the late Patsy Cline. She'd belted out heartbreaker songs, leaving the angels to cry on their harps. We got lost on the tapestry of streets made confusing by the lack of signs, but then we picked up our route. Further down the road just outside the wayside of Gore, Chet homed in on a neon road sign.

Bucy's Lodge
Members Only!

The Barracuda's screeching halt then made a whiplash turn into the median crossover, hurling me back in my seat.

"What's up?" I asked.

"Bucy's Lodge might tend a Sunday cash bar," replied Chet, speeding back the way we'd just come.

" 'Members only', the sign says," I pointed out.

"If you've got money, then you're a member."

"They'll card you."

"I turned eighteen and look twenty-one, but they'll never believe me." Chet's wad of money in a rubberband tumbled over the seat. "Pick up a fifth of bourbon."

"There's still that haul in front of us, Chet."

"Uh-huh. Wild Turkey will do. In fact I'll sip anything but a berry wine."

I knew from experience arguing with a Peyton, particularly Chet, was wasted breath. The Barracuda muscled into the Bucy's Lodge car lot and docked under a solitary streetlamp's pale, orange corona. The pay phone didn't appear vandalized.

"Here, watch my ferret and drop Sofia a call while I'm inside," I said before exiting the Barracuda.

Autumn had arrived. The air bracing me invoked a giddy remembrance of my high school's football games on frosty nights long ago. Ah, nostalgia. There was this car nuzzled over in a starlit corner. Inside the car, a blouse rustled. Hands fumbled and seams ripped. A bra clasp popped before coos escaped.

The spectators in the distant bleachers cheered my scoring a touchdown, but then Marty swung into my saddle and quashed reliving it all. I spat in disgust and ran a visual scan on the ten vehicles. Letters in smeary blue neon advertised, "Rolling Rock Sold Here". Chet hollered over the Barracuda's roof.

"I'm dying of thirst, Frank."

"Just phone Sofia." My strides doubled over to Bucy's Lodge, a squat, flat-roofed cavern. A caged light bulb over the entryway glimmered on the door's warnings, "Shirt and Shoes Required Inside" and "Must Be 18 Years Old To Enter." I was okay on all counts.

I braved taking on the tobacco haze. Brown paper topped the booth tables. The newspaper headline—*COP KILLER SOUGHT!*—in the vending box gave me a start. I went cold inside until I rejected the "cop killer" label. I'd never take one down without extreme provocation. My high school graduation portrait centered under the headline was a straggly mop.

Nowadays I went clean-shaven with a buzz cut to fit in a brain bucket I wore on construction gigs. Any casual stare had a less than average chance to make me, but I wasn't up for tempting the fates. I said screw Chet's dying of thirst and pivoted when a hammy wrist tapped my chest.

"Mind if I get my smokes from the machine, Holmes?"

I backed off to let the ex-linebacker by, and my eyes met the bartender's stare. Did he recognize me? A skinny bar bum glued to his stool no doubt since first call shouted in anger.

"Yo, Jeep, hit me."

"Can't. You've busted tonight's tab," said Jeep.

The bar bum dealt him a trenchant scowl as I padded over to the other end of the bar.

"Some crowd you got in here," I said.

"It's the usual Sunday night riffraff." Roly-poly and medium height, Jeep wiped his stubby fingers off on a Gatorade towel. I watched the bar bum do a telekinetic cigarette trick with his fingers. For the price of a drink, he'd reveal the secret, but I'd seen it done before at Fort Riley.

"Ring me up for a fifth of Wild Turkey?" I asked Jeep.

The same towel polished inside a glass tumbler, and I knew not to order any served liquor. Jeep snorted. "Hit the bricks, Holmes. Bottle sales from a bar are illegal in Virginia."

"I'm not out to jam you. What if I triple your going price?" Chet's wad—over sixty bucks, easy—appeared on the bartop.

Still Jeep didn't bite. "You a fucking cop, or what?"

Feigning disinterest, I edged toward the door. "Cops drink scotch. Bad asses drink bourbon."

Jeep gut-laughed. "Don't go off pissed, Bad Ass. That entire wad makes it yours, and we never talked."

The fifth of Wild Turkey tucked under my jacket, and Jeep stuck Chet's folded twenties into his white crew sock next to his ankle tats.

"What's tonight's big news?" I nodded at the muted TV held by brackets over the bar.

"A couple Pelham cops got capped. Good riddance, I say."

I didn't dispute his truculent glare but thanked him, and when I ducked out, the ex-linebacker smoking a cigarette slouched just outside the door.

"That's some mug shot in the paper, Holmes," he said.

My jaws worked but no words tripped out.

"Don't sweat it. My thanks, too. All Five-Os are cunt scabs."

"I better go help my friend," I said, wondering if he disliked ex-MPs.

The ex-linebacker flipped the butt and scattered sparks across the ground. "Uh-huh. Just watch your ass out there, Holmes."

Back in the Barracuda, Chet said he'd called Sofia. Virgil twisted until Chet took off his duct tape bindings.

"I need to piss," he said.

"The front bumper is clear. I just used it." Chet brandished the 9 mil. "Holler out or move screwy and I'll neuter you."

Virgil folded out, butted the car door closed, and shuffled to the Barracuda's front.

"I don't trust Virgil. He knows far more than he lets on to us."

"No, Virgil isn't too bright, but he can lead us to the Nazis," I said.

"But will he? Suppose Virgil still refuses to help us after we reach Little Salem?"

"I don't know," I replied.

"Do we pop him?"

"That works for me," I said.

"It might be too radical. This is all Cody's fault."

"Come on, don't start ragging on him again," I said.

"All right, but what I said stands. He was a Nazi."

"Suppose I accused Gerald of that? I know damn well it'd piss you off," I said.

"Gerald is a lot of things, but a Nazi? Hell no."

"But just suppose he was?" I asked.

"Well, if he crossed me, I'd whack him."

"No you wouldn't. He's family," I said.

"Probably not, but these Nazis are hardcore."

"They're amoral and deviant, sure, but they're also spineless and yellow underneath all the bluster."

"Sofia said she's ready to pitch in if we need her help."

"Good. Did you update Gerald, too?" I asked.

"Sofia will give him a ring."

After Virgil schlepped back to his seat in the Barracuda, Chet poked his finger into his chest. "No more lip out of you."

Virgil grunted.

We left Bucy's Lodge and polished off Jeep's overpriced Wild Turkey before cracking the Virginia-West Virginia state line. The bourbon's smoky flavor went down easy. Chet ditched the empty bottle out the window. Dialogue grew terse. The booze stupor left me feeling ugly and vengeful. The two-laner meandered up the flank of a bald mountain and then swooped into a valley before we launched into a climb up an even rockier ascent.

"Where is your Pelham gang?" I asked Virgil.

Virgil sighed. "How can I tell you what I don't know?"

The booze had eroded through my flimsy wall of patience. "You're a lying piece of shit, and I want some straight answers." A road sign flashing by inspired me. Chet had also seen the sign, and he was devious and cockeyed enough to collaborate with me.

"Haul it over, Chet. Virgil has more to tell us."

"No I don't," he said.

"But we think you do," said Chet.

He pumped the brakes and we slid to a stop on the summit. I jacked out my door as Chet sprang from his. My hustle beat him to Virgil's door and I yanked it wide. Virgil wanting nothing to do with us had managed to shimmy halfway out Chet's open door. We lunged in, grabbed Virgil's ankles, and dragged him out to us. Chet hooked Virgil by the right arm, and I snared his left, and we towed him back to the taillights' red illumination.

"Let me go." Virgil kicked and we dropped him.

"These mountain roads are perilous." I nodded up at the

dark outcroppings frowning down on us. "Rock slides."

"Huh? Rock slides?" Virgil turned from me to Chet, then to me again.

"Frank has it right." Chet pointed behind us. "That road sign back yon says 'Beware of Falling Rocks'."

"Be here at the wrong time, and an avalanche buries you," I said.

"I don't have the time for this shit."

I planted my 9 mil on Virgil, and he suddenly found the time.

Chet left us and clambered up to stand on a turtleback boulder. We watched his agile form cut between the laurel branches to eclipse the next higher up ledge.

"Time to leave," said Virgil, jumpy and irritated.

I shifted and my 9 mil checked his path. "Stay a while, Virgil. We haven't finished our powwow."

A stone came hurling down, its trajectory cloaked by the semi-darkness.

"Incoming," I said, stepping back a few paces.

The rock struck and rattled across the narrow pavement, crashing by Virgil. Realizing he played a human piñata, he shifted, but my 9 mil's cocking hammer petrified him in place. We heard Chet's scraping and stomping above us to dislodge more rocks.

"Better talk to us before the avalanche hits," I said.

Melon-sized projectiles flying down ricocheted off the pavement and bounded into the ravine behind us.

"Beware of falling rocks." Chet had a chuckle. "Get it, Virgil?"

An airborne stone whistled up and thunked into Virgil's shoulder. "Ouch." The next sailing rock tagged him on the hip. "Ouch. Fuck. What do you want to know?" He barely dodged another missile.

"Who went to Little Salem?" I asked.

"Make him quit it first."

Chet suspended his catapult act.

"Who's in Little Salem?" I repeated. "Did the punk-ass in the Rebel cap go?"

"They're a bunch of nut jobs."

"I already figured out that part," I said.

"Frank, the next load is primed to fly."

"Wait." Virgil's stricken eyes raised to Chet's treacherous shadow poised on the ledge above us.

I tried again. "Who's in Little Salem?"

"Yeah, a few are there, I guess."

"You can do better than that," I said.

"Whit wears the Confederate headgear."

"Whit who?" I asked.

"Whit Millard, spelled with two els."

"Good. Now, did you or this Whit Millard kill Cody Chapman?"

"Wasn't me. Don't put that on me." Virgil moved his head in emphatic denial. "Look, I started hanging with them for a few kicks. Life in a small town for a divorced man is the pits."

"Yet you inked a Nazi tat," I said.

Virgil wagged his head. "It's just a mean joke. One night in Little Salem, I got totally blitzed. The next morning I awoke with a migraine and this hideous tattoo. They'd paid for it, but I'm getting it lasered off."

"How did you get their pendant?" I asked.

"Millard gave everybody one. I guessed he bought them for pennies on the dollar from a fence somewhere."

"Who's the commandant?" asked Chet. A meteorite sailing down banged off Virgil's shin.

"Ouch. Hey, cool it." Virgil kneaded the newest bruise.

"Chet, rev up the avalanche," I said.

"No-no, wait. I'll tell you what I know. It's all Millard's bag," said Virgil, his words clipping out. "I've watched them act up enough. They don Nazi uniforms, strut around in military formations, and pop off automatic rifles. They stay in different camps like at the Pelham farmhouse. Only I was a hanger-on, never in the loop. I'd already quit attending their rallies."

"Bullshit. They'd grease any quitters like you," I said.

"They know I'm a screw-up, but I'll keep my mouth shut or else."

"Yeah, like you are now," said Chet.

"I'm not exactly volunteering this information to you guys," said Virgil, rubbing his shin bruise.

"What's up with this armory?" I asked.

"Beats me. Whit bragged he had something in mind, but I haven't the vaguest idea what. All I know is I had no part in their plans. You've got to believe me."

"Where's their armory now?" asked Chet.

"They never divulged its location to me."

"Who was their arms merchant?" I asked.

"I wasn't privy to that either. Look, I hate to waste your time, but I told you back in Pelham I'm a schlub. I know nothing. You've got to believe me." Virgil massaged his tender hip, and I'd had more than my fill of listening to his whiny excuses.

During Chet's scramble down, I broke it to Virgil. "I'm cutting you free. You sit tight until after we've left."

"You can't ditch me in bumfuck nowhere."

Chet laughed at him. "Can and will."

"A hard man who beats up his wife and kids can fend off man-eating bears," I said.

We sped off, leaving Virgil, a screaming lunatic, to shift for himself with the bears and rock slides. On the other side of the pinnacle, we pitstopped at an all-night Mexican joint, and chowed down on red menudo, pickle spears, and tart apple cider. The grub was better than the conversation turned.

"Virgil knows more than he spilled to us," said Chet.

I gave him a hard look. "You saw how Virgil is. He's nothing but a stupid thug. We've learned enough information to go round up Millard."

"Virgil played us, Frank. They've got something big and nasty in mind."

"Their shit, not mine," I said. "Nailing Cody's killer is my all."

"Then you shouldn't have ditched Virgil. He knows more."

"Maybe so, but what's done is done." I elevated from our booth. "Little Salem is still a ways off."

Chapter 26

Suburban sprawl hadn't metastasized in Little Salem. We cruised on its main stem, and I had a porthole into the mountain hamlet's heyday some five decades ago. The seams rich in anthracite "hard coal" had paid the miners' bills. In turn, slaving underground in the coal-face jobs rewarded them with asthma, bronchitis, emphysema, and pneumoconiosis, tarring their lungs black as doomsday. The coal took 250 million years to mineralize but a single generation of miners to excavate. Lyrics to the colliers' elegiac song "Dark as a Dungeon" by Merle Travis riffed in my head.

The played-out coal shafts brought lean days and the bulk of Little Salem's populace ejected. Only the diehards subsisting on church welfare and food stamps swore by their knolls. Familiarity bred fidelity. They stayed true to their roots. My dad's distant cousins, the Johnsons in southwest Virginia, copped a likeminded attitude. Called "coal crackers" and damn proud of it, they lived riveted to the same spot from cradle to coffin, no matter how bad the deprivations.

We trolled the crooked streets, vigilant for Rebby Cap's one-eyed white Chevy van. No dice. We expanded our net to encompass the outlying dirt roads, also futile. Chet pulled up by an unprepossessing garage, its signs touting "Semi-Used Chainsaws" and "Jesus Is Our Salvation".

"Get a motel room?" asked Chet.

"I'm too wired for any sleep. Try the next turn," I replied.

Chet cut the wheel left at the corner and ran us by Lawyers Row, its brass shingles the shade of weathered sculptures. (Where was my attorney Bob Gatlin? Still overseas championing the snow leopards?) The usual commerce—auto parts stores, barbecue rib joints, and a chiropractor's lair—went by us.

The oval sign over the Little Salem Savings and Loan digitized its messages: "38°F...12:48 a.m....Have a Snug, Safe Night!" Nice sentiment. Our next turn down Bear Wallow Road skirted the drive-in movie theater. I pointed out a deputy sheriff cruiser trawling through a strip mall. Chet pinned the gas pedal without attracting pursuit. Bear Wallow Road wended into switchbacks and my brain said, go back—this single route might leave us bottled up at the top. But the cruiser, a formidable threat below, forced us to press on.

"Aren't the Peytons from Keyser?" I asked.

"Not Keyser. Gerald and I are Paw Paw-born, but Dad moved us to Pelham before we started school," replied Chet.

"Do you go back?"

"Gerald hangs with a few shirttail cousins. You know, we should give Sofia in Apollo another call."

Chet's idea made sense. "Turn around at the top. We'll head down and find a phone."

"Solid. Gerald sleeps on his pager," said Chet.

Bear Wallow Road at the peak broadened into a blacktop paddock, and a radio tower staked its middle. An eight-foot chain-link fence with a top guard of razor wire protected the tower. Red beacons mounted at three successive heights pulsed at us. Signs on the chain-link fence read, "U.S. Government Property! Keep Out!"

As Chet scribed a U-turn, our headlights alit on a hieroglyph illustrating the radio tower. Seeing a crude, Day Glo-red swastika dumbfounded me. The tagger had somehow scaled over the razor wire to etch his ugly art.

"Looks like we came to the right place," I said.

"So it appears. Why did he risk castration to cross the razor wire?" asked Chet.

I shrugged. "He intended to make a statement."

A phone down below waited at the strip mall. Chet patched through our call to Sofia's phone as my eyes flitted about to catch any sign of the cop cruiser.

As he hung up, I said, "Bringing in Gerald might give us a lift. We're stuck in neutral here."

"He's still in North Carolina."

"Can Sofia get it done for us?" I asked.

"She says she works here in Little Salem, so she might know Millard."

Chapter 27

Apollo ("Population: 226"), Sofia's hometown, sat ten miles down the valley turnpike from Little Salem. Apollonites still left their houses and cars unlocked. Sofia's mobile home park was classy, and we took the right streets and parked. The mission-style ground lamps guided us on a beach pebble path to the porch deck off Sofia's doublewide. Chet thumbed the lit bell button.

"We'll crash here," he said.

"Coming into town, I saw a motel. Sofia won't let two strangers stay in her place," I said.

A porch light flaring on blinded us before a dachshund yapped behind the door swishing inward.

"Quick, come in guys. The mosquitoes are still terrible." The lady's papery voice upbraided her pet. "Hush, Nitro."

I trailed Chet into the living room and Nitro retreated behind the stove. Sofia flicked on a ginger jar lamp and signaled us to sit in the armchairs. She perched on the ottoman. I saw she'd just brushed her hair, but what impressed me were her large, mocha-brown eyes.

"You better lead me through it," she said.

After I recounted our story, she tugged the flaps to her terrycloth bathrobe, accentuating her breasts—there was a lot there to hold. "What do you need from me?"

"Do you know Whit Millard?" I said.

"He's born and bred here," replied Sofia.

"Does he head a gang of Nazi types?" I asked.

"Not to my knowledge. Who told you such a story?" asked Sofia.

"Virgil Sweeney," I replied.

"Yeah, he's another local and mean as a snake." Sofia made a face.

"We believe Millard and his gang are based up here," I said.

"Millard is obnoxious and arrogant. I know he's skipped bail for a grand theft auto, but I won't go after him alone."

"We can help you on that. Virgil claims after his divorce he got bored and started hanging out with Millard," I said.

"I've never seen them together." Sofia yawned into her palm.

"The last place we saw them was at a farmhouse near Pelham," I said.

"Why didn't they stay there?" asked Sofia.

"It went up in smoke," replied Chet, deadpan. "We know Millard has been stockpiling and concealing weapons."

Sofia put on a perplexed frown. "Why?"

"That's what we'd like to know," replied Chet.

I took the pendants out the baggie to display on her end table. The gold and diamonds glinted in the lamp's soft light, inciting Sofia's audible gasp.

"Are those things kosher?" she asked.

"They're crafted from 18-karat gold and three-karat solitaire stones and worth up to forty grand. Do they mean anything to you?"

"They're too rich for my blood. What, did you rip off a jewelry store?"

"I found them in the Nazi farmhouse," I lied, omitting any mention of my shootout with Dale and Lars until I trusted her better.

Sofia yawned again. "I'm off to work in a few hours. What else do you need?"

My tired bones replied. "Sleep will do us some good, too."

Kneeling, Sofia pressed her hand down to test the carpet. "This is cushiony and extra pillows are in my linen closet.

Sleep on my floor, if you like."

I nodded, surprised but grateful for her offer.

"Nice picture." Chet picked up a gold-framed 8x10 photograph from the end table. Gerald and Sofia had posed for the camera in a sunny place with lots of sand.

"Thanks. We took that at Cape May," said Sophia.

"Boss beaches?"

Sophia smiled at him. "We didn't venture out of our room so much."

Chet grinned but I didn't react when Sofia glanced at me. If Gerald and she were an item, I was happy for them.

After Sofia retrieved her pillows, Chet and I flaked out on her carpet. She gave Chet an extra cell phone.

"Depending on a pay phone is old school," she said.

Chet thanked her and his glance quelled my rising Luddite protest.

Nitro's sandpapery tongue scraped at my fingertips, and Mr. Bojangles, just tolerating the dachshund, squirmed out of my pocket and nuzzled into my knees. It was akin to sleeping in a damn stable.

I lay there on the floor in the dark, seeing Limpet close in on my ex and putting a cap in her. This time running the scenario didn't leave me feeling as fulfilled. I thrashed on the carpet. Too antsy for sleep, I found Chet's cell phone, ducked into the hall crapper, and closed the door. I moved a hairdryer and sat on the toilet seat. Gerald jumped on my call.

"The shit here is getting deeper," I told him.

"You're tangling with the Nazis?" said Gerald.

"You heard it right. Cody's murder set all this in motion."

Gerald grunted. "Get real, Frank. Cody Chapman was an asshole Nazi."

"So everybody keeps telling me," I said.

"I'm swamped here, but I'll bust this bail skip in a day or sooner and hook up with you."

"Any aid is appreciated. Meantime can we rely on Sofia?" I asked.

"She's rock solid. Is there anything else besides this Nazi

problem?"

His odd question stymied me. "What do you mean?"

"You got any other issues bugging you?"

"I hope not, Gerald. There's enough on my plate," I replied.

"Yo, some numb nuts is banging on my door. Stay cool. Catch you later."

Feeling a bit more upbeat, I poked out and curled up again with my menagerie. Sleep came, but before I knew it, rough hands jostled me awake. I struck out with my fists and Chet grabbed my wrists.

"Frank, we've got trouble."

A headshake didn't clear my grogginess. "Huh?"

"I just saw a cruiser's Christmas lights flash by the window."

"It's probably responding to a domestic disturbance report," I said.

"Probably, but do we chance it?"

More awake now, I sat up. "Better not. We'll split before they return."

I scooped up the jittery Mr. Bojangles. We barged out on the porch deck, and Nitro's paw nails snicked over the tile floor before he squiggled by my ankles to the deck. The October moon, fat and orange, cast sketchy shadows, and Nitro yipped at his.

My over-the-shoulder glance saw the windows brighten—Sofia was up. Chet under the Barracuda's wheel cranked the engine, and Sofia at the window flapped her hand, encouraging us to hurry off. No doubt she'd glimpsed the cruiser's lights, too. A pair of high beams flashed, and then skirted us.

We scribed a stealthy U-turn and sped up to follow the same pickup truck. We gained the main road with no mishaps. I checked my watch under the dome light.

"Gatlin expects me at his office in a few hours."

"He'll only tell you to bag it."

Resigned acceptance evoked my doleful shrug. "At some point that's inevitable, Chet."

"If it was me, dawg, I'd finish my business here. But it's your thing, not mine."

"Can't the cops now bring Millard to justice?" I asked.

"Why would they? The cops have no stake in this shit on Millard. But you allegedly nailed those two deputy sheriffs, and Sheriff Dmytryk wants your liver for lunch."

"Uh-huh. I guess dumping Virgil wasn't so smart. We're getting no closer to Millard and Sofia was little help," I said.

"Forget about Virgil. He ain't shit now."

"Sofia calls him 'mean as a snake'." A reminder of Virgil's smug boast rolled to the fore. "Back at the Pelham farmhouse, what did Virgil say on the Nazi's armory?"

"He bragged they'd enough weapons to outfit a castle, or some bullshit."

"Right. Suppose it was a slip of the tongue. Virgil's mention of the castle, I mean. Suppose a castle really exists."

Chet was skeptical. "I don't see how it's possible."

"I can. Rich eccentrics once erected castles like Garm did in Pelham," I said. "What if a coal tycoon put up one in Apollo or Little Salem? Then he croaked. Too pricey for upkeep, his castle sat empty and forgotten until now."

"How did Millard find it?"

"He's a native who knows the area," I replied.

"Nazis and castles don't mix."

"Himmler, I read, played a dark knight in Wewelsburg Castle," I said.

Argued out, Chet used Sofia's cell phone. "Sofia...thanks for your assist earlier...maybe we can tap you again...Frank figures Millard is at a castle, so does Apollo or Little Salem have one?...man, that's complicated...why don't we come and you can show us...just be ready to rumble." Chet punched off and dropped the cell phone on the gear console between us.

"What did you just do?" I asked.

"You're right on the castle, so I recruited us a guide." Chet nodded. "We're taking on a third partner."

"Great. Somebody else to get hurt," I said.

Chapter 28

I reached up to extinguish the Barracuda's dome light. Sofia in a dark outfit and carrying a bundle crawled into the rear seat. She frightened Mr. Bojangles awake to scamper along the gear console over the cell phone and to spill into my lap. I petted his fur to calm him.

"Hello, there," said Chet.

Sofia who'd put on her game face gave us a terse nod.

"Where to, ma'am?" asked Chet.

"Once out of my trailer park, make a right. This castle I have in mind is ten or so miles north. My parents picnicked there when I was a little girl. It was an exotic place."

"Could Millard use it now?" I asked her.

"It was a little ramshackle but if fixed up, it's habitable."

"Who built the castle?" asked Chet.

"A coal baron did back in the day. It's not so unique. A railroad president constructed an English castle up in Berkeley Springs. President Grant slept there."

"Awesome," said Chet.

But I bit my tongue. I resented taking on a third hand, especially one with untested abilities despite Gerald's guarantee. My next problem centered on how we'd destroy the found weapons. Chet's firebug mania was our last resort. Burning the castle and sending up a smoke plume didn't set well with me, but maybe no weapons or intact castle existed. Maybe I was certifiable.

Reminded of my morning appointment, I used the cell

phone to tap in Gatlin's number, but nobody grabbed my repeated rings and I signed off. The two-laner we followed crested a hogback ridge where the leafy thickets swallowed us. I felt like I'd only slept an hour over the last forty-eight. Sofia's handgun, butt first, pecked on my elbow.

"You're the gunsmith here, Frank. How about a weapon check?"

My fingers ran a mechanical inspection of her Beretta, the same model as mine back at the doublewide. The slide action on hers executed silky and precise while its steel clip held 15 rounds. I squeezed the Beretta's grips in my hand.

Just then, I gaped through my brain's mist and had a clear vision of the Jet Jackal stalking me. I recoiled from its hot, rancid breath mauling my face. The Jet Jackal flared its serrated fangs at me and blasted out a soul-shriveling howl. I stiffened at the chill spiking up my back, and I made a wish to go anywhere but to this damn castle in the mountains.

"You're good to go," I told her, returning the Beretta.

"Thanks, Frank. You can't be too careful." Sofia holstered her Beretta. "You sound bummed out."

"This thing could be bigger than us."

"Relax and it'll shake out fine."

Irritated nerves prickled me like an attack of shingles. Maybe it wasn't intentional on her part, and maybe the strife Marty had strewn through my mind exacerbated it, but Sofia's raspy voice similar to Marty's pushed my hot buttons.

"Things don't simply shake out fine. That's the sort of stupid thinking that gets you killed."

Nobody spoke during the frosty interval until Sofia's angry words. "Maybe I don't know these assholes like you do Frank, being as I'm new and a girl to boot. Just the same, I resent being called 'stupid'."

Chet intervened. "That's enough. First, Frank is right. Millard is vicious, and we'll stay on our guard. But Sofia isn't stupid. Her help is awesome. Frank, apologize to Sofia. Go on, dawg, do it. No more lip and lose the attitude, too."

"No." I turned in my seat to look at her. "Give me the

road map, and we'll finish this."

Sofia flung it at me. "Have at it, but you'll never find the castle up in the boonies."

"We'll manage it," I said.

Chet's elbow piked me in the side. "Cool it. You're gooning up things."

"No big loss. She didn't bring anything to the table," I said.

"Bullshit, Frank. You called me twice, remember? Millard is a bail skip, and I'm a bail bond enforcer, which lends you some legal standing. Or rather I should say did lend you, but I'm going home now. Turn this car around."

Like Gerald did when pissed, Chet growled. "Sofia stays, Frank, or else I'll also eject. Say hello to your one-man band. Which is it?"

Realizing I'd overstepped my bounds, I tried for a conciliatory note. "Apologies, Sofia. I'm just wound a little tight and shouldn't take it out on you."

Chet glanced back at her. "Well? Does Frank get a second chance, or is it back home?"

"I accept Frank's apology." Sofia paused. "I'll climb off my high horse, too."

"So good, we're a team again," said Chet.

The dome light flickered on, and a Kevlar vest fell into my lap. We donned the Kevlar. Chet leaned forward for Sofia to adjust his Velcro straps. As she did me, I grumbled how it felt like being clamped in a turtle shell.

"I read how eighty percent of cops killed would've pulled through if they'd worn armor, so we'll play those safe odds," said Sofia.

"Just wear the Kevlar," Chet told me.

Dogleg curves and near vertical climbs challenged us. We passed the antler alley sign, but the smarter deer were all off asleep. The orange hunter moon no longer burned over us, and the neo-Nazi castle we hunted out in the West Virginia wilds.

Chapter 29

"Just ahead, branch off to that logging road," said Sofia.

The Barracuda juddered off the blacktop, and its rear tires waffled in the loose blue stone until Chet's driving skill steadied us.

"Keep the rubber side down," I told him.

Our windows were down, and the yeasty odor of decay intensified as the yellow beams to our headlights penetrated the haze.

"See that fire trail?" Sofia pointed again. "Put us on it."

"Who uses these trails?" I asked her.

"Hunters mostly do."

The Barracuda cut along the high bevel to the ruts. Pointy rocks forced Chet's careful maneuvers to avoid bottoming out. For the better part of fifteen minutes we proceeded before our trek turned surreal. Ragged hemlock boughs swatted the headlights' glare back into our eyes. A detonation of pale wings and round shoulders smothered the windshield. Chet jerked the wheel and my pulse skittered for a few beats.

"Breathe easy, guys. It's just a snow owl. They fly quiet as a ghost," said Sofia.

"Uh-huh." Chet poked the black-framed glasses back up on the bridge of his nose. "As far as omens go, does a snow owl rate a plus or minus?"

She patted Chet on the shoulder. "It's just a snow owl."

"Sofia is right. No omens apply here. We make our own luck," I said.

"I'd say this is far enough before they can hear us. Nudge us in to hide behind the chinquapins. The castle is twenty minutes down through the trees," said Sofia.

We piled out and I didn't spot Orion the Hunter in the night sky. In fact, red and blue streaks broke through the sepia-toned eastern horizon. Daybreak waited on deck, and in the improved acuity I assessed Millard's level of security.

Did he deploy high tech minicams or vibration sensors? Or did he post sentries armed with automatic rifles? Guards were a basic protection, but electronic surveillance gizmos required some thinking and Millard, even if he had an animal cunning, was no mental giant. Booby traps also seemed improbable.

Mr. Bojangles scratched his claws at the Barracuda's windows, squeaking his gripes on his confinement. We waded into the rhododendron and witch hazel where aromatic toadstools and spongy pine needles paved the terrain. Not too far in, I detected a furtive hunchback troweling in the dirt behind a pulpit-shaped rock.

"That's Ole Jonah digging his 'sang," said Sofia, waving at him. "Leave him be."

I nodded, marveling at how Jonah the ginseng hunter, wily as a leprechaun, foraged for his keep under Millard's nose. Hope existed for us yet. The spiny seed balls of sweet gum trees resembling the battle maces that Crusaders once wielded crunched underfoot. We could use a few battle maces. Seeing a deadfall log where a black bear had clawed for bees and ants made my stomach growl. My liquid breakfast hadn't stuck to my ribs.

The undergrowth thinned out under a spreading crown of oaks where Chet walked point. I hoisted the sawed-off and trailed him by a few paces while Sofia toting her Beretta closed off our rear. We hiked by a ha-ha fence, a stone obstruction erected by Roosevelt's CCC for erosion control. They'd probably also explored the castle.

The soundtrack to Monday's sunup was the medley of birdsong trilling out in the trees. Our path sloped for a quarter-mile and then pancaked out. Chet led us until we breached a larger clearing, and I drew aside a beech tree branch. My jaws unhinged.

The castle loomed before us.

"Sorry I doubted you, Frank," said Chet, beside me.

I could discern each mortar line in the rows of red-stone blocks. *McMansion on steroids*, was my initial reaction. Pikestaffs crested the thirty-foot high ramparts while the ornate iron grillwork clad the V-arched windows. A crowned monolithic tower brooded over the new gate wide enough to admit a white Chevy van on the dirt lane. We'd stumbled in on the front side.

"It appears deserted," said Sofia.

Chet stood and reassessed before he ducked back down with us behind the beech. "No, the one set of tire ruts look fresh and makes it three or four at most inside."

"We might catch them asleep," I said.

My elbows braced on the branch and I tweaked the focus knob to the binoculars. My reaction was disbelief, chased by euphoria. Our first break had to be a mirage. The binoculars went to Chet.

"Get a slant at the gate," I said.

After thumbing up the nosepiece to his black-framed glasses, Chet fitted the binocular lenses to his eyes. Then he grinned at me.

"You must also see it," I said.

"The fools left open the fort door," said Chet.

"No need to knock. Let's invite ourselves in," I said.

Chet lit out for the gate, his footfall rustling over the dry leaves, but no gunfire disrupted the tranquil dawn. No Cujos bawled at our intrusion. I saw Chet halt and tuck down beside the gate. He maneuvered to peek inside at the courtyard and delivered us the all-clear sign. I shunted over, and Sofia trailed me. We crouched in a queue, urging Chet to poke out the gate several more inches.

"Assume hostile intent," I said, parroting Gerald's usual admonition.

"But so far, we're good," said Chet, before dodging through the gate's slot. I shadowed him, expecting all fresh hell to bust on us.

Chapter 30

It didn't. No sentries bellowed and no salvo rang out. We darted into the quince-fringed courtyard and saw the evidence of recent habitation—trampled grass and discarded beer cans. We saw no white Chevy van, just the tire ruts carved in the mud.

The tower's ajar door lured us in to see trappings gaudier than those Chet and I had inspected at the farmhouse. Direct lighting blazed down on the wall murals of neo-Nazi thugs lording over captured Bradley fighting vehicles, Tomahawk cruise missiles, and Army cargo planes. Millard in one vista, jaunty in his Rebel cap, posed beside a B-2 Stealth bomber. The murals glorified their perverted vision of a new world order. Their last attempt to establish it had kicked off in a beer hall, but I was certain a castle would serve as well.

"Millard has delusions of grandeur," said Chet.

"This is a total gross out," said Sofia.

The staircase corkscrewed up next to the inoperable cage elevator. Swastikas like the ones we'd seen at the radio tower and farmhouse glowered on the walls. Sofia's pretty features turned pasty, and she raised a window and propped it with a paint stick. The ventilation felt refreshing, but it'd never flush out the miasma of hate poisoning the rooms and seeping into our pores.

"Loads creepier than at the farmhouse," said Chet.

Millard had had interior renovations underway. Sunrays hammered down through the expansive windows on sawhorses, 2x4s, sacks of cement powder, and a mixing pan. A patina of brown filth covered the rooms reeking of cat piss. I saw no cats and recognized the odor of methamphetamine. I'd been in on a meth lab bust while in the MPs. It wasn't pretty—I'd shot and killed a dealer. I didn't sleep that night, fearful breathing the toxic meth fumes had rewired my brain in violent circuits.

The original carpenters had crafted the mantels and newel posts from a yellow-grained wood, now vestiges of a bygone luxury. I followed Chet up the corkscrew staircase, and my shotgun wound seared a spot on my calf. My wading up Mosby River to evade Sheriff Dmytryk's posse had infected the open sore. But the slimier horrors at the stair top sidetracked me.

We probed their inner sanctum, its lead crystal chandelier bedazzling the circular room. That spectacle was for openers. The central table built of plywood and 2x4s took the shape of an Iron Cross. A Confederate flag draped on each table end served as a tablecloth. An irony struck me—it was as if the two ideologies, neo-Nazi and neo-Confederate, had fused to create a modern hybrid of enmity. God only knew what new evils that brought us.

A flapping commotion arose over us. A bat flailed its wings against the ceiling medallions, frantic to use a nonexistent outlet. I resumed my study of the banquet table. Twelve chair backs bore a lion-and-shield coat-of-arms, underscoring the neo-Nazi's delight with medieval lore.

It got uglier. An ivory mug—actually a human skull—garnished each place setting. Teeth (human?) rimmed the dinner plates. I suspected the décor aped the dining hall at Herr Himmler's chateau. The laptop computer at one place setting was as incongruous as our recon through this castle.

Launching into a fit of fury, Chet plunged a shell into my sawed-off's chamber and cut loose on the chandelier. His lead pellets crushed the crystalline glass. Splinters prickled my forearms I threw up to shield my face. Electrical sparks crackled in hot, pink arcs along the ceiling. The chandelier swayed once, and then sank to bomb the Iron Cross at dead center. He jacked in a new shell.

"After seeing this, I want to shower with lye soap. I'd no idea this went on here." Sofia articulated my questions. "Just who are these fanatics, and what's their game?"

"We saw a swastika daubed on the radio tower," I said.

"A radio tower sits atop a hill down Bear Wallow Road," said Sofia.

I nodded. "What's the deal up there?"

"It has something to do with GPS gizmos," replied Sofia.

"That makes it a juicy target for a bomb," said Chet.

Shuffling footsteps on the corkscrew staircase drew our looks. A bearish man in a brown shirt with scruffy hair and pig eyes clenched an automatic rifle. He'd apparently been sleeping in a room downstairs we'd overlooked. He halted at the entryway, stared at us, and sliced up his automatic rifle.

"Are you the newbies?" he asked, lengthening his vowels in a mountaineer's dialect.

Chet leveled my sawed-off on him to put us in a stalemate.

I broke the ice. "Millard sent us."

"Uh-huh." He licked his sullen lips. His meth addiction had awarded him bloodshot eyes, facial lesions, and body tremors. "I see you're out of uniform."

"You're a palace guard, but we have to travel incognito. Cops, you know. Is that a demerit, Fritz?" asked Chet.

He wagged his head as if to dispel his chemical daze. "My name is Hans. Who are you again?"

"We drove up from Pelham," I replied.

"Did you bring me anything?" asked Hans, his crooked grin turning boyish.

Chet's head tip directed Han's gaze outside. "We didn't forget you, Hans. A few toys are locked up in the car."

Hans' grip on the automatic rifle relaxed. "Good. Dibs on the radio tower. I tagged it."

Quick on his feet, Chet nodded. "It's all yours, Hans."

"When we're given the order to strike, I mean," said Hans.

My throat tautened as my chest constricted. I gulped in

air to balloon my pair of lungs compressed by Kevlar armor.

"Right, Hans," said Chet.

A discrepancy only now occurring to Hans prompted him to frown and jerk his automatic rifle at us. "Car?" His pockmarked jaws set. "I was told you drove the big rig."

"Yeah. Well. The big rig leaves tomorrow," said Chet.

Han's eyes slanted at us. I saw his knuckles whiten to grip the automatic rifle. "I know for a fact the big rig has already left Pelham. Who the fuck are you?"

The explosive force rocked my ears.

Through the tangles of smoke I saw Chet had dropped Hans. The buckshot load had mangled his mid-chest into a bloody red mutilation. Chet handed me the sawed-off and dragged Hans into the hallway, smearing a blood trail over the floor. Chet's cool detachment amazed me, but then he'd been through it with his fatal shoot of Briones in the woods.

"They're taking out a radio tower," said Chet, back again.

"My gut tells me Millard has scads more in mind." I pointed the sawed-off at the blood smear into the hallway. "How do we get rid of that piece of shit evidence?"

Back downstairs after checking to find no more castle occupants, Chet briefed us on his corpse disposal solution. I wasn't sold on its merits, but its convenience was indisputable. Sofia nodded. Bags of cement powder rode on my shoulder, and Chet kicked the mixing pan out into the courtyard where Sofia followed us.

"First dump in half of that bag," he said.

The dry cement powder sifted into the mixing pan. Sofia filled a 5-gallon pail with rusty brown water drawn from a spigot and poured in the water. I found a hoe in the nearby tool shed and scraped it back and forth to stir the gooey mortar.

"That's the right idea," said Chet.

The crowbar he got from the tool shed pried apart the cellar doors. Sofia tied her jacket sleeves at her waist and poured in a little more water. I towed and bumped Hans down the corkscrew staircase, out of the tower, and into the morning sunlight where I tossed him down.

"Have you seen Hans before?" asked Sofia.

"No, he's a complete stranger to me," I said.

"Was he serious about destroying the radio tower?" asked Sofia.

"Yeah, I think so. Terrorists take a great zeal in blowing up Uncle Sam's property," I replied.

"What a waste." Sofia swiped her perspiring brow. "Such a terrible waste."

I saw Chet sidle down the steps into cellar's darkness. He shouted at me to come see the niche. I hated dark, dank places, but I went below and it was a fine niche, too, like something from Poe. I helped Chet salvage bricks from a debris pile in the courtyard, and I used an abandoned hod to tote the bricks down below to the niche.

Then I lugged Hans' balky corpse down the cellar steps. Breathing through my mouth didn't lessen his shit-and-piss stench. Chet retrieved Hans' automatic rifle and wiped off any incriminating prints we'd left on it. I knew a crime forensics lab discovering no prints on the too-clean rifle might raise a red flag, but I said nothing.

"Sofia has been giving me dirty looks," he said.

"No big mystery," I said.

"What did she expect by coming with us?"

"Our goal was to grab Millard and go. Instead a man ends up shot dead," I said.

"Did she have a better idea?"

"Let's just finish this and book," I said.

"I can't stand that bedpan odor," said Chet.

"Burning up Hans smells tons worse, believe me," I said, regurgitating the horror of my truck aflame incinerating Deputy Sheriff Dale.

The flashlight came from upstairs, and its beams sputtered inside the cellar. I experimented with stacking Hans to fit inside the niche, but he was an oversized Raggedy Ann doll flopping around. His slash for a mouth razzed me, and Chet muffled his chuckles.

"Quit dancing with the corpse," he said.

I dropped Hans. "You do it the right way."

"Cram him in sideways like you're nesting spoons." Chet put his idea into action while I wiped off my hands on a shop rag.

Sofia hollered down at us. "You need an extra hand?"

"Please come and hold this flashlight," I replied.

She did. Whacking the crowbar, Chet evened the rough sides to the bricks as I applied the stiffening mortar with a trowel and laid the uneven rows of bricks to reach the ceiling. The stench didn't abate. By nine-thirty we completed our rustic mausoleum. I stood back to admire it, when a cell phone's ring tone went off. I beamed the flashlight on Sofia's hands.

"It's not mine," she said.

Chet tapped on the bricks. "Somebody wants Hans."

We'd forgotten to frisk him and confiscate his cell phone.

"His battery will run down soon," I said.

We scurried out of the cellar, grateful to embrace the clean sunshine. Chet tamped down the cellar doors and heaved the crowbar. It landed in the quince shrubs. "After all that, I'm starved."

Sofia's hand clapped over her mouth. "No mention of food, please."

"I don't have an appetite either," I said.

Chapter 31

"We've found zilch," I said, feeling my frustration's bite.

"Maybe we haven't searched enough in the right spots," said Chet.

Fear widened Sofia's eyes. "I'm done working in that shark tank."

"No need to go back in the castle," I said. "Hans said the munitions had left Pelham on a truck en route here."

"Millard wouldn't risk running his truck by day," said Chet.

"Then their truck is hidden somewhere along the way," I said.

"We'll backtrack and find it," said Chet.

A near frantic gait took us through the woods. We boarded the Barracuda, and Mr. Bojangles wiggled from under the dashboard. As Chet nosed us down the fire trail, the furry traitor slithered over and nested in Sofia's lap.

"I call him Mr. Bojangles like in the song," I told her.

"How did you befriend Mr. Bojangles?"

"He was the only good I found at the Nazi farmhouse," I replied.

"That's important to you."

"You don't know by how much," I said.

"Everybody needs a pet. Pet owners live longer and happier."

The fire trail ended and Chet bumped down the dirt lane. I heard the gas tank scrape over the rocks and roots, but at least no snow owls dive-bombed us. Our ride on the paved road went smoother. A tiring daze sandbagged me, and I was content to slope back in the seat, mash my eyelids closed, and zone out to the songs playing on the radio.

Emmylou Harris, Leanne Rimes, and Alison Krause—those silver-piped ladies of the Appalachians—crooned us back to Apollo. I kept an ear attuned to Sofia accompanying the down-home ballads, her tenor pitch perfect. I enjoyed gentlemen blue-grass troubadours, but their wailing choruses lacked the soothing harmonies the ladies imparted. I started to ask Sofia if she'd ever sang professionally, but Chet had to break the spell.

"I see two things, Frank. One, the nosy cops force us to stick on the back routes only Sofia knows. Two, a full tractor-trailer will bog down at tackling the first steep grade."

"We can't impose on Sofia. She has her job," I said.

Unabashed, Chet called out to her in the rear seat. "Frank and I without a navigator will fly blind."

"Need you ask? Count me in. Absolutely," replied Sofia.

"Won't your boss gripe?" I asked her.

"Oh, I've got Earl by the short hairs. Now, don't go through town. A pig-in-the-poke sells coffee and Danish. Just go a quarter-mile past the turnoff to my mobile home park."

"So, what do you think happened to the tractor-trailer?" I asked.

"I think a truck pulling a full load hits trouble at the first steep grade," said Chet.

"That'd be at Paris Mountain. Their truck loses power and Millard freaks. He shuttles off the highway and parks his big rig out of sight. There he sits crippled, fuming to be off again."

"That's where we should hit him," said Chet.

I nodded.

The breakfast crowd, mostly blue-collar workers in bibs and hardhats, had jammed the mom-and-pop's grocer. "Kick Their Ass, Take Their Gas," taunted one bumper sticker. Chet and Sofia stretched from the Barracuda, but my queasiness wanted no food. Sofia called a neighbor to feed and walk her pet Nitro. Chet and she sidled into the grocer as I watched carefree gypsies in Jimmies tow their Airstreams by on the highway. My own freedom in peril compelled me to key in my absentee attorney's number.

A lady's prim tone responded. "Gatlin Law Offices, Ms. Reid speaking."

"This is Frank Johnson…"

She intruded, scolding me. "Where have you been, Mr. Johnson? Mr. Gatlin has been expecting your call. He's a busy attorney, you know. Please wait, and I'll try to find him."

I liked that, a well-connected attorney waiting for *my* phone call. Better yet, Gatlin had arrived in-country.

"Frank Johnson," said Gatlin with a trace of dry humor. "We go from discussing Cody Chapman's will to Sheriff Dmytryk's bounty on your head."

"I didn't just kill Dale and Lars. They charged me without provocation, their shotguns spraying lead, and I was unarmed, too."

"Sheriff Dmytryk doesn't reconstruct events that way," said Gatlin. "To hear him, you're a cop killer, pointblank. That's three strikes before you even go to bat."

"I've got no reason to lie to you."

"Watch your temper. I believe you. Now give me the abridged account."

I hit the highlights: my fatal gunfight with Dale and Lars at Mosby River; how fire had ravaged my truck and then gutted the neo-Nazi's farmhouse; my recruitment of Chet; our sojourn to Apollo; Sofia's able assist; and our dust-up at the neo-Nazi castle with Hans. I omitted our entombing Hans—Gatlin had enough to digest as it was.

"Where is this Millard?" asked Gatlin.

"We've taken on a couple of leads where to look."

"Don't tell me where you're going. If the authorities ask, all I can say is that you didn't show at my office this morning, and I've no idea of your whereabouts."

Ah, so the pragmatic Gatlin wasn't above flexing a few rules. He was my idea of a sharp lawyer. "Are you suggesting

I have to prove my innocence?"

"It sounds perverse but it's true. Track the logic with me. These pendants you found represent the commonality between Whit Millard, Virgil Sweeney, and Deputy Sheriffs Dale and Lars. We can assume they belonged to this Nazi junta. That's no crime since the First Amendment guarantees free speech, even for white supremacists."

"They weren't exactly upstanding citizens," I said.

"Precisely, and murder is a real crime. We can also lump in firearms violations and illicit weapons sales. Terrorist acts probably apply."

"Let my sheriff lock up the terrorists. Some low-rent killed Cody. All I wanted was to right that wrong, and before I can catch my breath, I'm the lead suspect for his murder."

"Apparently Cody was also a Nazi and a sneaky one at that. Even as his lawyer, I never picked up on it."

"The hell you say."

"But I do say. The facts fit. You recovered the same pendant from Cody's office. What's more, these Nazis ponied up the bucks for the armament Cody held a license to procure with ease. Did Hans also carry a pendant?"

"Maybe, but we lodged him behind a wall of mortar," I said.

Gatlin battled through a dry cough. "You did *what*?"

"Chet in self-defense shot Hans dead, and we had a corpse to make disappear. So we cemented up Hans inside the cellar wall."

"I see. Don't do that again."

"We didn't plan on it. But you weren't there and I was. 20/20 hindsight amounts to one-hundred percent bullshit."

"Calm down. Listen, my cousin Bill Ruffian lives in Shepherdstown. That's in your vicinity. He's at 13 German Street. Tattoo that address to your eyelids. If you get in a tight wicket, go see him and say Bob Gatlin sent you. He'll know what to do. Then call me when you apprehend Millard."

"First Millard owes me a few answers."

"That's your concern, not mine," said Gatlin. "Good-bye,

Frank. Stay in touch."

I tapped the cell phone on my chin, thinking. I dropped Dreema a call. She'd run the three names I'd given her (Cody Chapman, Virgil Sweeney, Randall Van Dotson) through the NCIC database without any record hits.

"That's odd. Randall Van Dotson did time for a property line dispute that turned a little rough."

"Contrary to popular TV cop shows, our databases aren't infallible," said Dreema. "Any other candidates to crank in?"

"Not now. I'll call you again in a day or so."

"Anytime but right now I'm late for a meeting," said Dreema.

Tapping the cell phone on my chin again, I mulled over the redlined map I'd discovered at the farmhouse. Had the neo-Nazis planned a protest march in Washington, D.C.? A door slapping in its frame drew my glance. Chet and Sofia ambled out, a six-pack in her hand. Chet toted a Styrofoam chest and ten-pound sack of ice. He dropped the sack of ice on the pavement to break it up before loading it and the beer into the Styrofoam chest.

"A few cold ones for the road," said Chet.

I frowned. "Beer isn't so smart."

"Then don't partake. It leaves more for us."

"Then I'll take over at the helm—" But Chet mashed in the door on me.

Sofia gave me some pogey bait, and Chet threaded us through the parked cars to the gas pumps. He hopped out and started filling our tank. A newspaper came out of the bag and Sofia opened to the front page.

"Kudos, Frank. Your picture ran in the paper. I see you go less hairy nowadays, an improvement I must admit."

"Let me see that."

I took her newspaper. The photo, my graduation portrait, was the same one I'd seen displayed in the newspaper vending box at Bucy's Lodge. This headline was also a doozy: "*Cop Killer Still at Large, Dragnet Closes In.*" Fear caused the newsprint to fuzz over.

Chapter 32

Sofia reclaimed the newspaper. "Frank, I'm sorry," she said, her tenor placating. "I didn't mean to upset you. Here, stick on these doodads."

She'd bought me a pair of inexpensive aviator sunshades and a black mesh cap. The Unabomber get-up I abhorred in the rearview mirror didn't reassure me, but I liked Sofia's thoughtfulness.

"Thanks," I said. "I'll use them if we go through town."

She nodded with an encouraging smile.

"Do you actually think I'm a cop killer?" I asked her.

"Not at all, Frank. I believe your story."

"At least Chet and you do," I said.

"Don't overlook Gerald."

"Right. How could I forget the big man?" I said.

Chet set us in motion again, and his eyes flagged mine in the rearview mirror. "Sofia knows a back route."

"The drawback is it'll take us twice the time," said Sofia.

I realized the Barracuda's conspicuous profile stuck out too much for us to use Highway 50. "Yeah, but the scenery is nicer. Better take it."

The overcast sky smelled coppery like rain and death as I espied a trio of PVC pipe crucifixes arrayed on a bald knoll. By the first mile I was thirsty enough for a cold one so I cracked three beers and distributed them. Chet leaned on the gas and the Mopar engine strutted up and down the bosky ridge lanes. Beer down the hatch bombed my sour gut.

Sofia read aloud from the article. "Listen to this bit: '*Authorities now believe the fugitive Frank Johnson is traveling in a classic 1967 Plymouth Barracuda. Mr. Larry Peyton admitted his prized antique car and youngest son Chet have both gone missing*.'"

"Gerald will be home soon and smooth Dad's feathers," said Chet. "Maybe nobody will notice us."

"Dream on. West Virginians pore over their newspapers only second to their Holy Scripture," said Sofia.

The road map was under the ice chest. "Gatlin said his cousin Bill Ruffian lives in Shepherdstown, and we can mooch on him for a favor like swapping out autos."

"Gerald can run me up later to fetch the Barracuda," said Chet.

Munching on a candy bar, I studied the road map, and Mr. Bojangles pranced across it to squat down in the middle and demand a pat. I did before picking him up. "Drive south on Route 5 and cut through the college. Two blocks down is German Street and look for Number Thirteen."

Chapter 33

Classes were in session at Shepherd College as we drove through it. I turned poetic and mushy. Tall, young vixens sashayed in form-accentuating sundresses exposing their long, lithe tans as if to stretch the summer's hot, bright limits. I'd missed out on the college experience, my loss it would now appear.

Just why I never went mystified me. I was a voracious reader, the majority of my books paperbacks, the keepers (Hammett, Macdonald, Lacy, etc.) stacked in my kitchenette cabinets at the doublewide. My writing was a minimalist style though I could stitch together more than a couple of sentences when I'd prepared my MP reports. My low funds had blocked my higher education, I decided.

"Frank, stay ducked down," said Chet.

I slumped further into my seat and saw Shepherdstown clung to a bluff overlooking the sluggish Potomac River. The rain began to slash down on us. In a few short minutes, the cloudburst dumped buckets of water to swill off the tin roofs, sluice through the gutters, and cascade into the drain sewers. Murat's Eatery, Esperanza's Taproom, and Aristotle's Pizzeria were the most profitable entrepreneurs on the diverse main drag. We heard the bell in the Trinity Church's tower gong out a single peal.

"One o'clock and all is well," said Sofia.

Chet gave a nod.

Not at all sure, I stayed mum.

Bill Ruffian lived over the Norfolk & Western Railroad

tracks where rack-rent landlords had subdivided the two and three-story houses into students' hovels. The ramshackle house we sought, Number 13, remained intact. Its limestone masonry complemented its limestone-bordered zinnia beds. A detached garage was also built of limestone. Chet parked us and we piled out into the rain, now a drizzle. Bracketing his hands, Chet gaped through the window glass into the garage bay, and we hovered off his shoulder.

"I can make out a big, black car. A Buick or Olds, maybe," reported Chet.

Sofia sounded nervous. "Should we call Mr. Gatlin?"

Ignoring her, Chet herded us to the garage door. "Damn, it's padlocked."

"That's to deter the punks," said an old man's quaver. We wheeled around to see he'd padded up stealthy as a big cat. "What do you want here?"

"Mr. Ruffian, I'm Frank Johnson."

Nodding, Bill blinked as if to say, *yeah, so fucking what?*

"Bob Gatlin gave me your name. He's my attorney. Mr. Gatlin said you were cousins, and you'd know how to help us."

I saw Bill's leathery face was pear-shaped. His slim physique couldn't shrivel another inch in the rain. Articulating words, his lips snapped under his liver-hued gums. "Are you Bob's gun-crazy kids?"

We nodded.

"Bob called me. What did you bring me in trade?"

Chet flicked the rainwater off his lenses. "My Barracuda is reliable."

Stretching his neck to scan past us, Bill appraised the Barracuda at the curb. With a nod, he undid the padlock and threw out the double garage doors to unveil a dark Buick LaSabre. We herded into the musty bay smelling of gasoline, and I saw the license plates running from 1956 and on screwed to the wall over Bill's cluttered work bench.

A ring of keys jingled from his pocket. "Pull it out. Slot your car inside. Be quick, before my neighbors start to gawk at us."

Bill's vehicle offered plush seats, and when I stroked its engine, a tiger's snarl poured out from under its hood. Chet ditched the Barracuda in the stall I'd vacated and Bill barred his garage doors. Sofia and Chet loaded into the Buick LeSabre. Bill at the open window released Mr. Bojangles into Sofia's care.

"I ordered the tinted windows installed. No FBI special agents spy on me. If the nosy cops ask, I'll cover for you. Meanwhile stay off the primary roads, but watch it. Push this chariot and it'll grow wings under you."

I yanked its shifter to put the transmission in first gear. German Street was a rain-slick tarmac, and Bill waving at us in the rearview mirror was a scarecrow pelted by the shower.

"Dad's Barracuda will stay unscratched parked in the garage." Chet turned to the rear seat. "Are any beers left?"

Sofia rattled the ice chest and looked inside it. "Sorry, we've only got empties."

The wipers scraped gritty smears over the windshield glass. Sofia used the road map and her memory to traverse the correct streets to leave Shepherdstown, and the West Virginia-Virginia state line waited some thirty miles off.

"I better report to Gatlin in case Mr. Ruffian hasn't told him we arrived."

"Oops."

My frown concentrated on Chet. "You left the cell phone in the Barracuda. Shit. Turn us back to go get it."

"But we're under way and Bucy's Lodge has a pay phone. Sofia knows a shortcut," said Chet.

"Bucy's Lodge also sells bourbon," I said.

Chet grinned. "So it does."

I watched as we lumbered by a field of cut corn. A covey of doves vaulted up from the honeysuckle fencerow as if to ridicule me, but fugitives from the law couldn't spare time to hunt for sport. Instead, they became the hunted.

"But then bourbon is good," said Chet.

My hooded eyes watched the doves vanish into the shadowy trees. "Staying clearheaded and getting home in one piece is better."

Chapter 34

I didn't spot my ex-linebacker pal hanging out at Bucy's Lodge. Chet and Sofia went in to replenish his bourbon from Jeep the bartender while I used the pay phone. Gatlin wasn't at his office, and I left no message with the starchy Ms. Reid. I checked my answering machine at the doublewide. Twyman had left a recording. He'd chased down the phone number for his old pal Mr. Zanzibar. I made a quick note of it, routed the call, and filled in Mr. Zanzibar.

"Right, Twyman phoned but I only vaguely recall a sketchbook. I divested all of my junk before I entered this geriatric gulag." Zanzibar used a frail, reedy voice, and my hand covered my other ear to shut out the road noise and hear him.

"Twyman said you ran across it in a Calais shop," I said.

"Okay, that part rings a bell. After the war, thousands of GIs waited for home transport so, bored, I hitchhiked to Calais. What a gas it was. A blind fräulein named Mallory—it means misfortune—ran a quaint whatnot shop."

"That's the one. One sketch shows a lady's pendant. They came as a set, and each features a big diamond and pearls in the shape of a daisy."

Zanzibar laughed with humor. "Sorry, but my memory comes and goes."

I hated brush-offs. "But who drew the sketches?"

"I've no earthly idea and doubt if we'll ever learn. Clearly you've never been in a war zone. It's pandemonium."

Film footage of the blitzkrieg steamrolling over Western

Europe flickered alive inside my head. "Did the Nazi Germans leave the sketchbook?"

"If I ever had one, I'd bet my wife on it."

"The pendants display tick marks, but they aren't detailed on the sketches," I said.

"No jewelry artisan would mar his creation. Nazi Germans stealing it might. I'd compare the tick marks to a gunslinger carving notches on the mother-of-pearl grips to his Smith and Wesson."

"That's a chilling analogy," I said.

Zanzibar sighed. "Yes, it is and this grisly topic of Nazis tires me. I fought them and once is enough. Good-bye and good luck, young detective." He rang off before I could thank him.

~~

The Buick LeSabre got us halfway up Paris Mountain. Eyes alert, we traveled at a cautious pace. A fresh set of tire tracks angling off Highway 50 cut down a sunken lane to an abandoned farmhouse. We figured it offered the neo-Nazis an overnight refuge. But the longer they sat there, the sooner the property owner might come snooping, or a trio of avengers bent on intercepting them.

Near Paris Mountain's summit, we found a turnoff to an old fruit stand to park. Chet flipped a quarter and I lost. So I left them and stalked off into the woods to loop in behind the neo-Nazis' suspected camp. Their heated argument guided me on where to steal up and hunch behind an old hay wagon.

Three Brown Shirts were griping to Millard that he should pitch in. Their logic was four men could accomplish more than three. Millard in his Rebel cap crafted a compromise. They'd smoke a cigarette while he shaved, then they'd all work in harness to finish restacking the wood crates into the trailer.

I sized up the gaunt Millard crouching in the knees and scraping a straight razor over his jaws. He used a hand mirror tied to a tree branch and reflecting silvery glints I saw in the late afternoon sun. Then he rinsed off the soap at a basin on an upended wood crate. He signaled the Brown Shirts to resume their loading the crates.

Sweeping right, I glassed the Brown Shirts puffing on their cigarettes. Their weapons I saw on the truck cab seat encouraged our chances. The wood crates looked spacious enough to transport automatic rifles. A garage and the old clapboard farmhouse sat a short sprint beyond the neo-Nazis.

Brown Shirt One, a cigarette screwed between his lips, came over. "What's up at the castle? I can't raise Hans on my cell phone," he said.

I had to smile.

"He's too busy working, something alien to you soldiers," replied Millard.

"I still say we better scratch this run."

"No soldier, we'll push on."

"Impossible. We can't reload by nightfall for another go at Paris Mountain."

"Bullshit." Millard jabbed the straight razor at Brown Shirt One. "I lost twenty-four hours due to your bungling, but no more."

I saw Brown Shirt One ball up his knuckles into mallet-like fists and hostility contorted his face. "The trouble is you've maxed out this trailer. The load is too heavy to overcome this grade and redistributing the weight will do nothing for us. I'm the driver, and I should know my big rig's capabilities."

"Figures lie, liars figure. So you figure out how to put us over Paris Mountain." Millard wiped off the straight razor on a rag. "We'll depart at nightfall and grind it out to Apollo. Next time has to go without a hitch. That's paramount, soldier."

"What next time is that? This big rig can't cut it now."

"You're flirting with insubordination, soldier."

Not hiding his contempt, Brown Shirt One rubbed the back of his neck. "You've racked on excessive tonnage. We ain't going anywhere soon."

Moving in a blur, Millard lashed out a simple judo kick and toppled Brown Shirt One from his feet to spill ass-first on the ground. Millard pounced to straddle Brown Shirt One's chest, gripped a hank of his hair, and wrenched back his head. Millard's straight razor flashed and Brown Shirt One tensed in horror. I saw its keen edge nick his Adam's apple. The trio of Brown Shirts gawked at their subdued leader's plight.

"Excessive tonnage, you say?" The bloodless Millard grinned. "Then you mules can haul it on your backs. One way or the other is no matter to me, but the entire cargo gets to Apollo."

Brown Shirt One's bug eyes riveted downward, watching.

Millard's razor swipe left a bead of blood. A demonic grin engraved his face. He liked it. "Tell your dough dick buddies to rack up the crates. No screw-ups, no emergency halts, and no backtalk, or I'll slit all your throats. Got it?"

Brown Shirt One, gulping, got it. Brown Shirts Two and Three snapped into action, wrestling the wood crates up the makeshift ramp. Brown Shirt One arose and dragged a wood crate over to the trailer as Millard buffed his clean-shaven jaws with a smelly cologne.

I crabbed away from behind the old hay wagon. Judging by the traffic's din, I put Highway 50 at thirty paces to their rear. Chet had calculated it right on where they'd maroon. My retreat into the woods sent me over a barbed wire fence. My boots tramped over the acorns carpeting the forest floor. A plan to subdue Millard took shape in my mind.

When I returned to the old fruit stand, the Buick LeSabre sat face out to Highway 50. Sofia and Chet sat on its hood sharing a cigarette and the bourbon bottle now two fingers from empty. Mr. Bojangles sitting on the front bumper preened in a swatch of sunlight, his catlike tail twitching.

"What's the score?" asked Chet.

"Better go easy on that stuff," I said.

"It's too late for that now. What's the score?" said Chet.

I nailed the final swallow. It scorched a tracer down my throat, and I pitched the bottle to smash on a rock.

"Their big rig couldn't lick the climb. They're at a derelict farmhouse squabbling over the workload. Millard and three men are repacking the trailer to redistribute the weight and take another crack at Paris Mountain. I saw no sentries or dogs, and it's ten minutes through the woods to reach them. We'll split up and trap them for capture."

"Armed?" asked Chet.

I nodded. "But their guns are on the truck cab seat."

"Sweet," said Chet.

My plan was a gem. Sofia and Chet would retrace my forest path and creep up to deploy behind the old hay wagon, tensed to strike. Meanwhile I'd move parallel to Highway 50, taking advantage of the cedar scrub as a screen. Once we were in position, Sofia and Chet would sweep in, and I'd cut off any jailbreak to Highway 50.

Scratching in the dirt, I completed the layout. Chet and Sofia nodded their approval, and I destroyed the sketch. The forest's shadows absorbed them leaving me. My nerves crackled with a snappy energy. I stuffed the squealing Mr. Bojangles, by now wise to me, inside the Buick. Tromping downslope took me into the tangy cedars. The evening sun was bowing behind Paris Mountain. The autumn leaf peepers and truck jocks thrummed by on Highway 50, and I could see snatches of moving vehicles through the cedar branches.

Sofia and Chet had taken a more circuitous route, and I wished to be in place first. My steps quickened. Tobacco smoke tickled my nose, and Millard's barked out orders came within earshot. I heard wood clack against metal, and my pulse notched up to a fiercer rate.

Chapter 35

I crouched behind the stone wall and peered over its top edge. Getting their truck packed and in gear by dusk grew more critical. They piled the wood crates just so inside the trailer. Why didn't Sofia and Chet hit them, my cue to close off our pincer movement? Waiting, I squirmed for comfort before I groaned at what I saw.

Sofia and Chet—their arms up and fingers interlaced behind their heads—had trudged into sight. A fifth Brown Shirt goaded them to march faster. He trained an automatic rifle at the nape of Chet's skull. My breath caught. Where had that sentry hidden when I'd scouted the woods?

"Look at what I bagged on our perimeter." Brown Shirt Four shared a malignant sneer with Millard. "They claimed they're out hunting. Shit. What's in season? Nailing dumb fucks with big noses, I'd say."

Millard flung down the crate lid and approached them. I turned and scanned through the cedars behind me. Did more sentries wearing brown shirts and brandishing automatic rifles circulate out there?

"Who are you?" asked Millard.

"Just a couple of hunters out in the woods. What's the big deal?" replied Chet.

Whap. Millard backhanded Chet across the nose.

"Hey, quit doing that," said Sofia.

"I'll repeat: who are you?" said Millard.

Chet, lying in the dirt, fumbled to retrieve his flung off

black-framed glasses. Blood streaked down his mouth and chin. He spat and coughed a little and that's when the bile flared into my throat, not a good sign. I stood up, ready to bag me a neo-Nazi or two.

"Why are you spying on us?" asked Millard.

My sawed-off rode at my hip. I saw only Brown Shirt Four was armed. Sofia, seeing me at a glance, reacted first, hoisting up Chet. I let fly a blast of buckshot and jacked in a second shell. Their heads jerked around, stunned to see me before they scattered, racing away.

My boot tripped on a loose fence stone as Millard romped off for the old garage. I hobbled up to chase him as the trailer loomed on my left. A scuffing noise caused me to look in that direction. Two Brown Shirts huffed around the corner, also making for the old garage.

My sawed-off's volley strafed the trailer's sidewall, missing them. I rechambered and shed my next round at them. Brown Shirt Four upping his automatic rifle sprayed rounds to kick up dust around me. Actioning in a new shell put me back in business. Brown Shirt Four created a clicking noise—he'd shot his wad.

Sofia waved at the old garage, shouting. Brown Shirt Four, screaming, heaved his empty automatic rifle. I looked back too late, and its muzzle speared my shoulder pit. Yelping, I jerked, and my 00-load dispersed skyward.

An engine squawked to life, and I saw the white Chevy van barrel out of the old garage. Now Sofia's shouts made sense. I'd also missed their van stored from sight. My last discharged shell had lodged in a stovepipe jam. Unable to shake it free, I stood powerless. Brown Shirt Four coordinated his sprint to vault through the van's open side door.

They streaked through a gap in the stone fence and steamed out to turn on Highway 50. The revved up van had tires squealing and glass pack mufflers thundering up Paris Mountain. We were too far away from the Buick to pursue them. My bruised shoulder and Chet's busted jaw were our only damage.

"The damn bourbon made us too sloppy," I said.

"We stay on top of our liquor," said Chet, defensive.

Sofia's headshake was emphatic. "Bullshit. That's it. No more booze. We almost got killed just now." She recovered our weapons dropped in the weeds.

Chet wasn't thrilled with our new alcohol ban.

My kick cracked a wood crate's lid where I inserted my fingers and pried it up. Ripping nails squeaked from the wood. I expected to see a raft of automatic rifles like the one lancing me in the shoulder, but what we encountered was a shock.

"Rocks…that's it?" Chet's mouth drooped.

Sofia bit her lip. "I don't get it either."

"Rocks," I said, hoping the incantation might tip me off with a plausible explanation. It didn't.

Chet gaped at me. "That's what we risked our necks for? They're crazy in the head."

"Are rocks in all of the wood crates?" asked Sofia.

We prized off the lids to the wood crates on the ground and then a sampling of those on the trailer. Their contents proved identical: rocks the size of medicine balls and similar to those in my doublewide's lunarscape yard. We found no automatic rifles, just the rocks.

"They hauled a truckload of rocks." Chet shook his head in exasperation.

I turned the lid over in my hands. It was unmarked on both sides. Millard's words, "the next time has to go without a hitch," echoed in my head, and this time it clicked. "Maybe it's not so weird."

"I don't follow you," said Chet.

"These crates aren't like those I've seen at the gun shop. I see no inked military markings, no warning stencils, and no explosive classifications. They're generic transportation crates you can find discarded behind any factory."

Chet toed aside a lid. "Get to your point."

"What we have here is a simulated run. I overheard Millard say their *next* haul has to go smoothly."

"Okay, so this haul might be a decoy," said Sofia.

"Millard won't let an underling transport the real munitions from Pelham," I said.

Chet nudged the black-framed glasses up on his nose. "So where are they in Pelham?"

"That's our new Easter egg hunt," I said.

Sofia climbed up into the truck cab. "I only see their personal weapons."

"Bust them up on the rocks. We're packing enough firepower," I said.

Chapter 36

Dusk had descended by the time we hiked back to the old fruit stand and filled the Buick LeSabre. Chet blazed up the twin beams and, more than ready to go home, mushed south to Pelham. For the first mile we said little as our pulses and breaths settled. Our good karma held, and no red-blue cop lights swirled up. No shrill sirens crushed the serene roadway.

Flexing his injured jaw, Chet caught my glance.

"Does your jaw feel broken?" I asked.

"I'll live. Just keep trucking," he replied.

※

Two hours later we hit Pelham County and sat snarled in traffic due to a three-car pileup at a stoplight. I ducked down and we slid by the cops. We then made a pit stop at a mini-mart, and Sofia went in to buy ice for Chet's aching jaw. I strode up to the pay phone and hit Gatlin for our next skull session.

"We botched our first go at Millard," I said.

I heard Gatlin smack his lips. "I see. Frank, my apprehension is mounting. Your manhunt has intensified. The state police ordered in a helicopter mounted with searchlights. They vow to comb every square inch of Pelham. Sheriff Dmytryk has interviewed me twice, and I blew him off, for now."

"What's gotten things so stoked?" I asked.

"Politics. Deputy Lars was the nephew of State Senator Reddman."

"Are you sure? I never heard that," I said.

"That's because they hated each other's guts. But Reddman is a politician first, and he's busy making political hay at your expense. Nothing whips up the voters more than salivating over a cop killer. The do-gooders established a reward fund for your arrest and conviction."

"This is crazy," I said.

"I dialed the tip line and they're quite serious."

"Where do we go from here?" I asked.

"For some reason, the authorities are under the impression you never left Pelham. That misinformation diverts their attention and buys us a little more time. Where did Millard flee?"

"West, but we're sure he'll circle back. They're squirreling away their munitions somewhere in Pelham."

"Locating these munitions is imperative. Now I phoned my lawyer friend at the Justice Department. She tells me this West Virginia group we're dealing with has recently drawn the Department's attention. The group is serious, determined, and worst of all, dangerous, she says."

I had a bitter laugh. "Your friend should try it on the front lines. What are the Nazis' goals?"

"She wasn't clear on that score. Because they're so secretive."

"I've discovered more than I want to know," I said.

"Right well, I see Millard is a bail skip, and Sofia holds a bail bond enforcer license so that sanctions your pursuit."

"What's the next step after I capture Millard? I also get busted?" I asked.

"Let's not get ahead of ourselves. By the way, I delved into additional facets of your case. Guess who rented the farmhouse you left in ashen ruins? Cody Chapman is who."

"No damn way," I said.

"Records don't lie. You keep deflecting the finger of blame pointing at Cody. Why are you so intent on protecting his sacred memory? Bury the dead, Frank. Their corpses always putrefy and stink."

"I hear you. Can we slip around this manhunt?" I asked.

"I'd say that's a crap shoot, so don't roll those dice right now."

"If we're to harpoon Millard, I have to stay up on his moves, including a jaunt into Pelham."

"Be smart then and stage it as a night raid. The manhunt is less active then but watch for the roving chopper's searchlights."

I hurried to the Buick LeSabre and reported on my conversation with Gatlin, concluding with, "So, our job is still to reel in Millard."

"No problem for me," said Chet, removing the ice pack from his sore jaw.

Sofia nodded.

"But we've got larger troubles," I said, striking up the engine and backing us from the mini-mart's parking lot. "Deputy Lars had relatives in high places. His uncle is a state senator who's been talking me up to the cameras as a psycho cop killer."

"Lars was the actual psycho," said Chet.

We returned to the highway, and I tacked our headlights in the direction of Pelham, my hometown under siege. Sofia shared her suspicions with me.

"Dale and Lars pulled shotguns on you, Frank. Why is that?"

"All I know is they had pendants, so I put them as Nazis."

"Good. Now who else owned the same pendant?" asked Sofia.

"Cody," I said, my voice tight.

"Then doesn't that link Cody with these Nazis?" asked Sofia.

I nodded. Chet, Gatlin, and now Sofia were all correct. I'd given Cody the benefit of a doubt for as long as I could in good faith. Besides my cousin, he'd been my closest friend. I hated to admit he had any part with the neo-Nazis, but it was an unavoidable fact. I let out a sigh.

Sofia glanced at Chet. "Gerald might be back from his

bail skip."

"Call him," said Chet.

The specter of adding Gerald's big man rage to this already volatile mix clenched my heart in mid-beat, but I didn't raise any objection, and Sofia updated Gerald. After listening, she thumbed off her cell phone, her smile turning wry.

"What did big bro say?" asked Chet.

"Gerald is back and his exact words were 'bring it on home'," replied Sofia, looking at me.

My heart resumed its pumping. "Fine, all. I'm up for it. Let's go see the big man."

Chapter 37

On my drive-by of Gerald's place just outside of town, we didn't spot any deputy sheriff cruisers, marked or unmarked, lurking on his road or nestling in a side lane. I heard no ghetto bird rumbling overhead, and our shunting into Gerald's gravel driveway blazed on his porch lights.

Gerald, barefoot and in a tank top and jeans, stalked out the front door. Where Chet was compact and wiry, Gerald towered near six-six and had bulked up to squat 800 pounds, bench 425, and power clean something off the charts. He mainlined the steroid called "attitude". I didn't miss the .45 Mag he tucked behind his thigh. His head was a massive cue ball and his flat, hard eyes softened only when he heard Sofia's ebullient greeting.

"What's up, hon?"

He stuck the .45 Mag into a pocket. "I'll show you what's up, hon."

Gerald ripped out the Buick door and lifted up Sofia, both hungry for a kiss. His hands sliding to her rump pinioned her curves between his hips. My little soldier twitched. Here I'd been fighting the devil by Sofia's side for the past twenty-four hours, and I'd missed the erotic delight of her femininity.

Then I felt a pang of warm emotion for Rennie Van Dotson. I missed her for reasons I lacked the energy and time to analyze. I construed my mushy feelings were shallow, but my affection for Rennie felt profounder than any emotion I'd ever squandered on Marty. A circuit of fear left my nerve endings to tingle. I'd last heard Rennie was with Mr. Van Dotson, but where was she now? Was she safe and away from danger?

"Yo bro, give us some time," said Chet.

Gerald broke off their kiss saying, "Why? I can see you any time."

Sofia's nod went to me. "Frank is in a jam."

"Your surveillance car is made to order for us," said Chet.

Only Gerald wasn't having any of it. "First you swipe Dad's pride and joy, and I do some fast talking to pacify him. Then you pull up in this broke-dick Buick, asking me to lend you my surveillance car. Dream on, bro."

"But you can drive your Mustang," said Chet.

"Besides, you already agreed to help Frank," said Sofia.

"Fine then, take it, but I can't go with you. My boss just called in a hot bond jumper."

"I'll pitch in with you, and then we'll join Frank," said Sofia.

"I like it," said Gerald, tossing Chet the key ring.

"Go grab our stuff, Frank," said Chet.

The four-door hoopty Chet drove up in was a nondescript champagne color. You'd passed a dozen of them in a day and wouldn't recall a single one, which was the general idea. Any parked surveillance had to blend in like a fire hydrant or a cable box on the subject's street. The car also had no hope of outrunning or even eluding a deputy sheriff cruiser. Gerald tapped me on the wrist with something.

"Take this cell. Keep your shit tight, but if you hit any turbulence, call me. Frank, don't sweat it. It's all good." Gerald dished me a cagey wink and a slap on the shoulder. Somehow, despite the manhunt rocking Pelham off its foundation, his tough-as-Shaft swagger gave me hope.

My head propped against the car window frame as Chet accelerated away from Gerald's house. I watched Gerald chase Sofia to the lit porch. They were laughing like young lovers do, and maybe I was a little envious of them.

"Aw go on and phone her." Chet scoffed louder. "I mean it. Talk to that damn Van Dotson girl. Do it now before your moping depresses the shit out of me."

"Okay you twisted my arm."

Right off Rennie answered, her voice tentative. "You haven't, I guess, watched much TV," she said. "But Senator Reddman is anxious to catch you. Now tell me the truth. Did you do it? Did you shoot the two deputy sheriffs in cold blood like he keeps harping on? One was his nephew. That's his family, and this is awful. My stomach is tied in knots."

The pair of accusations, Senator Reddman's and hers, tied my nerves in knots. Anger renewed my gut churn. "I told you before Dale and Lars came dealing death. What was I supposed to do? Stand there like a mannequin and play their target? Hell no, I used self-defense. Believe me, that's the true story of Mosby River."

"How did Pelham plunge into this bedlam? Roadblocks are set up on the outskirts of town. Troopers patrol our streets. Helicopters fly like a scourge of locusts. You're a wanted fugitive."

"Rennie, ignore what this Reddman says. He's just playing to the cameras. I'll gut through this. It won't hurt me, or you." In that crystalline instant, I could snatch a glimpse of our possible future together residing in Pelham, and I added. "Or us. You'll see if you just give it a fair chance."

"Were the two deputy sheriffs responsible for Cody's murder?"

"In part, yes, I believe so."

"I see. Anyway, you missed Cody's viewing tonight. I tried to postpone it, but Sheriff Dmytryk said, no way. It was nice. I saw lots of mums and gladiolas, and everybody there signed the registry. Cody was well-liked. We used a walnut and not maple casket."

"That's swell. Again, thanks. I'll pay you back the money."

"I know you will. Sheriff Dmytryk ordered a cordon of his men around Fincham's."

"I figured as much."

"Have you spoken to Mr. Gatlin?"

"I keep him in the loop."

"Good, good. But do you have enough help, Frank?"

"We just enlisted Gerald Peyton. He's a bounty hunter."

"A bounty hunter helps you?" She hesitated. "But is Gerald any good?"

Her query made me smile. "Put it this way. Gerald is a force to reckon with."

"Wait a second, Frank. Here's Dad."

Mr. Van Dotson came on the connection. "Virgil Sweeney drove up a couple of hours ago."

"Fuck. What did he want?"

"Hunting for you, he said. Rennie and the grandkids stayed inside, the doors deadbolted. She wouldn't let me take him off at the head, so I just ran him off."

"That's probably a good idea. Did Virgil come alone?"

"Yeah, he did."

"Have you seen the white Chevy van or Rebby Cap?"

"Our only visitors have been Virgil and the deputy sheriffs."

"Okay that's good. I better go." I folded the cell phone shut.

"You've got it bad for this girl," said Chet.

I nodded. "Guilty as charged. She's definite wife material."

"Oh fuck, here we go again," said Chet, no humor in it, but I had to smile.

Chapter 38

Gerald lived out of the surveillance car for nights at a time sitting on a bail skip's crib. That accounted for the Chubb handcuffs, Aquafina bottled water, and the pair of binoculars I saw in the rear seat. I found a stack of various business cards (for a fake identity) and a dog leash (for a cover story) in the glove compartment. We rambled on through the night.

Mr. Bojangles poked his bullet-head snout under my fingers, acting all cute. I acquiesced and scratched between his pointy ears. He chattered at me, and we were becoming fast road buddies. I indulged a mental picture. Virgil at the neo-Nazi's farmhouse had rolled up his sleeves. A distinctive forearm tattoo showed a swastika overlaying a Confederate flag. I had to verify if Cody sported the same tattooed logo on his forearm, if he was a full member of the neo-Nazis.

"Cody's viewing was tonight," I said.

Chet scoffed. "SWAT covered Fincham's. You'd never get within pissing distance."

"True enough, but it's going on eleven o'clock." I inserted an afterthought. "Everybody went home hours ago."

"So?"

"So we can go pay our respects now."

"Better forget about it. Fincham won't let you in."

"Who said jack about Fincham?"

Chet reacted to hearing my shrewd cadence. "You're fried, dawg. I ain't—and I'll repeat it—I *ain't* busting in there to disturb the corpses."

I ignored Chet's vow. "We'll peep in the coffin, too. Cody deserves a final salute. It's only right. I was his next-of-kin, after all."

"Doesn't cracking open a coffin holding a dead dude freak you?"

"If Gerald was the dead dude in the coffin instead of Cody, wouldn't you expect my aid if you asked me?"

Chet reconsidered. "Right, right."

"That sounds better. Let's get to it," I said.

The moonlight eliminated any need for using flashlights. Our tired legs at a long day's end demanded we drive into Pelham, not park on the outskirts and walk into town. Chet took a seldom-used alley, and we hit no flak. He slotted the car between the three grain silos at the Farmers Co-op just off Main Street.

"Are your lock picks in the glove compartment?" I asked.

"Gerald's lock picks, not mine. They're his Ebay swag."

I didn't express my skepticism that Ebay would sell illegal lock picks online.

We darted down the ill-lit streets hushed as ghost-ridden canyons. The street lamps' buzz serenaded us until we spotted two uniformed figures armed with automatic rifles loitering under a cone of light. They murmured and smoked cigarettes, the epitome of a lax night guard. Going the other way gave us the shortcut alley between the old bank and drugstore, and we reached Main Street.

A look from a corner showed us the washerette's open door. No night owls trucked in baskets of dirty clothes, and we continued prowling on to Fincham's Funeral Home, a brownstone rambler with matching yellow shutters and doors. It shared a common parking lot with a scab barbershop and a contemptible pay-day loan store.

Orange cones and barricades had directed the conga lines of gawkers attending Cody's bon voyage party. We hefted up to the loading dock, and Chet knelt to fiddle at the lock. I leaned my forearms on the hearse, its hood glossy black.

"My cousin in Paw Paw did a stretch for a b-and-e."

"We'll be careful. Can't you hurry it?" I said.

I saw Chet lick a third steel pick and test it. "We're in, dawg."

Inside the yellow door the chilled draft hit us, its fumes of embalming fluid leaving me light-headed. The ceiling lamplight caromed off the shiny, arched lids of different coffin models, all arranged by rows in the undertaker's sales room.

"Mucking around in here will tick off Fincham."

I grinned at Chet's apparent heebie-jeebies. "Just stick close to me. Safety in numbers."

"No argument here."

The double doors in the far alcove bore the warning, "No Patrons Permitted Beyond Here!" We entered anyway. Refrigerated display cases preserved showy flowers like gladiolas, chrysanthemums, and baby's breath sold to the bereaved. My shuddering glance at another closed door identified where Fincham had pickled Cody's body for interment.

"Cody must be upstairs in the chapel," said Chet.

"Lead on, Macduff," I said.

A flight of stairs led us into the reception area wallpapered in mellow gold. The chairs looked stiff and medieval. A retro telephone booth by a columnar ashtray stand stood empty, and I saw no telephone. The electric candelabras and fern green carpet added touches of elegance I doubted if mourners even noticed. I didn't see the registry with signatures and figured Rennie had it.

Chet paused by the door with the black-gilded I.D. card: CHAPMAN, J. "The chapel is through there."

I led us inside where the center aisle guided us to the raised altar verdant with a subtropical jungle of flowers and ferns. Overhead fluorescents bounced light off the polished walnut coffin riding on a catafalque aproned in green baize. A dirty-wicked candle staked each corner of the altar.

"You'll want a little privacy."

"Nice try but get back here and help me tip up these coffin lids," I said.

Chapter 39

Cody Chapman's 350 pounds filled out the coffin. Even in death his lips ticked at the mouth corners, conspiring to grin up at us. Fincham had decked out Cody in his tropical worsted suit the dutiful Rennie had probably brought over.

Chet rubbed his nose. "Cody looks peaceful enough."

My head motion disagreed. "Look, he's laughing at us."

"You shouldn't knock the dead."

"Paying the freight entitles me to say what I see." I actioned out a 9 mil slug from my Browning and tucked it into Cody's breast pocket. "You can't have enough bullets," I told Chet.

Chet swallowed to lubricate his words. "Do we say a prayer?"

"Who for, Cody or us?" I asked.

"Cody. It's too late for us."

Really? Cody lies flat out. We're still standing, I thought, but I didn't try to top Chet.

Instead I reached down and lifted Cody's heavy wrist. Chet hissed out "don't" as I peeled up Cody's sleeve. No tattoo decorated his exposed forearm skin.

"At least Cody didn't ink a Nazi tat," I said.

A shrug hunched Chet's bony shoulders. "So?"

"It was important for my sanity to know if he did," I replied.

The coffin lid falling into place created a thunk. As far as I was concerned, Cody was ready for the worm-work farm.

"What's that?" Chet went to the chapel window and

canted his ear. "Hear it?"

A *thwunk-thwunk* pulsated through the walls, catafalque, and candlestick holders. Then a powerful exterior light whorled in the frosted glass windows. I knew the state police's ghetto bird Gatlin had mentioned was flying in low to strafe its 500-watt searchlight over Pelham. Our glances locked in alarm.

"We're safe in here," said Chet.

"Think again," I said. "These are ex-military. The ground units coordinate with the air patrol." As if to underscore my point, we heard vehicles roar up out back, parking behind the hearse. "With any luck they'll rattle the doors and leave us alone."

Chet cracked a window. "Four uniforms are rolling out of two lit up cruisers. All tote riot shotguns."

"Any K-9 scent dogs?"

"None are in sight. They paired off, one to the front and the other to the back."

"They're shaking down the place," I said.

A side exit voided to the stairs we hammered down. Chet spilled to the steps and dragged himself up.

"Don't stop. I'm hot on your heels," he said.

The coffin display room was too bright. I heard a thump and, looking over, knew they'd grouped on the loading dock. One snorted out, cursing the lock Chet had just picked. They had us cornered, but I wasn't willing to give up yet.

"Hide out in their coffins. Act quickly."

Chet's hand snared my wrist. "We'll asphyxiate."

"No Chet, the seals aren't that airtight," I lied.

Chet, plainly displeased, nodded and went off to find his coffin.

I halted at a white model, flipped up the half-couch lid, and hitched aboard. "Whoa." The coffin mounted on a set of coasters drifted a few inches over the hard floor. My boots probing underneath the lid into the coffin tore the white satin liner. My glance went across the aisle. Chet slinking his wiry body into a black enamel model had an easier time. My shoulders bumped into the sides as I wormed my way downward.

A man-cough followed stomps and colorful expletives. I yanked down the half-couch lid on top of me. Slapping shut, its bang coincided with the funeral home's rear door clanking open. Hot, black tar oozed into my eyes. I blinked.

Right off, my dark berth also grew claustrophobic and lumpy. I worried I might black out on my next breath. How did Cody expect to go through eternity hemmed in like this? Marty my ex deserved this tight fit buried under six feet of dirt. Noises outside the coffin seeped through its walls with enough clarity for me to eavesdrop.

"Jesse, you and Woodrow go check out upstairs," said Sheriff Dmytryk. "Erskine, we'll sweep this level."

"Sorry, I can't, Sheriff."

"What is it now, Jesse?"

"The chapel is off-limits for me. I suffer severe allergies from the flower pollen."

Sheriff Dmytryk grunted. "Then you two canvass down here, and we'll secure the upstairs. You find anything, sing out."

"Just like the fat lady, Sheriff."

Sheriff Dmytryk grunted again.

After the footfall tramped by me in the coffin, Jesse resumed talking.

"I say let the sheriff go fraternize with the stiffs. He pulls down the big bucks."

Woodrow groaned. "The quicker we work, the sooner we go home."

"It's colder than an Eskimo's dick in here."

"Do you see anything, Jesse?"

"No, this damn coffin is locked up tight."

"Then let's just say they all are," said Woodrow.

"Works for me. This fucking joint creeps me. What's taking Dmytryk so damn long? There ain't anything to see. Johnson is sleeping somewhere."

"Thank God this is our last patrol. I'm dog-tired," said Woodrow.

One deputy sheriff jogged into my coffin. My hands

pressed to the sides as it rolled a short ways. My air supply seemed to dwindle. To ward off panic, I controlled my breathing to also conserve oxygen. My imagination kicked into overdrive. That gnawing noise came from dung beetles feasting on my protein. I couldn't stay cooped up like this for much longer and remain sane. The nearby deputy sheriffs talked again.

"I'm sick and tired of Senator Reddman ordering in outsiders. We can manage this problem ourselves."

"I have to disagree, Jesse. Outside resources give us a boost, and Reddman has the juice to get them."

"Either way, Johnson is dog meat," said Jesse.

I frowned at hearing that comment.

"The top floor is secure," said Sheriff Dmytryk, now back with them.

"We got zip down here," said Jesse.

"Radio the chopper we're all-clear and will suspend all operations until daybreak."

"I'm all over it, Sheriff."

The four lawmen, their utility belts squeaking and boot soles scuffing on the floor, exited Fincham's. I did a slow count to ten, but nobody returned to fetch a forgotten radio or flashlight. My arms hoisted the half-couch lid to allow in life-affirming light and air, and I hefted myself from the coffin to stand on the floor. Chet had already ejected from his coffin. We heard the departing ghetto bird's noise diminish and the cruisers droned off. The walls ceased vibrating and the exterior lights faded away to darken in the windows again.

Chapter 40

Chet went over to crack a window and said the coast was clear. We eased out Fincham's rear door, humped by the black hearse, and followed the same alleyways across Pelham. The gum-chomping custodian mopping the washerette's tile floor gave us her wide back. We crossed the doorway and hurried to get in our car still parked between the silos.

Chet coaxed fire into the cylinders and off we rolled. Seeing Cody had gratified me but linking him with the neo-Nazis didn't. I had to accept that he scored arms deals with them to inflict a big hurt on innocent people. I'd had some exposure to suicide car bombers while stationed overseas in the MPs, and these terrorists operating in Pelham re-engaged my old jitters.

I let Gatlin's hypothesis—Cody sold black-market guns—take center stage in my mind. So, if Cody was selling illegal munitions in volume, wouldn't he keep a dirty business ledger and not record the transactions in his legitimate books? I decided to act on my hunch (*P.I.s got those, Dreema*) on Cody's dirty business ledger and go chase it down.

"Drop us by the gun shop," I said.

Chet gave me a covert glance but drove us in that direction.

I had put down my car window. The early killer frosts had zapped the fiddler crickets, and the nocturnal world held an eerie hush. Mr. Bojangles wiggled out of my pocket and curled up to nap on the warm transmission hump. On our flyby of the gun shop I saw the deputy sheriff sitting in his cruiser parked by the fireworks stand. Their dragnet had slacked off, but by daybreak a few hours away it'd ramp up again. We had to investigate with alacrity.

"Make the left up ahead," I said.

The vacant lot was used by working stiffs in their car pools commuting to distant jobs. A pair of raccoon bandits pillaging the brimming dumpster chattered at us.

"Dock over there." I motioned to behind the dumpster. "We'll cut through the woods and come in on the rear side."

"Can I ask you something first?"

"I already know what it is, Chet. What's at the gun shop? God's truth, I can't say."

"No, an idea buzzes in that head of yours. I can tell, so just lay it on me."

"I want to go search for Cody's dirty business ledger."

"You figure Cody is who sold the contraband arms to the Nazis?"

"He was a terrorist profiteer, but I've got no proof. Rennie saw strange shipments arriving at the gun shop, so I think some records on the illegal sales must exist."

"That's our Easter egg."

We tramped into the woods where the slash pines dripped with a dank turpentine smell needling my nose lining. My first step in the black gunk oozed up to my ankles, but we slogged on. Foxfire embers—the morsels of phosphorus wood rotting in the wet marsh—glimmered a pale orange.

I let Chet take a long lead and inserted my boots in the sucked out impressions he left. I made an association, putting the black gunk as the dirt Marty tracked into my life. I couldn't step anywhere without it clinging to me, but not for much longer. My consolation was overpaying Limpet to cleanse away all traces of her messy backstabbing.

When the slash pines phased out, we emerged from the black lagoon at the firing range and surveilled our front. The cruiser I'd spotted sat under a street light, and I made out the deputy sheriff was sleeping, quite possibly stoned. His forehead slumped to rest against the steering wheel's upper arc.

We wiped the gunk from our feet on the jute doormat. Chet sprung Sheriff Dmytryk's new padlock, and I inserted my old door key, and we ducked inside the gun shop's back area.

Motion lights in the electric sockets, Rennie's crime deterrent, generated a meager light. Our eyes adjusted as I greeted the comforting aroma of gun oil. I was back in my element and now as the gun shop's owner, I incurred Cody's debts, both the legal and illegal ones. Right off, I nullified Cody's dirty deals and that went double for any he'd brokered with Millard and the neo-Nazis.

Cody stored an emergency flashlight under the work bench. My fingers masked its direct light as my old bearings reasserted themselves. My flashlight beam played over the bench clutter: a plumber's bench vise, metal files, whetstones, and a bevy of pliers I'd bought from a shoe repairman's widow. I grunted in disgust, tossing aside the hand-lettered poster, "Cody's Ten Commandments for Shooting Safety". Chet glanced at me as we moved in deeper.

The smaller room was brighter. The bookshelf stocked our gun guild literature: Colt's *Illustrated Firearms Disassembly Bible*, Stackpole's *Small Arms of the World*, and Braverman's *Firearms Encyclopedia*. I'd borrowed the handgun repair manual to do my freelance work at the doublewide.

Damn but didn't Cody have a racket going? A niche market always thrived for weapon customizations. We could crop, lengthen, or doctor your guns to any spec your little heart desired. For the right price, Cody fudged on what was legal. Such projects were popular hobbies for blue collar do-it-yourselfers. But enthusiasts with money to burn preferred to hire a pro gunsmith, and Cody, breaking into a smarmy grin, loved to grab their easy money.

I didn't see any Marlin rifles Cody had alluded to at Leona's. I did see the finishing wheels in an alcove behind the air compressor. I'd used the finishing wheels to polish the metal surfaces to the various gun components: cylinders, barrels, back straps, frames, and hammers. Polishing steel was grimy scut work.

An air duct tried to vacuum up the particles of black friction compound spewed off the spinning wheel, but the flung compound still blackened my face. The gun parts I polished on the spinning wheel heated up in my hands. The new sisal, Scotchbrite, and buffing wheels sat stacked on the shelf where I'd left them on the day I'd quit working here.

My beam glided over to illuminate the crusty slag covering the baths in the three bluing vats I'd once maintained. The red and blue slag resembled the salt crystal gardens that school kids like to grow in science classes. It'd been months since the electric coils under the bluing vats had heated the slag to create the corrosive baths. I paused. How many steel firearms had I cooked in the bluing vats and pulled out with their black oxide finish looking store-bought new?

I grew astonished to see Cody had let things go to pot, and this neglect didn't make sense. Then I recalled Cody's major obsession was making money, and I realized that fact explained the disorder around us.

"Cody didn't run a very tidy ship," said Chet.

"The gun shop fronted Cody's new lucrative business he took up after I left."

"I don't follow you."

"His revenue streamed in from somewhere, and I figure it was his black-market gun sales. Rennie took care of the usual customers up front, but back here was Cody's domain." I tamped my heel on the floor. "I searched under his office rug and found the pendant in a cavity. We'll comb the entire floor to search for the dirty business ledger."

"You mean a second hidey-hole?"

"Cody created one. Why not two?" I moved past the gun display counters and put myself in Cody's skin. His photo gallery of trophy kills on the knotty pine wall panels reminded me how he was a big kid at heart. The gumball machines just inside the front door drew my second glance. Kids nagged their parents for quarters and *ka-ching* sounded Cody's cash register. We'd search that floor area first.

It took us no effort to scoot over the gumball machines

and peel away the fake grass carpet not glued down. No sawed or cracked concrete lines suggested another niche as the one in Cody's office. Stung by disappointment, I replaced the fake grass carpet and scraped out its wrinkles.

"His dirty business ledger could be kept offsite," said Chet.

"I can buy that idea, but where?" I said.

"I'd rent a safe-deposit box. Does Rennie know anything?"

"She's smart to give Cody's underhanded shit a wide berth," I replied.

Chet rapped his bony knuckles on the display counter's glass. "Do we check the floor under here?"

I grabbed an end and we grunted to shove the display counter flush up against the wall. Chet hit the exposed concrete floor with the flashlight to reveal the square outline that a pavement saw had cut in the concrete.

"We'll take that," said Chet.

I crouched and pried out the square concrete flap to expose a dark cavity. I peered down into it, and a Mosler floor safe the size of a car battery gleamed in my flashlight beam.

"Is safecracker on your résumé?" asked Chet.

"No, but Cody was big on memory aids," I replied. "Slide out his office desk drawers, pitch the contents, and bring back any drawers with numbers written on the underside."

"Your cousin wasn't that stupid."

"I just knew Cody well enough to understand what made him tick," I said.

While Chet ransacked Cody's desk, I ran a window check. The deputy sheriff's shadow hadn't moved in his cruiser. Chet returned with a grin and a desk drawer. He flipped it over and read aloud, "4xR to 25, 2xR to 30, and 1xR to 0."

Cody's instructions set how I twirled the knurled brass dial. Tumblers clicked and I hefted up the safe door to grope inside the dark cavity. "I hit the mother lode, Chet." A black ledger appeared in my hands. I used the flashlight and my eyes skimmed over the columns of written figures entered in a half-scribble, half-print style as unique to Cody as his Size 13 work boots. He hadn't bothered to encrypt his clientele and used his personal shorthand. I saw "Suggs", the drunk who'd pawed Rennie, had bought a grenade launcher, maybe for deer season.

Entries for Millard's neo-Nazis ("Millard, Knights") cropped up with alarming regularity. Their twenty or so buys included automatic rifles and frag grenades. Reading the "C4 explosive" entry hiked my eyebrow. An explosive suggested they'd something more ambitious in mind than popping off automatic rifles. Despite my reluctance, I knew one thing more than ever. Cody had armed the neo-Nazis and I felt responsible enough to take on stopping them. Frustrated, I snapped the ledger shut. We hadn't found squat at the Pelham farmhouse or Apollo castle.

"Uh, it gets rougher, Frank."

His young, dark face set in hard edges, Chet slipped color photos from a manila envelope, and they fanned to the floor. One gape down wrenched my gut. But it was true. Marty and Cody did the mattress mambo. Yes, my cousin Cody shagged my ex Marty doggie style, and, shit-faced, they leered into the camera lens.

The red heat flushing from my neck into my ears incited a new level of rage over Cody's betrayal. I stewed over how long their tryst had gone on. I now had the actual reason Cody had dropped by the doublewide the day Marty had seduced yet another stud. Or maybe they'd made it a threesome.

I knew Marty had to be liquidated. Limpet was taking too much time. For a moment I wondered if he'd skipped town with my money. But then he'd never collect the second half, and something told me the scar-faced bastard was too greedy to forgo making the hit.

"I wasn't going to show you, but you deserve to know," said Chet.

I shredded the photos to pile in an ashtray and set fire to destroy the lurid evidence.

"Get Millard and at least end this shit," said Chet.

My thoughts pinballed inside my head until I settled them. The neo-Nazis had shifted their pyrotechnics from the farmhouse to a new staging area. But where were they in Pelham? I used the ledger to fan the tendrils of smoke away from me. Rennie's face materialized, and it developed into Mr. Van Dotson's.

I gazed off at Cody's photo gallery on the wall, waiting. A brain synapse fired to make the correct link. Mr. Van Dotson had enlightened me on Pelham's Nazi POW camp, and that's how I knew where next to aim our quest. So obvious, it'd sat in plain view all the time. I motioned at Chet I was ready to leave.

Chapter 41

Bill Clinton had signed off on mothballing a slate of military bases, and Pelham's satellite farm had fallen victim. No local gave a monkey's fart since it didn't impact us. Nobody I knew had worked there, and the armed sentries at the gatehouse used to run off hopeful job applicants showing up with hat in hand.

A twelve-foot chain-link fence crested by concertina wire corralled the satellite farm's weedy acres populated with dishes, towers, and antennas of all shapes and sizes. The fence didn't look electrified though it probably once was. "U.S. Government Property! Keep Out!" signs appeared at even intervals along the chain-link fence. The Nazi POW barracks fifty-odd years back had occupied the same site, and I wagered that supreme irony alone enticed Millard to adopt the satellite farm as his new base.

Chet and I arriving in Gerald's surveillance car taxied into the satellite farm's entranceway. Our headlamps fell on the roofless gatehouse and bent up gate. A case-hardened steel padlock connected the rusty, double-link chains securing the gate. I hopped out and spotted my flashlight beam down to study our obstruction.

Fresh scratches marred the padlock's steel. Some mortal, not a phantom, had used this entry point in recent nights. A new awareness spooked me, but I saw no video cameras, infrared motion detectors, or trip wires installed to secure the main gate. No Doberman pinschers or pit-bulls howled to oppose us, and I saw no swastika graffiti. But I knew this was the right coliseum.

"New key scratches show on the padlock," I told Chet back at the car.

"Spring it?"

I shook my head. "Not this new one. A hacksaw might cut it."

"We're short one hacksaw."

"Then that's a problem and we're stuck," I said.

"Forget the photos. Marty was bad news."

"She was at that. But let's just drop it," I said.

My bleary eyes roved through the main gate to a quadrant of cinderblock structures maybe the distance of a football field inside the fence. Moonlight outlined their boxy dimensions. Red signals on the twin radio towers winked down at us. Uncle Sam still supplied electricity to the ghost facility.

This was no reprise of our Paris Mountain debacle, and Millard spoiled for battle. I didn't care if he heard or saw us. The gauntlet had been slapped down, and this dogfight left only the top dog standing. The larger posse giving Millard the bulge left me grim. A drone buzzed down the dark road before the headlights glittered into view like nuggets of foxfire, and I had a sudden suspicion.

"Tell me you didn't call him," I said.

"Damn right I did. Why should we go it alone?" said Chet.

"But he was busy on a hot bounty hunt," I said.

"Gerald was busy getting that hot girl's booty. I told him the poontang party is done. It's time to get real. They're licensed bounty agents, and that keeps this official."

"Does that mean this is wide open?" I said.

"Will you just chill? Gerald is in unless you uninvite him."

Fat chance. Relief soothing me said Chet was right. Gerald more than evened up the odds, and he kept a cool head under duress. At least I clung to that reassuring thought. The headlights closing in left us squinting. The car stopped, and Sofia's head bobbed up before Gerald hulked there in the semi-dark, a gladiator amped to kick serious butt.

"Yo road dawgs, what's up?"

Chet, then I bumped knuckles with him.

"The gate is locked up tight," said Chet.

"Is this manhunt buttoned up for the night?" asked Gerald.

"That's what we overheard the sheriff say," replied Chet.

After stomping back to scrounge in his trunk, Gerald lit an oxy-acetylene torch to sizzle at a low-tipped, blue flame and with a swordfighter's aplomb sliced the blue flame across the padlock. I also heard the chains jingle free and clink on the pavement.

Chet toed aside the padlock and chain. "We're back in action."

Gerald heaved the sliding gate wide. Bathed in the car's twin cones of illumination, his imposing profile strutted back to us. Little wonder Gerald stalking down an alley scared any sane man pissless. He stabbed the hissing oxy-acetylene torch down at our target.

"Head count?"

"Frank hasn't an exact tally. Ten, maybe twelve," replied Sofia.

"Do you think? Not that many. I'd say four at most, counting Millard." Low-balling the odds netted me false assurances we might pull this off. My strained voice didn't ring with confidence. Gerald closed the snuff valve on the oxy-acetylene torch and chucked it.

We strapped into our Kevlar hulls. Gerald issued 16-gauge Mossberg shotguns from his trunk to arm Chet and Sofia. His shotgun was a 12-gauge. No weapon outdid shotguns at close-quarter combat and knowing that offered comfort. I tipped in a full magazine load and lined my pockets with extra 00-buckshot cartridges.

I also cached Cody's dirty business ledger under my Kevlar vest while Chet hid our cars inside the chain-link fence. Mr. Bojangles, abandoned again, romped back and forth over the dashboard. Tough. Squeaky ferrets had no role in my immediate plans.

Sofia shunted me aside the gate. "Frank, you're awfully quiet."

I replied with fake conviction. "Millard has slipped through too many fingers but not this damn time."

"We could wait and go in at daylight," said Sofia.

"I can't wait that long," I said.

Gerald had come over and he clamped his hand to my shoulder. "No big thing, Frank."

Disgust sharpened Chet's words. "It's just a cake job, huh, bro? What if it's dark? What if they lay in wait? What if it's three-to-one sides? No big thing."

Turning, Gerald growled. "Cut the bullshit. We fight."

I broke in. "Let's start it up."

Our fire team skulked in along the gatehouse lane, using the bulkiest satellite dishes to mask our approach. Adrenaline steeled my frazzled nerves, or an overdose of stupidity numbed me. Either way, I ran on a pair of rubbery legs.

Gerald drew up to me. "Have you been inside here?"

"Just to scope it from the state road," I replied.

"Me, too, so we'll just feel our way along," said Gerald.

The gatehouse lane ended at the first rectangular building silhouetted by the moonlight. Closing in, we doubled our gait when a fusillade of automatic rifle fire made us disperse. Racing forward and cycling my 12-gauge's slide action, I threw a round of retaliatory blasts downrange. The gun barks pummeled my eardrums.

Chet and I pounced into a ditch. Just at that instant, their gunfire flattened. Sweat oozing out my pores soaked me. I humped forward and then fired to cover Chet pulling up behind the concrete abutment.

"I see 'em hunkered down on the second floor," he said.

"Me and my bad ideas," I said.

"It's not so bad, Frank. We'll sprint to the courtyard and infiltrate their rear. Then bust into the building and cap them."

"That's as good a plan as any."

Their volley screamed down on us. Hot, blue whistlers chiseled the concrete and flying fragments prickled my scalp.

I tried to aim and counteract the fiery discharge points, but their barrage pinned us down. Cold sweat dripped down the skin of my back. I cast over a glance. Sofia and Gerald, prone behind a concrete abutment, also hung on by their toenails.

The snipers, it dawned me, were scoring high and right in the dark. I saw a ray of hope: they weren't crack shots and, most likely, didn't use night vision hardware. Sofia hollered over to us.

"Say what?" I bellowed.

Gerald had vaulted up to jitterbug over the turf, cutting hard for the first building. I grasped her strategy: go on offense. Chet and I used Gerald's zigzag route, drawing their cannonade as Sofia anted up with her racket. Gerald lobbed in 12-gauge rounds, a heat big enough to protect us.

We charged by the first building to a new position in the courtyard behind them. Sofia came on even faster to clear the building. Next we edged along its cinderblock wall and reached a door. Gerald kicked it into splinters, and we poured inside after him. The fluorescent lights beamed down on a hodgepodge of switches, gauges, and buttons. Breathing hard, we stood in a utility room.

"No airborne choppers will see us until morning. Flip on every light you can find," said Gerald. "If nothing else, we'll flush them out into the bright open. Chet, nail down this exit. Nobody goes in or out."

"I'm all over it," said Chet.

He activated a main switch. I saw mercury vapor lamps on steel poles blossom across the courtyard, an orange illumination bathing everything in sight. The scene put me in mind of parading back and forth on the klieg-lit drill fields at Fort Riley.

"You two back up Gerald. I've got this," said Chet.

Gerald had hit the interior doorway into an ill-lit hallway. As we advanced, my ears strained. This was a hairy room-to-room operation. I scrunched up my nose at a cat piss stench, damn likely crystal meth. We were dealing with drug-addled crazies, no white flags.

I let Sofia lag off my right shoulder and we padded ahead. At each closed door, we jumped in and cleared out the space, repeating the maneuver until we secured the hallway. Gerald guarded the central stairway's bottom.

"Did you spot any elevators?" I asked.

"No elevators." Gerald's glance scoped each side. "The only way out is these stairs."

We ascended, spacing a conservative gap between us. Our feet crept up the concrete treads. My pulse jackhammered behind my ears. An abrupt chatter of gunfire erupted below us—Chet was taking hot rounds.

"We better get back to Chet," said Sofia.

"Take out these snipers first. We can't get sandwiched between them," said Gerald.

We fanned out from the stairhead, probing the second-floor corridor. Gerald hit the offices on the right and we swept the left. Doors sailed inward. The chairs and desks had been stacked for the candy ass generals to choreograph our next high tech war from their laptops. Rank had its privileges.

Somebody sneezed. I craned up my neck. A Brown Shirt, stomping out the ceiling tiles, rained down a lead spurt on us. Gerald, backpedaling, fired underhanded. His pellet cluster mauled Brown Shirt from the ceiling, and he did a head plant to the floor.

"That's whack." Gerald pumped his 12-gauge, ejecting the spent shell. "The motherfuckers pop out of the woodwork."

I recognized Brown Shirt from our dustup at Paris Mountain. Gerald scooped up the groaning Brown Shirt in his arms and heaved the load down the stairwell. Gerald winked at me. "Make sure they're good and dead."

I didn't miss seeing the shudder travel down Sofia's back.

Gerald leading, we snaked up a second flight of stairs. The third floor gave way to a cavernous warehouse, its skeletal metal rafters naked in the grainy light. I saw bats swoop through a hole. No snipers had forted up on this tier. The bombardment down below us intensified.

"They've ganged up on Chet," I said.

"Fall back," said Gerald.

Sofia went first. We barreled down the same stairs and hallways to the ground floor. The gunfire staccato fell slack, and they were probably marshalling for an all-out assault. I rushed into the utility room and saw Chet flat out on the floor. His hand tilted, a warning. I wheeled on my heels.

Brown Shirt lurched into the open, his automatic rifle at port. We squared off. His rounds shredded my jacket sleeve, but my shotgun spewing a tight pattern of 00-buckshot pierced solid meat. From the doorway, I saw another Brown Shirt scurrying through the smoke. I pumped and fired, leading him, but he bugged out of my kill zone. He lunged through the next building's door where they took their next stand.

My 12-gauge lowered and I pulled Chet from the exposed doorway. I looked but didn't find his black-framed glasses. Indecision teetering on panic debilitated me. Sofia knelt by us and she knew what to do.

She detached Chet's bloods-soaked Kevlar and, searching, we saw where the slug had gouged a two-inch tunnel in his upper thigh. Blood puddled on the floor. So much blood. I wanted her to rule out a nicked artery, always fatal. Sofia's thumb at Chet's neck gauged his pulse. She pinched her lips. Gerald, crumbling to his knees, shoveled his hands under Chet's head to cradle it.

"Chet? Can you hear me, bro?"

"Gerald, he can't hear you," said Sofia.

Chet's glassy eyes ogled the ceiling. I sucked in air. Blood smeared Sofia's fingers. Blood splotched Chet's Kevlar vest. Gerald using a rifle sling created a bulky but effective tourniquet.

"We need a doctor." Sofia tightened the tourniquet.

A cross breeze had dissipated the densest gun smoke. My glance at the state road saw no cop lights. I appraised the courtyard and mapped out our possible exit routes under the harsh artificial light. No egress looked safe or promising enough.

"We can't evacuate Chet. Too slow. The snipers will decimate us," I said.

Gerald stalked to the doorway, hefted up my Brown Shirt kill, and hurled him out to land in the courtyard. "Where did the fuckers go?" Rage caused the veins in Gerald's bullish neck to quiver, and his eyes gleamed like a snake-handling preacher.

"Keep your head screwed on," I told him.

"I'm cool." Wiping his bloody hands off on his pants, Gerald squinted out into the courtyard's luminous, smoky depths. "Point me to the snipers."

My hand addressed the next building. "I saw them tear across the quad and duck through that door."

"That's where we attack." A chin tip was Gerald's "go" sign.

Chapter 42

After diving into the smoke-laced arena, we hugged the dirt and snaked ahead. The rounds shot from the sniper nests in the next building whizzed by inches over our heads.

"Yo, move it."

"Shoot out the lights," I said.

"No time for that. Don't stop."

We did a salamander crawl, our tucked-in elbows and forearms digging over the courtyard. The door, our objective twenty paces away, laughed at us. A concrete abutment at half the distance gave us some cover. Once there, I peered out down low and could trace the outlines of the man-shadows at the second story's bright windows.

A spat of rifle fire drove me back, but my recon had spotted three snipers, and I knew Millard led them. Gerald flexed upright, and his 12-gauge belched out buckshot to pound out the windows, and the crescendo plunged into quiet. He nudged my shoulder.

"Charge them," he said

We sprang up from the concrete abutment, dashed to the building, and pressed against its cinderblock wall. Gerald's kicks walloped in the door and, bellowing, he lumbered into the dark hellhole. I hustled to keep up with the big man's romp through a hallway.

We huddled at the central stairwell. Rifle fire stitched the floor, scarring the concrete in front of us. No dummy, Millard wanted to leave his line of retreat uncontested. We had different ideas and lay low from the ricochets zinging off the walls and ceiling.

"If we hurl up enough hot lead, they'll hunker down. We zip up, corner the snipers, and grease 'em."

The pleasing image incited my nod.

We chocked our magazines to full capacity before we hurtled into the stairwell and worked our triggers to spew up the 00-brimstone. Spent shotgun hulls jacked out but none jammed. I commanded my boots to stamp up the steps.

Wheezes racked my chest, and my head felt swimmy, but I didn't slow or stop. A hit like a left jab punched me below the collarbone. I did a rope-a-dope off the stair railing and tripped on my boots. Gerald one step below steadied me in his grasp.

"Hang tough, Frank," he said. "We're just a cunt hair away."

I nodded. Gerald had the right feel. I didn't. But the savage in me focused. We emptied our chambers and prized them off the stairs to establish a toehold on the next floor. Concrete pylons protected us from their volleys strafing the hallway.

My thumb tip traced the perforation under my collarbone. I startled to feel the projectile's jagged nub. I'd taken a hit. Only a scrim of Kevlar had stood between me and death. I credited Sofia's insistence we wear the Kevlar for saving my life.

My mental snapshot showed Chet's red, pulpy gash. I jabbed 12-gauge shells into the magazine's loading port as if they were sausages. The barrel steel hot from rapid firing scorched my palm calluses. I liked feeling the burn.

Gerald grinned at me. "You rocking, dawg?"

I shrugged. "It's all in a day's work for an MP."

That quip got a hearty laugh from Gerald. "We'll split up. I'll hear the gunfire if you hit trouble."

"One shot, one kill," I mantraed.

Gerald scoured the north wing; I went south. While hunkered outside behind the concrete abutment, I'd recorded sniper perches based along here. I bashed in the first office door and slapped on the toggle switch. Beams spilled down on the yellow patina of filth. "Christ." I recoiled. Meth fumes caustic as napalm threatened to melt out my eyes. I rubbed them. It didn't help.

My sawed-off shotgun thrust out sliced in a 180, left to right. I heard a grating noise. A blonde giant in a brown shirt charged out from behind a bookshelf. Our eyes clashed. I saw crystal meth powered his rage. He shrieked a curse and heaved over the row of bookshelves, wanting to crush me under them. I was a matador dodging the tumbling dominoes. My trigger knuckle flicked, and my shotgun volley roared and cored out the giant's sternum. He plummeted with a final thud on the floor.

A blissful narcotic sang through my veins. It felt too much like fun. But I shrugged off my smug languor, and I eyed the grimy sheetrock. I espied no mouse-hole that urban snipers use to move between rooms on upper floors. The dead giant didn't impede my progress. My pause leaning at the next shut door detected no interior sounds. The knob twisted, and I cut into what passed for a library.

The cat piss vapors seared my face like a burst of pepper spray. Evil seethed in here. Brutal scenes kaleidoscoped before my mind's eye: my truck as a lit pyre, death at the neo-Nazi's castle, and Cody blasted to the shop floor. My boots crunched over the CD cases. Manuals lined the shelves on metal stacks. I felt a draft rattling the loose corner of a world map thumbtacked to a corkboard.

My peripheral vision flagged a movement. I pivoted. The shaft of sallow light landed on Millard, and I startled. Spit flecked the grin warping his skull face. Then in a surreal turn, the Stars and Bars on his cap shivered alive. I gaped at it. The bar endings bent down, and a swastika was born as if entwining the two dogmas, neo-Confederate with neo-Nazi, and throwing the latest homebred terrorist at us. I envisioned an ominous crematorium burning in every county, and the air redolent with bone ash and dense smoke.

Millard whooped out a Rebel yell. The automatic rifle at his side clacked, but my rebuttal fire pried him off me. One shot whapped into my Kevlar shoulder, hurtling me back. My stagger landed on the floor. The slug's impact socked the wind from me.

I gasped in gulps of air to revive, or I'd cash out while flat on my ass. Like Pelham, Johnson fell here, but he sure as hell wasn't ready to die here riddled with neo-Nazi bullet holes.

Millard called out. "Johnson, hear me?"

Dizzy and nauseous, I hitched upright and faded to the end of the metal stack, avoiding any tromp on the piles of CD cases.

"Cody Chapman was one of us. Face it, Johnson. You are, too."

Silence.

"Why not join our elite ranks?"

More silence.

Millard lashed out his words. "Johnson, that's my offer. What's your answer?"

"Fuck you."

I stepped out, going with my reflexes honed on the firing range. My sawed-off shotgun flew up. Millard's sneer and grommets for eyes cut to me the second before my trigger finger crooked. The sawed-off jolted, flared, and smoked in my hands.

The thunderclap explosion plowed Millard into the wall. His Rebel cap tumbled off his head and rolled across the floor. He caved at the knees and pitched forward into a bloody slump. His outstretched fingers clutched at the high arches to his ribs, then went slack.

Endorphins, the brain's joy juice, gave me a head rush. I felt giddy. It was almost done. I went to Millard, removed his wallet fastened to a chain, and peeled out a grungy banknote.

"I lent you a sawbuck for gas," I told the corpse, flinging the wallet to his chest. Millard's colorless eyes watched the dark-haloed angels descending to harvest his dark soul. They'd be back to cull out mine, but not this morning.

"Frank! Frank!"

Gerald's hollers reverberated over his footfall in the hallway. I turned as he rushed through the library's doorway. "I heard shooting. What's up?"

"Things got sticky. I bagged two," I replied. "What's your body count?"

"One. The other sniper smashed out a window, leaped to the ground, and deuced out before I could cap his ass."

"Or did you throw him still alive through the window?" I asked.

"Man, I don't do that kind of shit," said Gerald.

"Never mind. Getting an ambulance is more important," I said.

"Phew, what's that godawful stink?"

"A crystal meth lab," I replied.

Gerald's scowl darkened. "Let's get the fuck out of here."

We returned to the utility room in the first building. Sofia nodded at us. She'd dialed 911 from her cell phone. Chet, laboring for breath, had turned ashen and lines of pain crazed his face. We conferred. Sofia and Gerald said they'd get Chet to a doctor. My task was to go nail the fleeing gunman. He'd be easy to track with the big streak of yellow running up his back.

"I know Chet looks in bad shape," said Sofia. "His pulse is strong. At least I've closed off the bleeding. That's vital."

"Will you guys make out okay?" I asked.

"We hold bail recovery licenses, and shit happens to us, even if this turned a bit messier," said Gerald.

"Just a bit," said Sofia.

Waving off her sarcasm, Gerald continued. "We pursued Millard, a legit fugitive. His buddy snipers helped him resist apprehension, and we applied due force. It's a cut-and-dry operation. Now go tie up this stray end, and then we'll go see Mr. Gatlin to straighten out things."

I choked on the welter of emotion boiling up in me. "I can't leave Chet like this."

Gerald ripping apart the Velcro straps to his Kevlar vest grunted. "He'll pull through. I believe it, and so should you."

Sofia turned her head. "Listen all, is that a siren?"

It was, distant but articulate. Was it our ambulance or a deputy sheriff cruiser? I ditched my Kevlar and stuck the dirty business ledger under my shirt. Traveling light and fast was essential. I struck out the doorway at a brisk pace, leaving Chet in their ministrations, dubious I'd see him alive again.

Chapter 43

I trotted through the satellite farm's weedy field. A hasty glance over my shoulder put a picture with the banshee sirens I heard. The red-blue strobes glinted on two deputy sheriff cruisers cantering down the state road. Three cruisers had already turned at the main gate we'd left open.

The defunct satellites, once our nation's ears tilted to the skies, I darted around covered my trek in the budding daylight. My lungs and wounded calf were on fire, but I didn't stop until at the rear chain-link fence. My crabbing downslope into a shallow ravine discovered where storms had eroded a hole under the fence.

It was a challenge but, sucking in my gut, I piped through, dragging the sawed-off behind me. Then my eyes alit on a wallet. A previous traveler had lost it. I scooped up the wallet and riffled through its contents.

"I'll be a son of a bitch."

Virgil Sweeney, said the credit card. So he'd hidden out with the neo-Nazi snipers, their automatic rifles firing to waste us. My rage heaved out in vapors. Virgil had a head start on me. I cast a 360, appraising the possibilities he'd faced. Two hundred yards to my left was a deciduous forest.

Flight into the sticks bestowed advantages on Virgil. He could elude pursuit. Trees offered him shelter. Jumbles of boulders provided crafty ambush sites. Creeks, springs, and bogs dissolved his scent. Once reaching the high, rocky ridges, he could stay on the dodge for weeks. But it all didn't tote up that way for me. No, Virgil knew their munitions had fallen into the authorities' hands and his commandant, Millard, lay among the casualties. My shotgun blast had decked him.

My suspicions narrowing on Virgil lit up more questions. Who'd happened by the Pelham farmhouse Chet and I had staked out? It wasn't Millard. No, Virgil had put in an appearance. He'd doubled back after we'd dumped him at the rock slide. Did he return to harass Rennie? I doubted it with me set to chop out his kneecaps.

Chet had told me Virgil played us and I agreed. Virgil was no damn hanger-on or wannabe. He'd beat it back to Pelham to guard his precious munitions, and only the boss would care so much. For all his lip, Millard was the hatchet man. Making Virgil the neo-Nazis' ringleader dejected me. I'd underrated him and made a colossal blunder by cutting him adrift. Darker questions assailed me.

Why did a guy married to Rennie Van Dotson decide to lead a hatemongering cult? The harder I mulled it over, the knottier it tangled my logic, so I quit. Who could decipher whack jobs? I ditched the wallet and took up my pursuit.

I stretched through the barbed wire fence at Doc Edwards' place. Crouched at a black gum tree, I assessed what I faced. Doc provided a means for escape Virgil hadn't missed. I smelled and then spotted the grayish smoke wriggling up from the stone chimney to Doc's cabin, a pre-fab model. A plum-colored Crown Victoria lolled under his lean-to. No doubt Virgil had zeroed in on the Crown Vic as his getaway car.

I saw a glow in the window next to the door. Doc had greeted a hostile guest. I skidded downslope and prowled up the next hillside. My neck craned from behind the raspberry canes.

A blue tick didn't yap at me. No wonder. I saw the deep purple splotch. Virgil had popped the hound between the ears. This atrocity stoked my rage past its combustion point. This defenseless dog had been slaughtered out of spite. My clenched teeth gritted to contain the lava of bile flushing into my throat and mouth.

I wanted to hurt Virgil—badly.

Chapter 44

My first steps edged into Doc's yard before I ran at a crouch to the bright window. The cabin's wood had a smooth texture like cedar. Feeling like a cheap spy, I chinned up from the windowsill.

Doc in his pajamas sat bound and gagged to a kitchen chair. I also saw a Wheaties cereal box and a milk carton out on the tabletop. Doc had been eating an early breakfast. Virgil munching on a doughnut strode into my field of view. The automatic rifle, the only weapon in sight, draped from Virgil's arm. His mouth flapped, but his words were unintelligible to me.

I detached from the windowsill and boogied off again, ducking under the electric meter. I ran another recon from the next corner. The open front door invited entry, but first I checked my full chamber load. My hope was to use it up on Virgil.

The grass muffled my swift tread, and I knifed into to the cabin's foyer. I listened. Virgil was ranting how his world had gone to smash. My taut lips smiled. He didn't know the half of it. Yet.

The oak floor planks underfoot were squeak-free. I saw the two men and cut into the room. My sawed-off's muzzle prodded, and Virgil stiffened in mid-sentence.

"Rifle goes on the floor. Slow. Or I shred your kidneys into Jell-O. Nothing would give me a greater pleasure." After Virgil did so, my boot slid his automatic rifle away from us.

"Johnson, you aren't going to spoil my little joke, are you? We've been through all this."

My sawed-off speared Virgil again. "Shut up and free Doc."

Doc once untied balled up his fist and clipped Virgil on the chin.

"That'll teach you. If Johnson wasn't here, I'd drop you on the spot."

Virgil with an agonizing groan swooned but righted himself. His eyes, black holes of hate, swiveled to me. "Johnson, we can strike a deal."

My reply was more incisive. The sawed-off's stock, an age-hardened walnut, thwacked into Virgil's midsection. Eyeballs bulging from their orbits, Virgil doubled at the waist, grappling to prevent his guts from squirting out. He wheezed, attempting to enunciate words.

"That's for hitting Rennie and sapping me," I said. "No deals either."

"Let me get in all my licks, too."

"Better get dressed, Doc. We've got a tight timeline."

Doc, muttering oaths, hustled down the hallway. Virgil retreated to the sofa and collapsed on it. His rasps inflated his lungs as I took up his automatic rifle.

"What you just got a taste of, Virgil, is my bullshit detector. When it detects bullshit, this club springs into action. If you bullshit me like you did in West Virginia, it'll dash out your brains."

"I did in your shrimpy pal," said Virgil, still haughty. "Bullets always trump rock slides."

"You just scratched Chet," I said.

Dressed in jeans and tucking in a work shirt, Doc reappeared, and I handed Virgil's automatic rifle to him. Doc speared its muzzle in the narrow wad separating Virgil's eyes.

"*Bang!*" Virgil flinched. Enjoying it, Doc laughed and yelled again. "*Bang!* One Nazi motherfucker is dead as lead. *Bang!*"

Virgil's features blanched to a fish-scale color. I thought

he'd piss his britches.

"I'll pop you, motherfucker. Nobody fucks with my dogs. Nobody." The deadliness to Doc's growled threat darkened the room, inciting even my shudder.

Virgil's wild eyes cut to me, a frenzied appeal. "Do something, Johnson."

I shrugged. "You popped the man's dog, and he's gone postal. Understandable."

Doc prodded the automatic rifle. "Spill your guts, or I blow out your brains."

"Millard killed Cody Chapman at the gun shop. Millard pried out the cash register drawer and rigged it to look like robbery."

"Bullshit. You killed Cody, Virgil. What was he to you?" I asked.

"Cody supplied automatic rifles, grenades, or whatever I ordered. He'd ship the big stuff further down the line."

"Your line ended this morning. So, Millard went to meet Cody," I said, seeing Millard coming into Leona's. I knew he hadn't kept a hot, young thing in his van stalled at the stoplight but a trove of automatic rifles.

"They met somewhere in Pelham." Virgil scraped his tongue over his lips.

"We haven't got all morning," said Doc.

"I discovered Cody and Millard had skimmed off the top and was set to deal with them when one got greedier, and they argued. Cody ended up dead. I told Millard it was stupid. He could direct the soldiers, but when it came to the grand strategy..."

"Yeah, all right," I horned in. "Speed this along. What's up at the castle in Apollo?"

"Cody rented the farmhouse for us, but it was too damn near Pelham. Millard's plan was to transfer our operations to the satellite farm. It was safe enough. Nobody has been near the place in years."

"Not to mention the original Nazi hard-cases had been imprisoned there," I said.

"Not all the Nazis returned to postwar Germany. My grandfather was one who stayed behind." My stunned reaction made the cadaverous Virgil smile. "That's right. He was a ghost slipping off to West Virginia. Chameleons, we became Sweeney instead of Schwartz—"

Doc jabbed Virgil. "Screw the family tree. Get on with your main story."

"Millard got antsy when the Feds started talking about reopening the military bases. We needed our own site and seeing the Garm castle reminded me of the old one in Apollo. So I bought it outright."

"Not for a few paltry bucks, you didn't. Who bankrolls you?" I asked.

Virgil smirked. "We can tap our lucrative sources. And I'm broken up over you burning down our farmhouse. 'Evidence, Your Honor? What evidence?' Yep, you outdid yourselves there."

I shook my head. "Nothing of evidentiary value was there. I combed it." Then I yanked the parcel from my pocket. "What are these?"

Virgil's eyes caressed the pendants glimmering in the baggie I held up. "They came off the rich Jew-pigs from the glorious death camps. I presented one to each soldier in my loyal service."

The erupting acrid bile swam between my teeth. I spat. "These tick marks record their number of hits."

"We're not playing around. How did you get the pendants?" asked Virgil.

"Funny thing. I keep picking them off dead Nazis. Spoils of war, I guess. Now they're evidence for the Commonwealth's Attorney." I recalled the swastika we'd seen tagged on the government radio tower in Little Salem. "Hans had a hard-on to level the radio tower. What big plans did you cook up?"

Virgil wagged his head. "I've said my last to you."

The baleful cackle was Doc's. "Be careful or it might be for good. You railed enough before Frank came. Virgil claims their castle was a training camp."

"Training for what? Sabotage?" I asked.

"No. They've marked political targets," said Doc.

"Assassinations—"

Virgil's scoff interrupted me. "Assassinations are onesy-twosy. Explosives are our league. Oklahoma City was the warm-up act."

"Your targets are in Charleston and Richmond?" I asked.

"We go for the jugular. Washington, D.C.," said Virgil.

I laughed at the idiocy of his grandiose boast. "Tall talk, Virgil. You're not nearly clever enough."

"Aren't I? McVeigh had a 126 IQ, a bit above average," said Virgil. "All we need is a panel truck, ammonium nitrate fertilizer, and an imaginative plan."

The stark reality he presented beat down my words. My fatigued brain dredged up a grisly detail. The redlined map I'd dug out of their farmhouse basement in Pelham had marked Washington, D.C.

"All we need is my gravel crusher," said Doc.

"You better explain before I let Doc act on his idea," I told Virgil.

Virgil slapped away Doc's automatic rifle. I signaled for Doc to back off a step.

"Life in a democracy is truly magnificent," said Virgil, priming his speech. "We harnessed it to foster our aims. The key was identifying and recruiting our kindred souls living here. Did you know racists flourish in your free speech society? We united with them, and they make good soldiers.

"We started off by buying arms, but recently, I saw automatic rifles and grenades are too limited in scope. Detonating government installations has the biggest impact. So, my agile mind asked, why not pick the juiciest plum? And they don't come any juicier than in Washington, D.C."

"What happens after that?" I asked him.

Virgil smiled at my obtuseness. "It's a simple plan, Johnson. Anarchy foments revolution. We stand ready to step in and fill the leadership void. A bloody putsch ensues, and then one bright morning you look out, and see a new swastika flapping on every flagpole in America."

Even if unoriginal and unattainable ideas, listening to Virgil spell them out in his conversational tone as if discussing today's weather chilled the bile in my gut.

"Enough of your crazy talk," said Doc.

We marched Virgil out to Doc's rear yard. The morning sun was a hot, red wafer. All at once, Virgil bolted for the raspberry canes. He might've made it, too, except the lead slug I flamed from my 9 mil gnawed a second shank from his leg. Grimacing, he crumbled to the turf. Doc and I towed him over to the Crown Vic and dumped him in a writhing heap.

"Use my dog chain and hook the Nazi behind us. Fly over some dirt routes. We'll put down the windows and catch a joyous earful."

"Tempting, but Gatlin will arrange turning over Virgil."

"Is Gatlin your attorney, too?"

I nodded. "He's the only one I can afford."

"Same here. Gatlin pulled me from a legal jam, and I repaid him with a carpentry job. Good man."

Doc found a spool of bailer twine. Virgil wasn't ecstatic over our plan, but he'd no input. Blood from my gunshot wetted a dark patch on his pants leg. Doc cut sections of the bailer twine. He tied Virgil's wrists and ankles before he muffled Virgil's gripes with a gag. We shoved him into the Crown Vic's trunk, slammed down its lid, and ignored his head butts thudding the metal.

"Be right with you. Let me go round up my keys," said Doc.

"Do me a favor, too." I tugged out Cody's dirty business ledger and the pendants in the baggie. "Stash this evidence and ensure it gets to Gatlin."

"But we're going there now, Frank," said Doc.

"We're delivering Virgil to Sheriff Dmytryk, but I don't want him to grab and bury this evidence," I said.

"I know just the place," said Doc, leaving.

I used Doc's cell phone I found on the Crown Vic's seat to thumb in Gatlin's home number.

"Robert Gatlin, Attorney-at-Law," he said, accenting the final three words.

"I'm coming in. Doc Edwards is my chauffeur."

"Wait. Tell me you're on a landline and not conversing over the unsecured airwaves," said Gatlin.

"At this late inning, it hardly matters. You just stay put," I said.

Gatlin clucked his tongue. "You didn't do as we discussed, did you Frank?"

"Millard is now a cold stiff, so get off that damn kick," I said.

"Christ Frank, what's happened now?"

My flat voice summarized our predawn battle at the satellite farm for him.

"Hang up and drive straight over. Doc knows the way," said Gatlin.

"What do you have in mind for next?" I asked.

"We'll play it by ear," said Gatlin, a true lawyer's evasive reply.

Sirens behind me at the satellite farm hurried my hang up before Doc returned, his car keys jingling. His thumbnail scratched his gray throat stubble.

"Do you know anything about that pandemonium I heard earlier this morning? It jarred me awake, and I finally had to call the sheriff."

That accounted for the deputy sheriff cruisers at the main gate.

"Chet, Gerald, his girlfriend Sofia, and I pursued a fugitive into the satellite farm," I replied.

Doc rolled his eyes.

"It was a legit op. Gerald and Sofia are bail enforcers. We flew into a hail of sniper fire but won the nasty firefight. Chet took a hot round in the thigh, and I hope it isn't serious. Then Virgil turned rabbit, and I dogged him here. You know the rest."

"I'm sure glad you did. Thanks for your help."

"We're not out of the woods yet, Doc."

We climbed into the Crown Vic and Doc spat out the window. He reversed the Crown Vic from the lean-to, and I relaxed in the bucket seat. My nerve endings burned raw as lit kerosene as we coasted down his driveway.

"Just lay low, Frank, and we'll ace it just fine," said Doc.

Doc grabbed a right at the state road, straddled a pothole, and we jetted off, making for Mr. Gatlin's swanky digs. We didn't catch Virgil's head thumps, and I could only deduce he'd brained himself senseless.

I scrunched down when an SUV in the opposite lane whipped by us. It was ten o'clock, and my battered mind sought a warm, numb port. That was a short-lived fantasy. A double shriek bolted me upright in the seat. I wrenched around, incredulous to see a deputy sheriff cruiser, its grille wig-wag lights flaring red, crowding our rear bumper.

"Where the hell did she pop up?" Doc shot his rearview mirror a hostile glance. "Hang on tight, Frank. I can shake her."

"Nope, hold up, Doc."

Rational logic governed my thoughts. Those twin whip aerials I saw on her cruiser powered a radio, and she'd alerted her dragnet. The ghetto bird and a swarm of cruisers were closing in. Tensile-taut nerves might snap. A hot pursuit fueled by adrenaline might result in fatalities. I banked on the two advantages I had: Virgil Sweeney, Cody's killer, and Robert Gatlin, my lawyer.

"Did you hide that evidence I gave you?" I asked Doc.

"No breathing soul except me will ever touch it."

"Good show. For now, pull it over, Doc."

"Toss in the towel? Are you sure, Frank?"

"Sure as dirt. Just do it, please, and nobody gets hurt."

Doc's foot lifted off the accelerator as we drifted to a slowing roll. His Crown Vic's tires bounced off the asphalt to the road's muddy shoulder and we halted. Doc engaged his four-way blinkers, flipped off the key, and I threw on the emergency brake. The deputy sheriff cruisers lashed in behind us. Our hands lifted to convey our docile intentions. Our rearview mirror showed the lady deputy sheriff vaulting out, the Glock 9 mil grasped in her two fists training on us.

She belted out her orders at us. "Out slowly. Keep up your hands."

"Frank, this is last call to bolt off."

"Just do as she says."

"You better put Gatlin in the picture."

"I'm not reaching down for the cell phone, or she'll open fire on us."

"Wait until she finds your sawed-off shotgun and prisoner."

We yanked at the door handles and edged out. Eager hands wrangled me spread-eagle up against the Crown Vic to frisk and cuff. I squirmed but I'd no chance to slip my bracelets. In their exuberance, our arresting officers neglected to inventory Doc's Crown Vic and its trunk transporting the unconscious Virgil.

A burly state cop with three stripes and a hatchet face dunked me in their transport cage. It reeked of vomit. He seatbelted me in, and I warded off a spasm of nausea. Yammering excited the radio up front. The rookie deputy sheriff looking all of eighteen gave me the Miranda spiel. No specific charge was given.

"Do you understand these rights I've just read to you?" he asked me.

"You recited them like a real pro," I told him.

"Cooperation facilitates communication," said the rookie deputy sheriff.

My grunt dismissed his police academy slogan. My glance out the side window saw Doc grinning in another cruiser's cage as we roared off.

"I want to call my lawyer," I told the cops.

They snorted in derision. Now made the prisoner, I had a taste of how it felt from the other side.

Chapter 45

This was my first arrest and, so far, it wasn't bad. My interrogation room wasn't as fly-specked or cramped as those I'd seen. I didn't glower at a one-way mirror or an ashtray of butted cigarettes. I hauled out a groan. Fatigue had burned out my core, but I didn't dare rest my eyes.

My barred window framed the outlying, hazy Blue Ridge Mountains. A flashback of our blood opera at the Apollo castle marched goose bumps down my back. The manacles left my ankles and wrists to ache. I had more acute problems. My temple sapped at the farmhouse throbbed. Did concussions throb? My calf wounded at Mosby River was a white-hot brand. Did gangrene burn? My noise-wrecked ears whistled. I had to suck it up.

A pair of brawny deputy sheriffs looking as if they wanted to tear me a new asshole hulked outside the door. I sat alone with my thoughts. From the outset, I'd dummied up and invoked my right to counsel. "Lawyered up," as the faddish jargon went. My pleas weren't denied so much as they went unheard. My harping wore them down.

"Who do you have in mind?" asked the rookie deputy sheriff.

"Robert Gatlin," I replied.

The rookie deputy sheriff left the interrogation room saying, "You just sit tight, cop killer." His final two words—"cop killer"—dropped the temperature by more than a few degrees. A rancid mood told me I had few friends in here, and I'd never get word to Gatlin any time soon.

What stewed me were the photographs Chet had dredged from Cody's desk. He'd forked Marty. I'd heard extreme anger leaves you seeing red, and I experienced that phenomenon. I sat seething, unable to see or think straight. It was a race at who I was more pissed, Cody or Marty. I even gloated over the shotgunned Cody getting his just desserts.

Marty still had hers coming. I pondered on how I'd learn of her demise. At least I had a valid reason not to pay off Limpet when he sent the delivery instructions for his second installment. But did he have any bloodthirsty pals on the inside to shiv me in the neck?

The door batted wide, fanning the air, and Sheriff Dmytryk ambled into the interrogation room. I squirmed up in my plastic molded chair.

"Hello, Sheriff," I said.

Sheriff Dmytryk ignored me.

I saw behind him a stranger, a six-footer carrying a husky bricklayer's physique. However his jet black beard and pork chop sideburns denoted a hip shrink. Christ, I'd undergo an evaluation by the state psychiatrist. His three-piece suit was brushed brown corduroy, and a showy silver-braided watch chain lined his vest pocket. My disdain for him shot up. I'd bullshit him right back.

They settled into the seats across the oblong table to face me tethered to the O-bolt. The stranger, sighing as if this was all in long day's work, fiddled with the gold-plated latches to an elegant attaché case. His right hand extended to me.

"Bob Gatlin," he said, his tenor the articulate baritone I recognized from our phone conversations. "I'll serve as your legal advocate, Mr. Johnson."

"Sorry, being hog-tied here prevents me from shaking your hand," I said. "But I'm pleased to make your acquaintance."

"They've got you hooked?" Gatlin's jasper eyes skewered Sheriff Dmytryk. "My client sits in cuffs. Explain."

"But of course, Counselor." Sheriff Dmytryk tapped his

Masonic ring on the tabletop. "That's by the book to restrain mass killers."

"I see. There's no chance to undo the cuffs?" said Gatlin.

Sheriff Dmytryk failed to contain his smug superiority. "Pigs fly first, Counselor. Are you ready? I've got paperwork mounded on my desk. I'd advise your client to come clean."

"Luckily, you're not his lawyer. I am." Gatlin turned to me. "What have they charged you with?"

"Nothing," I replied.

"Nothing? Why, this must be a new police technique." Gatlin's black, bristly eyebrows worked over Sheriff Dmytryk. "Well…?"

"Right now we're, um, detaining Mr. Johnson as a material witness in a double homicide," said Sheriff Dmytryk.

Gatlin's fierce eyebrows didn't relax. "That doesn't sound like a mass killer to me."

"We recovered Johnson's pickup truck at the murder scene of my two deputy sheriffs. That's for starters. I've every confidence we'll develop solid physical evidence as soon as our lab reports arrive."

"I see. But as of this moment, my client is only a material witness." Gatlin's style turned audacious. "Have you developed any proof Mr. Johnson operated this pickup truck? Can you produce an eyewitness, for instance? Can you produce photos, prints, DNA, Tarot cards, or tea leaves? Perhaps you'll decipher chicken entrails as an investigative tool."

Sheriff Dmytryk, beet-cheeked, jabbed his finger but didn't quite touch Gatlin. "Push me so far. You've been warned."

"I'll see my client in private," said Gatlin.

"Ten minutes." Sheriff Dmytryk tapped his fingernail on his wristwatch's bezel. "Not a second more."

"Better make it fifteen." Gatlin paused. "Plus twenty this afternoon if need be."

The obstinate Sheriff Dmytryk's head wagged as a "no".

"Then I'll complain to Judge Gonzalez how I'm not permitted reasonable access to my client, what our Constitution defines as 'due process'. You've read the Constitution, right?"

"That's cute. Do you know what you are? Let me spell it out. You're a pompous prick. I've watched your showboating on *Court TV*, but no slick tricks go on in my jurisdiction. I won't tolerate them."

Sheriff Dmytryk's bombast didn't faze Gatlin. "Have you finished your tirade? I mean with all that paperwork mounded on your desk, surely..."

"I'm not finished. Your client is a shitty, little polyp. How many stiffs lie in my cooler? So many I've lost count. Johnson is on the block for them. Worst of all, he's a cop killer. Dale and Lars were first-rate deputy sheriffs. Their grieving families scream for justice, and as long as I'm Pelham County's sheriff, I'll see to it they do."

Gatlin grunted for effect.

"But here you sit champing at the bit all bright and eager to help Johnson. What will people say? I'll tell you this much. Folks detest cop killers, and they won't think too complimentary of you for defending one."

The impassive Gatlin shrugged his heavy-set shoulders. "The jury has the final say. Not you. Not me."

"Suit yourself. Go to trial and spin the roulette wheel, but you'll lose. Mark my words, Johnson will go down hard," said Sheriff Dmytryk.

Still Gatlin sat unmoved. The shrewd glint I detected in his eyes triggered my memory to add a cogent detail.

"That's not what you told me," I said to Sheriff Dmytryk. "Saturday morning you drove out to the doublewide and told me to retain Mr. Gatlin as my lawyer."

Astonishment lit up Gatlin's face. "What? Did you instruct Mr. Johnson to contact me, Sheriff?"

The wishy-washy Sheriff Dmytryk rubbed his nose. "I said it was off the record. But Johnson isn't why I came. I knew his dad Harmon is all."

"But you gave Frank explicit advice to call me. I just heard you admit it."

"So? I don't see any relevance," said Sheriff Dmytryk.

"I'll show you the relevance in my opening trial statement."

"Gatlin, don't try and badger me..."

Gatlin's hand gave a cavalier flourish. "Cut to the chase. What's your best evidence? Is it Mr. Johnson's shotgun? Will your ballistics prove it was used in the commission of Mr. Chapman's homicide?"

Sheriff Dmytryk's eyes narrowed into quartz flecks. "My lab results will be in soon."

Gatlin folded his arms high up on his chest. "Ballistics on the shotgun will be imprecise at best. The results are virtually worthless."

"Well, account for the carnage at the satellite farm." This time Sheriff Dmytryk crossed his arms on his chest. "Go ahead, I'm waiting."

I bridled my tongue and watched Gatlin.

Gatlin tossed off a shrug inside his corduroy jacket. "They perished during the legal apprehension of a fugitive."

Sheriff Dmytryk jutted his chin at us. "No sir, that big blowdown counts as a multiple homicide, and I'm treating it as such."

"The media carnival you brought in wants you to treat it as such," said Gatlin.

"Freedom of the press guaranteed by our Constitution brought in the reporters. I can't help how they spin Johnson," said Sheriff Dmytryk.

"A court of law will view it with a different spin after I've presented our side," said Gatlin.

"Uh-huh." Sheriff Dmytryk elevated from his chair, his posture jerky and combative. "Ten minutes, Counselor. Better make it count." The door slam punctuated his stormy exit.

"I haven't told them dick," I said.

"Smart thinking. I'll do all the speaking," said Gatlin. "Did you recover the munitions at the satellite farm?"

"No time to search." My swallow felt lumpy and dry. "Is Chet bearing up?"

"He's in stable condition." Gatlin looked thoughtful. "Let's spool it back to the beginning. Why did Dale and Lars draw down on you?"

"My manhunt was an excuse to smoke me while I allegedly resisted arrest." I added an afterthought. "They were all Nazis."

Gatlin's eyebrows scrunched up. "Ah, I just spotted the glimmer to our silver lining. We'll cast the late deputy sheriffs in that pernicious light and woo the jury's empathy. Headlines will trumpet, 'Lone man's battle waged against a hate group'. Worst case scenario, we'll lock up a hung jury and live to litigate another day."

"We'll never pull it off," I said.

"Don't be so pessimistic. We'll spin Sheriff Dmytryk's media carnival and roll you out as our big small-town hero. The patriotic public will eat it up."

I nodded. "You know Felham's history includes a Nazi POW camp where the satellite farm now stands."

"That's a scary thought," said Gatlin.

"A few POWs escaped before Uncle Sam flew them back to postwar Germany. They assimilated into our melting pot, and their descendents live among us. Virgil's grandfather was one."

"That suggests something else. What ensures you got them all? Suppose more Nazis than Virgil slipped under the rear fence?"

I cocked my head at Gatlin. "That's even a scarier thought."

Chapter 46

After my godsent shower and shave, the deputy sheriffs tossed me in a cell. At 7x14, it felt a skoesh roomier than Fincham's coffin. Amenities included a concrete bunk and a combo toilet/sink (cold water only). They'd appropriated my belt, shoelaces, and pocket wares such as my wallet and keys. Lunch arrived but the ptomaine meatloaf earned a surly glance before I nudged it away.

Sprawled back on the concrete bunk, I wondered if my earliest possible release date lay somewhere off in the new century. My brain reworked my past few days. I cracked my knuckles and hopped up to pace in my rathole.

The irony of funding Limpet with Cody's blood money to bump off Marty hectored my thoughts. The stressful part was not learning the news on when, or if, my hit went off. I couldn't quiz anybody in here. I couldn't reach out and light a blowtorch under my lethargic hit man. My angst almost sent me bouncing off the steel bars until I had some company.

My visitor was Mr. Van Dotson. The jaded deputy sheriffs left us alone. We sat on the concrete bunk in my cell, murmuring. Sheriff Dmytryk had deemed the visitors' kiosks were too risky to meet in. I didn't object. The only bugs here were roaches. I'd already checked.

Mr. Van Dotson's unshaven, craggy face drooped, aging him by ten years. My lodging had to evoke unpleasant memories of his jailbird days. His dirt-brown ringlets were caught in a ponytail. I was a liar if I didn't admit Rennie's sad eyes had crossed my mind.

"Are you going bananas yet?" he asked me.

I shrugged. "I've got no real kick."

"Frank, you've got a slew of friends."

After a nod and some hesitation, I asked, "How's Rennie?"

He played deaf by updating me. "Doc Edwards made bail yesterday. He told me certain major items in his possession made it to Gatlin."

I thrilled—Doc Edwards had delivered Cody's dirty business ledger and the neo-Nazi pendants to Gatlin. He'd know what to do with them.

"How's the gang?" I asked, this time sort of backing into my Rennie questions.

"Sofia and her dachshund bunk with Gerald. Chet is recovering well. The sheriff fished Virgil Sweeney out of Doc's Crown Vic. Virgil's fingerprints smothered the meth lab they found at the satellite farm. He's at the hospital under armed guard."

"Why did Rennie marry a goon like Virgil?"

"Mule-headed. Like all young people, Rennie knew what was best. I couldn't tell her anything, and she went ahead and married him."

I recalled Virgil's uber-Nazi grandfather was a POW camp escapee living in West Virginia. Bad blood sure flowed in Virgil's veins. "What did she see in him?"

"Virgil always had a wild hair. That bad boy charm is what allured Rennie. Things went south fast when his true self shined through. He went on binges and turned abusive. Fed up, Rennie took the kids and split."

My slow nod filled the pause. I didn't tell Mr. Van Dotson about Virgil's direct lineage to the Nazi POWs. I didn't know if Rennie had learned the extent of Virgil's dark past, or how she'd disclose it to their kids. Virgil's story would shake out soon enough at my trial. I felt sorry for the Van Dotsons.

"What's your transgression?" asked Mr. Van Dotson.

"The homicide of Dale and Lars," I replied.

"All I can say is don't plead guilty. No jury will convict

you. Tell them to stick any plea bargains. Stand up and plenty, including me, will rally behind you. We've started a pass-the-hat deal."

"Thanks, but I can earn my own way." I still had Cody's $25,000 earmarked for Limpet, but that fat wad could also buy me a ton of attorney hours.

"What comes next?" asked Mr. Van Dotson.

My shoulders flexed up. "Keep the faith, I guess. Not for nothing, but you just now ignored my question about Rennie."

"So I did." Mr. Van Dotson groaned up from the concrete bunk and clutched his hands to the steel bars. "That was done on purpose, Frank. I don't know how Rennie is doing. She says damn little to me."

"Is she staying at your place?"

"For the time being, she is. All this uproar scared her."

"She told me as much, but it's finished now. Tell her that."

"Uh-huh." Mr. Van Dotson turned to me. "Frank, level with me. Was Cody Chapman really a Nazi?"

"I don't think so in any official capacity. You need to understand Cody loved to hustle a dollar, and you'd never convince me he backed their aims. But their money was too green for Cody to pass up."

"Gatlin is a legal whiz. He got me in to see you. Let him quarterback your defense."

"That's my game plan," I said, anxious whether this fast-tracked trial worked to benefit me or the Commonwealth, but Gatlin had said we were ready to rock.

"Doc Edwards left your pet rat with me."

Mr. Bojangles I'd left cooped up in Gerald's surveillance car before we assailed the satellite farm had slipped my mind. "Watch him until I can get home."

"Now that's the right positive thinking," said Mr. Van Dotson, smiling for the first time.

Chapter 47

Events trundled along for three weeks. I slept a lot as a pretrial detainee, Judge Gonzalez having denied my bail. The prison physician fixed my shotgun wound. I missed but didn't miss attending Cody's funeral. Mr. Van Dotson, my crusty neighbor Mr. Farok (had he reclaimed his tomcat at the doublewide?), Gerald, Doc Edwards, Mr. Birdsong (from the apple orchard), and even Bob Gatlin played my stand-in pallbearers.

The next day Gatlin finagled the deputy sheriffs to forward me a care package of dog-eared paperbacks, but the meager light in my cell made reading difficult. I could've used a portable radio to tune in WKQK and catch some bluegrass music.

Then Gatlin goofed up big time. After all the hype, I couldn't believe it, especially with my neck on the line. We conspired in my jail cell. He was leaning against the steel bars, his flabbergasted expression regarding me.

I sat in a leaden daze on the concrete bunk. "But that was our best evidence."

"I feel your dismay," said Gatlin.

"The judge leaves us no wiggle room?" I said.

"Not Judge Gonzalez. The chain of custody issue is sacrosanct with him. My turning over Cody's dirty business ledger and the Nazi pendants cast enough serious doubt for His Honor to exclude them as evidence."

"Chain of custody. I should've seen that truck coming," I

said.

"You've had a few distractions. Even I missed it." Gatlin took a breath. "Your arrest report is half-literate. Maybe I can attack the deputies' credibility and cast doubt on them."

"That angle never works."

"Well, Judge Gonzalez's honesty forces us to attack from a more creative angle."

"What do you mean?" I asked.

"Never mind. Leave the brainwork to me," replied Gatlin.

"Uh-huh. What shot do I now have at an acquittal?" I asked.

Not as upbeat, Gatlin had lost his bravado. His jasper eyes showed a matte glaze. "Fair, I'd say. We'll revamp our game plan and grind it out. The jury pool is culled from your neck of the woods. Do you enjoy a solid reputation in Pelham?"

I shrugged. "No worse or better than most. That makes it a toss up, I guess."

❧❦

My trial nicked the taxpayers of Pelham County for a half-day. The telegenic Gatlin, as always, oozed his robust charm in front of the *Court TV* cameras while delivering his opening statement. As he spoke, I studied each juror's face and noticed a smile twitching on the two older ladies'. But things soured.

Gatlin executing our strategy did his best to tar Deputy Sheriffs Dale and Lars as neo-Nazis cranked on meth. The Feds had already located a trailer chocked with weaponry at the satellite farm. Their discovery of the C4 plastic explosives in a panel truck as well as the meth lab was more perturbing. But the Commonwealth's Attorney objected, saying nothing definitively connected Lars or Dale to the neo-Nazis. Judge Gonzalez agreed, and Gatlin plodded on. Mr. Birdsong testified he'd seen a Nazi flag in Lars' trunk.

"Objection. Circumstantial," said the C.A.

"Sustained," said Judge Gonzalez.

And so it went. Our side lost on the major points, and I

felt any momentum flowing away. I slouched more in my chair. After his closing argument, Gatlin with a groan flopped down next to me at the defense table. His metallic voice betrayed his low confidence in our percentages. He brushed off his jacket sleeve as if to dismiss my case.

"The jury is now in recess," said Judge Gonzalez.

The sober jury filed out of their box into their deliberation chamber, and Gatlin bailed to go grab some fresh air outdoors. Gerald strolled up, his hard squint fending off the pair of courtroom deputies stirring to pace over and intercept him. He patted me on the shoulder.

"How's Chet making it?" I asked.

"He's a tough kid."

"How are you at busting into jails?" I asked.

"My oxy-acetylene torch cuts steel just fine. But you aren't going to jail."

"Say what? Gatlin got trounced and we hit the skids," I said.

"So maybe Gatlin wasn't as flashy. Maybe this jury doesn't dig flashy. Hang tough, Frank, and let's see how it washes out."

"Just keep your oxy-acetylene torch handy," I said.

∞

The jury burned thirty-two minutes by my watch before they trooped back to their thrones. An ashen-faced Gatlin, his necktie now unloosened and collar undone, had a heavy seat beside me. The full-hipped, gum-chomping forelady I'd last seen mopping the washerette's floor the night Chet and I visited Fincham's to see Cody was the only standing juror.

"Is the jury prepared to render a verdict?"

"We are, Your Honor."

"How say ye?"

"Not guilty, Your Honor."

Judge Gonzalez's gavel rap over the outburst of cheers made it official. "Mr. Johnson, you're free to go."

I heard Gatlin's heaved out snort of relief. He slapped my hand in his giant mitt and shook it. We'd triumphed and kudos flew all around. Nobody was more incredulous than me how I got a walk, maybe as a recompense for the lush who'd T-boned my parents' auto and went free. I could stroll out Pelham's courthouse doors as any citizen. But Gatlin had spotted the paparazzi back from the media carnival trawling on the steps, and he spirited me to the freight elevator.

"Ho, Frank Johnson! I say wait up!"

Sheriff Dmytryk took authoritative strides down the carpeted hallway. He barked as the elevator doors rattled to close and shook his fist at us.

"You'll be back. I'll hold your rat cage. Hear me?"

Gatlin's meaty palm swatted to block the elevator door. He rumbled from deep in his chest. "Sheriff, you better back off. Or else you'll deal with my harassment suit."

"I don't give a fuzzy fuck how the jury voted." Sheriff Dmytryk tapped his Masonic ring on the elevator door. "And you're no better than your dirtbag client."

Gatlin chuckled in Sheriff Dmytryk's face. "Sticks and stones."

"Yeah well, you heard me."

"I only hear a sore loser blowing off steam," said Gatlin.

Sheriff Dmytryk, fists on his hips, glared at us until the elevator door finished collapsing into its slot.

"Asshole," said Gatlin with apt succinctness.

We dropped fast in the elevator car to the first floor and bustled through a side exit. I saw Gatlin's red Chrysler LeBaron at the curbside and felt ecstatic not to curse any steel bars enclosing me. No autumn morning smelled sweeter—I vacuumed in a lungful of crisp, liberating air.

Doc Edwards, Gatlin's new wheelman, sat under the controls. Gatlin flumped down up front, and I shrugged into the rear seat, this ride made without a transport partition or manacles to restrain me.

"This trial couldn't have gone any better. I love it when I'm at the top of my game." His jasper eyes dancing, Gatlin kissed his fingertips.

I followed Doc's lead rolling his eyes the rearview mirror

at Gatlin's schtick. He'd almost blown it, but only almost, and I liked him okay. Doc floored the gas and, tires chirping, he hammered us down the nearest side street.

"Going home, Frank?" asked Doc.

"No, let me off at Mr. Van Dotson's house," I replied.

"Mr. Van Dotson's it is." Doc winked at me in the mirror except my drop-in was anything but for a lewd or romantic encounter.

Gatlin pivoted in his seat and dealt me a congenial smile. "Frank, are you too young to remember Perry Mason and Paul Drake?"

"I sure do. They're the old lawyer and P.I. tandem."

"Correct. Have you ever considered the private investigation racket?"

"Me? Hell, I can't find my ass using both hands and a flashlight."

My quip invoked Doc's grin and Gatlin chuckled.

"A P.I. is an immeasurable asset to me."

I realized snubbing any lead for gainful employment bordered on reckless if not stupid. "Sounds intriguing. I'll call you next week."

"Make it tomorrow. Ms. Reid will arrange a convenient time."

"Uh-huh," I said, dreading my encounter with Ms. Reid.

"Don't look so skeptical." Gatlin gave his wheelman a curious glance. "Doc, don't you concur Frank possesses the acumen and talent to excel as a private investigator?"

"Frank gets the job done, and I know he likes to help folks," replied Doc. "Plus, his MP record isn't too shabby."

"You were an MP? That's so much the better. Call me tomorrow, Frank."

I knew Gatlin's autocratic demeanor would drive me berserk, but I sat there like a moron bobbing my head. "I'll need a backup, and I have just the sidekick in mind. Gerald Peyton is a good guy to have in a jam."

"Stellar. And I have just the project in mind. Middleburg despite its façade as something out of Gatsby isn't all genteel.

We also bare a seedy underbelly."

Seedy underbelly. Oh jolly, I can hardly wait, I thought before something occurred to me. "What's your salary?"

"Competitive, Frank."

"Can you spot me a couple of C-notes?" I asked.

An engraved billfold appeared from Gatlin's inner jacket pocket, and he slipped me the earnest money. "Great fringe benefits, too," he said.

Before I could get clarification, Doc Edwards glided up to stop in full view of Mr. Van Dotson's house. I disembarked. Gatlin waved once in his offhand way, and Doc grinned at me again as they sailed up the state road. Talk about your two peas in a pod. I tucked back my cuff: a few minutes shy of noon.

I hadn't eaten a square meal in three weeks, and my gut tied in a knot as I tramped down the gravel driveway. The porchside pumpkin carved in a Halloween leer greeted me. Before my knuckles rapped, I heard a shuffle inside, and the doorknob turned. Mr. Van Dotson brought out a broad smile.

"Gerald just broke the news to me. You beat the bastards."

"By the skin of my teeth," I said.

"That skins close enough. Do we share a celebratory toast?"

"It's still early, but what the hell?" I replied.

Coltrane's soprano sax crooned on the MP3 player as a slinky furball skittered over the rug to me. Jabbering, Mr. Bojangles nudged his whiskered snout at my boot tops, insisting I pick up and love him. I obliged.

Mr. Van Dotson laughed as he splashed our shot glasses. "The little bugger has missed you, and now I'll miss him. Did you go to a pet store for him?"

"No, I rescued him from the Nazis," I replied.

"Then you better hang on to him."

The whiskey streaked a blaze of lightning down my throat. "Is Rennie around?" I asked, faking nonchalance while my heart did acrobatic moves under my ribs.

His grin flattening, Mr. Van Dotson gave me an envelope

creased in thirds. "Rennie and the grandkids cut out yesterday, towing a U-Haul."

She didn't waste any damn time, I thought.

"She's off to stay with her Aunt Erin, my kid sister. I can't say where. I wish I could, but a promise is a promise. Anyway, Rennie told me this is for you."

I accepted the envelope, and Mr. Van Dotson retreated through a doorway to decrease the volume of Coltrane's eloquent sax solo. I tore apart the envelope and removed the folded sheet of paper. Rennie's note penned in a prim cursive was laconic.

Hi Frank,

I hope when you read this, your trial has ended, and you're free to live your life.

After much deep thinking on all that has happened, I've decided to leave Pelham and make a clean break with the past, and try out with a fresh start of things.

Violence can hold no place in my duty to raise my family. I hope you can see what I mean. I expect in the end you'll come to understand and agree with me.

Please, please don't follow me. I don't see it working out between us. Ever. Please forgive any hurt reading this may've caused you.

~ R ~

The stain I saw in the page's lower corner could be from a teardrop. I doubted it. Fury compounded by a feeling of betrayal flushed the red patch up my neck and ears. I mused on where Rennie might flee to evade the unremitting violence she deplored. It crashed in on us from all sides. Wandering in quest of a safer womb to live and raise a family made no sense, but I didn't share my misgivings with her father, my friend still.

"Sorry to be the messenger of more bad news." Mr. Van Dotson who'd returned to the room handed me the signed registry brought back from Cody's funeral.

"Thanks." I made a mental note to mail him a check to reimburse Rennie for Cody's funeral expenses.

Then I brought up my trial. "I'm sorry you had to hear Virgil's dirty Nazi past—"

"Rain off a duck's ass, Frank." Mr. Van Dotson did an accompanying hand motion. "We're all better off to forget it, and him."

"You said it," I said.

Mr. Van Dotson slapped me on the shoulder. "Frank, if I were you, I'd take a vacation. Things should cool off here, and by then you can return with no fuss to Pelham."

"I'll think on it," I said, uptight over how I'd stave off the repo man much less go off on any vacation.

I didn't dare tap the $25K even if after Mormons gave me the ax, and I had a stack of overdue bills at the doublewide. So, how did I earn a paycheck? I was a leper at any law enforcement unit, and I'd no wish to touch another firearm except for self-protection. A correctional officer job at a prison was off the table. Did railroads still hire private cops? Security guard was tempting—plenty of time to read, but the pay sucked. My viable employment options had dwindled to Gatlin's lone offer. For richer or poorer, better or worse, I was married to my new career path as a full-time private investigator.

Chapter 48

Unannounced the next morning, Gerald dropped by the doublewide. I was out on the cinderblock stoop feeding my tomcat as he pulled up in his champagne-colored surveillance car. I strolled out into the yard, watching the big man stretch out into the sunlight. I'd a notion he'd knocked out a few iron sets on the bench before driving over.

Gerald threw me a short nod. "I thought I'd check in."

"I'm good. How's Chet making it?"

"He'll be fine."

"Sofia?"

"She says yo but, Frank, we need to talk."

My sidelong glance didn't like seeing the steely gleam hardening Gerald's eyes.

"What's up?"

"Let's take it inside."

I let Gerald shift by me as I fought off my qualms to follow him into my kitchenette. I almost broke out in hives, and my heart slowed to a chug. I moved a paperback I'd been reading and shooed Mr. Bojangles off the other chair. Gerald sat down at one end of the table facing me.

A flashback came of that morning Cody and I had huddled here. This time I'd no Beretta or hollow-point slug in a salt shaker. The Jet Jackal, dragging his dark chains from Hell's kennels, hadn't returned to bite me in the ass for months. I knocked on wood.

"Frank, we've been road dogs for years," was Gerald's

sappy preamble.

"Uh-huh." A bolt of anger left me irritated. "Get to it. Why are you here?"

Gerald's eyes didn't flicker. He was locked on what he had to say. "I bumped into Bexley. Have you seen him lately?"

I nodded. Bexley was the conduit to Limpet, my hit man.

"Bexley as usual started his nipping early in the day."

"Bexley has diarrhea of the mouth." I now had an idea where our plane wreck of a conversation would crash.

"What he dropped on me sure stinks." Gerald stopped.

Rubbing the back of my neck is how I broke off engaging his incendiary glare.

"I want the no-bullshit truth, Frank."

I put him off. "What truth?"

"The truth on this hit you put out on your ex."

I clenched my fists. "Why are you up in my business?"

"Yo, dial it back. I'm here as your friend, remember?"

"Why?" I asked again, less intense.

"Because I'll have to live with it, and I already deal with enough dark shit on my soul."

Nodding, I unknotted my fists. I hadn't taken into account how my hit might foul up my friends. "As far as I know, it's in progress."

"You best hope so. Now, you go tell Bexley to call off the dogs." Gerald's frown sagged. He sighed. He looked like riding on the tail end of an all-night surveillance. "Frank, I love you like a kid brother, then I hear this bullshit. What the fuck is going on? You can do better than this stupid thinking."

Mr. Bojangles chittered, demanding attention, and I picked him up to hold and pet in my lap. My throat tightened with emotion. In truth, reading Rennie's letter yesterday had stopped me cold. All night I'd done some heavy-duty soul searching. Second thoughts had eroded my resolve to even the scales with Marty. An icy douse of reality told me I'd crack up from dealing with my guilt over instigating the hit I paid for on her.

Murder was murder. Killers and killers' accomplices perched on their concrete bunks, watching death row's interminable clock, and I had to cancel the hit as soon as possible. I didn't want to dwell on what if it was too late. Besides, if I didn't contribute to the local violence, Rennie might have her own second thoughts and with a change of heart move her family back to our small, imperfect town.

"My thinking did slide sideways, but I'll go see Bexley."

Gerald nodded. "We've done enough shooting."

"Sorry to throw you into the Nazi firefight, too."

"It was no big thing, and I'd do it again." Gerald went to the doorway where he made a half-turn, grinning for the first time. "You know your hit man is a phony."

Hearing that stunner almost dismantled me. "What the hell?" I didn't believe Gerald, but he continued nodding, and I knew it was no joke. How had I been duped without a sliver of suspicion on Limpet's credibility?

"How do you know?" I asked.

"This ugly scammer has bilked desperate types like you for years. What's more, Bexley is wise to the grift. Thank god he sent you off on a goose chase."

So my hit man was a con man. Then Limpet saying he'd disguise Marty's hit as a hunting accident at one in the morning echoed in my head. That flaky bit alone should've tipped me off he was a fraud.

"What about my pot of money?" I asked.

Gerald hiked his shoulders. "I bet he's tooting it up down in Miami. Chalk this one up to lessons learned." Gerald's good-natured wink defused my rising anger.

"Shit, you knew all along. How did you find out?" I asked.

"Like you said, Bexley has a big mouth. He knows we're friends and called me early on."

"How early on?" I asked.

"Early on enough to keep a sharp eye on you. I asked you over the phone at Sofia's place if you had other issues. Remember?"

"Yeah, I do. Now I'll go settle a certain score. Bexley probably got a cut of my money," I said.

"You ain't doing shit. Bexley did you a favor."

"Was Chet in on it, too?" I asked.

"We both accept your thanks. But the big question you now face is what comes next for Frank Johnson?"

"Gatlin wants me as his private investigator," I replied.

"Take it."

"I'm not cut out for P.I. work," I said.

"Don't worry. If you slide sideways again, I'll kick your ass straight."

"Well damn, how can I turn down his offer?" I said.

"You can't. Have you called Dr. Bob's folks at AA?"

"It tops my list. I've been sober since our big blowdown," I said.

"So has Chet. You both keep it going that way."

Gerald strutted out my door, and I heard him drive off before I chuckled. My ineptness dealing with the flaky con/hit man Limpet had saved me from making a terrible mistake. I dropped a dime on Gatlin to discuss his first project, and he posed a question.

"Has Gerald conferred with you?"

Another jolt of disbelief rocked me. "You knew about my hit man, too?"

"Don't get bent, Frank. I'm your attorney and Gerald consulted me. I'm never too modest to express my opinion, personal or professional."

"I've got so many guardian angels it hurts," I said.

"Amen to that," said Gatlin. "If your vendetta is over, maybe we can get some work done."

Chapter 49

Gatlin had wondered if more neo-Nazis than Virgil had slipped under the rear fence, but no Day Glo-red swastikas desecrated a church, boxcar, or overpass. I grew a pair of eyes in my rear skull. Something malignant befouling the air warned me they bided their time as a terrorists' sleeper cell, poised to wreak some fresh hell. They'd resort to today's sneaky crap like driving suicide car bombs or brandishing box-cutters in close quarters. Plus which, Dale and Lars' antagonistic families wanted to nail me to the wall.

I repaired the Beretta I'd offered as trade bait to Cody for the Luger, and the Beretta rode in my sling holster. A .32 semi-automatic was my backup piece. My Kevlar was kept handy along with a half-dozen frag grenades. I even practiced hurling my well-balanced knife at a dead tree. *"If you don't own a dagger, sell your cloak and buy one,"* to quote from Luke. I also hid two sawed-offs stoked with home defense loads at the doublewide.

"Hell Frank, you're a hardcore paranoid," Gerald told me.

"How many sawed-offs do you hide in your cave?" I asked him.

He put on a sheepish grin. "Three."

Additional vita on the dead neo-Nazis came to light. They'd been trained while in the Army at sniper school. Why didn't hearing that fact shock me? Hans, the neo-Nazi we'd plastered up in the Apollo castle, still dozed and his cell phone went on chirping until Satan answered it. Pelham buried the neo-Nazis from the satellite farm in unmarked graves at our town cemetery.

I never shared the neo-Nazis' plans Virgil had divulged to me at Doc's house. I can't say why. Maybe it was unfinished personal business. The Feds found Virgil Sweeney's fingerprints all over the munitions. After his trial, he would ship off downstate to grow old behind bars. I made myself a promise. If he scored an early parole, a distinct possibility with time off for good behavior, I'd go after the bastard.

Senator Reddman never groused in public during and after my trial. I'm certain he accepted Lars' neo-Nazi affiliation and, for political expediency, sought to distance himself from his dead nephew, a sworn lawman. Or perhaps Reddman feared Lars had put him on their enemies list. At any rate, we'd vote Senator Reddman out of a job, and he'd retire to San Paulo.

I mailed in the completed paperwork I'd received from Dreema with the requisite fee to the Virginia Department of Criminal Justice Services. My qualifications were impeccable and, twenty-four hours later, I was an official P.I. with my own photo I.D.

Gatlin phoned me on Wednesday afternoons to hear my progress reports and to complain about dealing with our prickly clients. Better him than me. He told me another bloody Middleburg divorce perked in the pipeline, and this incensed wife demanded proof of infidelity, something up my alley.

"Did the owner renting the farmhouse to Cody have any kids?" I asked Gatlin during one phone call.

"Twin girls lived there. Their father accepted a computer job in Houston. Why?" said Gatlin.

"I just had to know that house of horrors was once normal," I said, picturing the Hot Wheels toys I'd seen abandoned in the yard.

"A big box store is slated to go up there," said Gatlin.

"So it goes," I said.

The gun shop's contents went at auction. Gatlin oversaw the gun shop's sale, and the IRS garnished the profits to retire

Cody's delinquent taxes and penalties. The opportunistic developer demolished the gun shop, bulldozed the dirt berms on the firing range, and slapped up three McMansions, the inaugural units to a new gated enclave with a golf course. I bought a cast-off Prizm (like Rennie's car) and rerouted my trips to avoid any sight of our latest blemish.

Rumors percolated how Gatlin's deep pockets and Doc Edwards' kibitzing had bought off several jury members, perhaps the two older ladies I'd seen smile. My surprise "not guilty" verdict had left me wondering, but what was done was done. Gerald and I returned the Buick LeSabre to Bill Ruffian, Gatlin's cousin in Shepherdstown. Bill had a conspiracy theory, but running late, we split in the Barracuda.

Stonesiffer our county coroner suffered a chainsaw mishap while pruning high up in his giant maple, and bled out to death. I felt sorry for his wife and three kids. On a brighter note, I heard Lenny Curtis who'd cleaned up Cody's viscera off the gun shop floor embarked on his Holy Land pilgrimage. I never had a yen to go visit Cody's grave. I found he'd been wrong on one thing in our final conversation at Leona's: blood isn't always thicker than water.

Right after recovering from his gunshot wound, Chet quit at McDavid's. Sober as a choirboy, he attended a school for operating heavy equipment and hatched a scheme to bulldoze new bridle trails through the woods. The spoiled daughters of the horse barons liked shady paths to trot their thoroughbreds on. I laughed until he showed me his first check stub. No doubt Gatlin had landed Chet several cushy contracts from his affluent but troubled Middleburg clients.

From time to time, I bumped into Mr. Van Dotson, and we exchanged banal pleasantries. I trembled on the inside to ask after Rennie. A P.I. could trace her easy enough, but we'd moved on. Or I should say Rennie had. Late on insomniac nights, I prowled by the old Shepherd place on Main Street. I spotted a warm, amber glow in Rennie's old bedroom window, and the loss stabbed me. I should've known it—the sad-eyed girls always crack your heart in half. I finally admitted that I'd fallen in love, and then lost it, a first for me. But my radar went on red alert.

A brown-wrapped packet, no return address on it, arrived in the mail. The wedding ring in the box had a familiar flash. So Marty had a decent bone in her body after all. She also didn't include a poison pen letter. The diamond ring with the twenty-five grand (minus Cody's funeral expenses) and my valid passport went into a safe-deposit box as my rainy day fund.

Every other day or so, Sheriff Dmytryk sent out his deputies. Their cruiser shambled up the cul-de-sac and braked to idle in front of the doublewide. They sat watching behind tinted glass before burning rubber. Their harassment was a poke in the eye. But my crusty neighbor Mr. Farok had some *cojones*. He'd lounge in his front lawn chair, swig on a beer, and ogle the deputy sheriffs right back. I got the impression Sheriff Dmytryk was already turning skittish at his election rolling up the November after next.

Dreema Atkins, my friend in Richmond, took my call.

"You better treat Mr. Gatlin right," she said. "He needs a detective, but more importantly, you need a lawyer."

Irritated at how she was right, I let my silence imply assent.

"Frank, get back to taking care of business. Moping around is bad for you. Take any cases you can find, even pro bono. I'll lend you lab support."

"Thanks. We did a good job partnering on this case."

"No, you did the legwork, Frank. Now, what are your Thanksgiving plans? Are you headed anywhere special?"

I consulted my mental day planner. Marooned at the doublewide with my two pets was same old same old. A late turkey-and-cranberry dinner at Leona's Bar & Grill in town with Gerald and Chet felt a little cheerier. Conducting a holiday stakeout for Gatlin flat out sucked.

"Nothing special. Why do you ask?"

"Richmond is gorgeous in late November."

Something blipped, then buzzed on my radar screen. "Is

this, like, a date, Dreema?"

She laughed that coy, sweet way girls do. "Then is that, like, a yes?"

"A resounding yes, and I'll bring the vino."

"You better let me select the wine, Frank."

"Actually I've quit drinking."

"That's even better."

"Then shoot me a time before I die here," I said, enjoying our flirtation.

Dreema made it early morning.

Gerald and Sofia announced their nuptials amid much fanfare and within three days broke it off. Cold feet, I figured. So Gerald wasn't the invincible iron man. I drove Sofia at her insistence just to the Greyhound depot in town.

"Thanks for everything," I told her.

"You're most welcome." Her large, mocha-brown eyes teared up. "And Frank, stick with the P.I. gig."

"I'm sort of stuck with it."

She kissed me on the cheek, exited with her dachshund Nitro, and I saw them board the bus to Little Salem. That night I slept on thorns, brooding over the break-up. Love is so goddamn fickle.

Finally, one night a few days before Thanksgiving and feeling restless, I stepped outside the doublewide. The cinderblock stoop under the porch light was my seat where I lit a crumpled cigarette. Exhaling smoke, I noticed the blue spruce in the patchy shadows looked scruffy. I'd trim it up within the week.

By the time I extinguished the butt, I resolved all the recent bloodshed had atoned for the rage I'd heaped on Marty. Enough was enough. I took stock in something important. With no close family left now, I'd have to depend on my friends—Gerald, Chet, Doc Edwards, Mr. Farok, Dreema Atkins, and now Bob Gatlin. I'd never repay all the favors I owed them, but then I knew they didn't care.

All at once, a red-eye shine emerged across the lawn from the direction of the old limestone quarry. My pulse flatlined until I saw it was a neighbor's collie, not the Jet Jackal. The collie padded over and sniffed at my coat pocket. Mr. Bojangles peeped out, and I had to laugh.

A memory chipped loose. I'd waited while smoking a cigarette on a certain porch on a similar clear, cold night not long ago. Ah Rennie, I'd miss her. But I understood her reasons for leaving Pelham, and I didn't much blame her. Hey, I still had Richmond with Dreema.

The End

Acknowledgements

Chapter 1 in an earlier version ("Like a Fox") appeared in the literary magazine *RE:AL* (Vol. 26, No. 2, Fall 2001) (Stephen F. Austin University, Texas).

Chapter 2 in an earlier version ("Gearing Up") appeared in the literary ezine *Samsara Quarterly* (Winter 2002).

Chapters 1 through 6 originally appear on Allan Guthrie's NOIR ORIGINALS website (Issue #2, August 2003) (Scotland). Many thanks to Al.

The text from the John Pelham highway historic marker used with the permission of the Virginia Department of Historic Resources.

John Pelham's death and funeral are loosely based on the accounts described in *Lee's Lieutenants* by Douglas Southall Freeman (Scribners, 1944) and "Major John Pelham—Arms and the Boy," *Richmond Times-Dispatch*, March 26, 1939.

The Nazi POW camps background information is derived from "Sahuarita Once Had POW Camp," by Tim Ellis, *Arizona Daily Star*, May 25, 2006.

Grateful thanks for technical assistance extended to Jay Mason (Forensic Scientist Supervisor, Virginia Department of Forensic Science), Dr. James I. Robertson, Jr. (Alumni Distinguished Professor in History, Virginia Polytechnic Institute and State University), and Kimberly Freiberger (Virginia Department of Criminal Justice Services).

Appreciation expressed to the Military Police of the Vietnam War web site for supporting Frank Johnson and his adventures.

The background for Frank's gunsmithing profession is based on my work experience at Interarms, Midland, VA, manufacturing .357 and .44 Magnum handguns.

About the Author

Ed Lynskey's short collection, *Out of Town a Few Days*, appeared in 2004, and a novel titled *The Blue Cheer* was released in 2006.

Ed's next PI Frank Johnson novel, *Troglodytes* is scheduled for release in Fall 2008 from Mundania Press.